Brutal SAINT

VICIOUS EMPIRE: TWO

LUNA KAYNE

Brutal Saint by Luna Kayne

Copyright © 2022 by Luna Kayne

All rights reserved.

No part of this book may be reproduced in any form or by any electronic or mechanical means, including information storage and retrieval systems, without written permission from the author, except for the use of brief quotations in a book review.

This book is fiction. Any similarity between the characters and situations within its pages and places or persons, living or dead, is unintentional and coincidental.

Book cover design: Pretty Little Design Co.

Cover model photographer: Wander Aguiar

Cover model: Josh Mario

Editor: Caroline Knecht

First Printing, 2022

ISBN (eBook) 978-1-989366-32-5

ISBN (paperback) 978-1-989366-33-2

Luna Kayne, Kayne Publishing

Brutal Saint is the second book in the Vicious Empire series. It is NOT recommended that the books in this series be read as standalones as there is an ongoing story that begins in the first book, **CRUEL SAINT**, and will continue through the four books in this series.

Despair is when your pretty smile is the only thing
holding the pain in and no one knows you well enough
to know the difference.

— LUNA KAYNE

1

HARLOW

Everything I own is in my backpack.

It's an old habit that has worked for me ever since I got out of the system eight years ago.

I learned early in life to keep my valuables close and not to plant roots.

Growing up in foster care meant I moved around when I least expected it. People came and went, and I got used to taking care of myself.

I'm not completely on my own now. I have my brother, James, down in Oregon and my sister, Genie, here in Seattle. We were lucky enough to find each other again, but it hasn't been easy. We grew up apart, and reconciling the close siblings we once were to the damaged adults we've become hurts my heart. This is why I dropped everything to come to Seattle when my sister called me a week ago.

She was in a bad place with a shitty boyfriend, and she was scared. She'd had enough and wanted to get out.

"Why are we going to meet this person? Do you know

them? Why don't we just leave?" My questions pour out of me, one after the other, from the driver's seat of my car.

I should probably shut up. Genie is already showing signs of withdrawal, and I shouldn't agitate her until I can get her home and to the help she needs, but something isn't sitting right in my head.

Everything inside of me is yelling at me to cut and run.

"Just—I need to do this, or he'll come after me. I've got to hand something off, then he said I'm done and he'll let me go this time." Her hands tremble in her lap as she looks down the street before pointing in front of us. "Park over here; it's a few blocks away."

The whites in my knuckles, which are clenched around the steering wheel, glare at me when we drive under a streetlight, and I park in the first spot I see.

Neither of us has much of a jacket on, and I twist from my spot in the driver's seat to pull out an extra pair of mittens that I picked up for Genie at a secondhand store last week.

Her hands stop shaking for a brief moment as she looks at them, and I wonder if the mittens bring back the same memory as they do for me. As soon as I saw them, I had to get them. They match the outfit her favorite television character wore when we were little. I remember she wanted a pair so bad when we were kids. They had even smelled like strawberries when they were brand new.

The ghost of a smile haunts her features as she puts them on and lifts one hand to her nose. Inhaling deeply, she closes her eyes.

She remembers, and I'm sad all over again. I wish I could take her back and give her the childhood we all should have had.

I can't go back, but I can go forward.

As soon as we leave this city, I'll be there for her every step of the way. I won't give up on her. Out of the three of us, she fought the hardest for our family, and now I'll fight for her.

Turning the car off, I look over to the passenger seat, and her expression worries me.

Empty eyes stare down a dark road into the distance, and I wonder if she feels like running away as well. Maybe I could convince her to leave with me right now if I pushed a little.

"I love you, my little Harley." Her voice is a whisper. "I don't remember if I said that when you came to get me. My brain isn't working right."

I whisper right back, "I know, Genie. I love you too."

I want to cry.

I want to let it all out.

Years of being separated.

Years of feeling alone—but I hold it in, and I smile.

I always smile. Even through the pain.

I smile.

When she turns her head to face me, her eyes are glassy, and I swallow a lump in my throat. "Thank you for rescuing me."

I choke back all of my words and nod sharply.

"Let's do this and leave tonight. I'll have us home in five hours." I smile—again.

We have everything we need in the car anyway. I made sure she packed her belongings before we left. There's no way I'm taking her near that asshole ever again.

Her lips thin into a tight grin before something else flashes across her face. "Can I get the keys to the trunk?" She reaches her hand out, and I drop them into her upturned palm.

The cold air slaps me as we step out, and I lock my door the old-fashioned way since the car was built decades earlier.

When I look over the top of the car at my sister, her eyes are lowered to the side.

"Those flowers." She shakes her head before she circles to the trunk and opens it.

While she rummages through the contents, I glance down to what she was looking at.

There is no mistaking my beater in this city. I bought this car from a flower shop that went out of business last month, and you can't miss it—it's got large daisies and roses painted all over it.

It was all I could afford.

Genie shuts the trunk and joins me with nothing in her hands.

"Everything okay?" I ask.

"Yeah, just checking on our things. We need to get going. I texted the address a few minutes ago. She said she's coming." Genie tightens her thin coat around herself to keep the chill out, and I follow her across the street and down an alley.

My nerves settle a fraction when I realize we are meeting a *she* and not a *he*.

We approach an office building, and alarm bells go off in my mind when Genie pulls out a key and opens a back door in the loading area. I hold my question back. I don't want to stress her out any further.

The building looks like it isn't finished, or maybe it's being renovated, but at least it's warm. I follow her into the main area, where she unlocks the front door to the street before turning and walking down the hall.

She stops abruptly, then spins to look at me, and her expression catches me by surprise.

She looks lost. The sister I remember is gone, and I hope she's only hidden away while we get this done.

"You'll wait in here." She turns to what looks like an office and urges me through the doorway. "Hide if you need to, but don't let anyone see you no matter what. Do you understand?"

She's anxious all over again, and I nod, hoping not to push her any further. I step into the room, my own nerves firing on all cylinders, and she turns to walk further down the hall into the next room.

I stand still, waiting, staring at the hall for what feels like an hour when I finally hear the front door open, and it's just now I realize this office doesn't have a door on it yet.

I take five steps back into a corner and cloak myself in the shadows as a man walks by and glances into the room without stopping. There is no recognition on his face. I'm sure he hasn't seen me, and I release my breath in a deep sigh.

My sister's voice travels through the wall when a chill runs up my spine.

She said she was meeting a woman.

Panic grips my heart, and I take a step out of the shadows without thinking when a gunshot sucks the air out of the room.

I don't know if I screamed, but my hand is over my mouth as I take a step back into the corner and freeze, my body going numb.

Less than twenty seconds later, a second gunshot echoes in the empty building around me, and tears burst from my eyes in the silence.

Heavy footsteps thud into the hall and past the room I'm in without stopping.

I wasn't seen.

As soon as the front door closes, I run as fast as I can into the next room.

It's a larger, open area, but I find my sister right away. She's lying on the floor.

She looks like she's sleeping, but I know she's gone.

A pool of blood swells around her, and her vacant eyes stare up at the ceiling.

I reach for her hands. Everything slips away from me as I touch the mittens I just gave her to keep her warm.

I remember seeing a phone in the room I was hiding in, and I stand to hurry back to it when the front door opens again.

I waste no time. I can't be found here, so I run back to the only hiding spot I know.

A different man stops at the entrance to the room and looks in. I stay still in the shadows, knowing my life depends on it. He glances down the hall toward the other room and pauses before turning and heading toward Genie.

Taking a deep breath, I look around the area. The phone sits on the desk, just out of my reach, but it isn't plugged in. The cord is wrapped around the handset, and I'll make too much noise trying to set it up—if the lines are even working.

I consider using my own phone, but I know these things can be tracked now. I glance at the hall.

I have to assume more people are coming, and someone will eventually walk in here and find me.

I'm not ready to leave Genie like this. I have a couple of places to lie low until I figure out what to do.

Right now, I need to get out of here.

I remember seeing an emergency exit just before this room. If I run into the hall and back out, maybe I'll get away before anyone sees me.

I pad quietly to the office entrance and glance once down the hall toward the room where Genie is. My heart aches that I have to leave her here.

I didn't rescue her.

I hid in a corner while she was murdered.

I couldn't save her.

She needed me, and I let her down.

My emotions build to the point of explosion. I use my anger to push me around the corner, and I slam my body against the door.

The sound is loud.

I'm sure I was heard, but if I run fast enough I should be around the first corner before anyone gets out of the building.

The cold air hits me, cooling my tears, and I run away and into the night as fast as I can. Each building I pass and every alley I clear takes me closer to my car, and I jump in and start it up, peeling down the street without looking back.

Once I'm far enough away, I pull out my phone and send off a message. I'll find a place to hide out, then I'll leave town in a few days and go home.

Home.

The place where we should all feel safe and loved.

Genie doesn't get to go home.

Tears pour down my face, and I finally let myself sob. I want to hear my pain, and I cry and scream as I drive toward the little hole I'll hide in.

From there, I'll get a message to James and make my way back to him in Portland.

James was the one who told me not to come here.

He said Genie was mixed up with the wrong crowd and she was too far gone, but I know she wanted to come home.

I didn't listen to him. I waited until he went to work, then I snuck away and drove up here against his wishes. He's been texting me almost every hour since.

I wanted my family back, like it used to be before our mother died and we all got pulled apart. I barely remember her now. She wasn't present when she was alive, but I know she loved us. She put herself out there, worked twenty-hour days and did everything she could to keep us fed. Her life was a losing game, and she did just that. Then we all lost each other.

When my mother was gone, Genie filled her void. She made sure I ate and went to bed. She took care of me, and now I've let her down when she needed me most.

I love you, my little Harley.

I'll never hear that again.

2

COLE

*L*eaving my brothers to pick up the pieces and take care of Amara was the last thing I wanted to do, but I was needed at our businesses in Portland. If I didn't show my face, my father would find out, and he'd start asking questions.

We can't bring him in until we know more about what Lennox is up to, or he'll just call another family meeting and insist we sort our shit out.

My guy on the force in Seattle tells me the woman found in the office building is still listed as Jane Doe. No one has come forward to claim her body.

I would beat the information out of Steevers, but the guy disappeared into thin air after his woman was murdered. I'd rather see him lying dead on the ground. It was a cowardly thing to send her in his place. If I ever see him again, I'll make him pay for sacrificing her to settle his sins.

My mind circles back to Dagen's account of what he saw when he got to the address Amara gave him that night. My knee-jerk reaction is to discount his recollection that Lennox was there—it was dark, he was running on adrenaline—but I know he saw what he saw.

Dagen is the most levelheaded of all my brothers, myself included. I think it's because he got out of the family business early. He made the decision to go out on his own, and he was able to truly get out from under my father's thumb.

I don't know why we all didn't follow suit. I remember I had thought about going out on my own once, but some things had happened, and I got sucked back in.

As for my oldest brother standing over the girl's body? My jury is still out.

I know Lennox is capable of killing someone. I've seen him do it right in front of my own eyes, but that situation was different.

He's still my brother, and I know in his heart we are still his, but he put up a wall, and for some reason the three of us younger brothers all seemed to get tossed onto the other side of it.

I've checked in with the last of our companies and set myself up with some time off so I can head back to Seattle and relieve Dagen. Now I'm back at my penthouse with a bag of fast food, and I don't want to be here. I want to be back in Seattle, near my family.

Missing the monotony of a scheduled life is the first sign I'm burning out. These past few weeks have been one long ride on a crazy train. I haven't allowed myself the time to sit back and think about everything we've all been through.

Amara really put herself out there for Ryder, Sloane, and Henry, and I'm itching to get back to properly thank her.

The universe aligns with my thoughts, and my phone rings. Dagen's name registers on the call display.

"Hey, man." Wedging the phone between my shoulder and

my ear, I grab a plate from the cupboard and start serving my food. "Everything okay?"

"As good as can be expected. The nurse says the doctor is stopping sedation overnight. They expect Amara to wake up sometime tomorrow. Ryder is a hot mess about it all." His chuckle follows his words, and Ryder yells something at him in the background, making Dagen laugh harder before he stops himself with a deep breath. "Listen, the cops still have nothing on the woman, but our guys got a lead on her. It's not much, just a name, but I should have more soon. An auto body shop picked up footage of her parked outside of their store with someone else that night. I should have it for you by tomorrow. I'll text when it comes in."

I take a bite of my burger—it tastes dry and overcooked. The tough meat rolls around on my tongue, and it's a struggle to swallow it down. I could make a better meal strung out on speedballs. Not that I've ever touched the stuff.

"No. Leave it off our phones. Get the information together. I'm driving up tomorrow. I'm not needed here for a bit, and I'm getting antsy." I glance down at my meal, and my stomach turns. I package up my uneaten junk and toss the whole thing in the garbage.

"I'll let Ryder know to expect you. Hey, any word on Elia Lucciano?" Dagen asks.

"His health is about the same. Nothing's changed on my end."

The entire organization has been quiet since I saw them at Eros in Seattle. It's unsettling. It feels like the calm before the storm, and I don't like it when things aren't happening where I can see them. It means they are going on behind closed doors, and I don't like not being invited into the room.

Dagen's hummed response tells me he feels the same.

"Look, I'm going to go. I'll be there in the early afternoon. Call me if anything changes. If not, I'll see you tomorrow."

Dagen says his goodbyes, and I hang up, looking at my pathetic dinner in the trash.

I need to get out of Portland, but I'm not ready to be in Seattle. I pull out my laptop and look up some places for rent along my drive to our family home. A couple of remote listings pop up, and I pick the one farthest from the road. I need to be off the grid for a night.

I dial the number and ask about last-minute availability. The guy on the other end tells me it's free, and ten minutes later I've sent him the funds for one night and he's texted me instructions to access the place.

There are a couple of grocery stores and gas stations on the road out, so I pack a bag and make plans to pick up what I need on the way.

The farther out of town I get, the more my neck muscles seem to relax.

My people in Portland have been told I'm heading out for some time off, and Ryder isn't expecting me until tomorrow. Tonight is all mine, and I need the time to regroup.

The sun is setting when I pull my truck up to the little cabin. I'm missing my bike, but the weather took a turn for the worse about a week ago, so it's waiting for me at our parents' old house. If the skies are clear when I leave, I may trade my truck for the bike for my ride back to Portland.

The old guy on the phone was right: this place is as old school as you can get.

My cell toggled between one and no bars on the little

walkway leading to the front door, and there is no television or phone in the main room.

Five stars.

I love it already.

I chuckle to myself. Dagen would hate it here, which means I love it even more.

I drop my bag. It takes four steps to get to the bedroom. It's the only other door leading off the main room. A wooden chair sits in the corner. It's used as a nightstand beside a small-framed bed that looks like it's seen better days. From there, it's another three steps into the small bathroom, and I start heating water for a quick shower, following the instructions I saved from my welcome email before I lost service.

Once I'm set up, I return to the main room and start a fire to get the heat up before I freeze to death out here. The owners aren't big on lamps in the living area, so I light a few candles as well as one lantern before returning to the little light in the kitchen to prepare a decent meal.

I've been so busy lately that I haven't had time to cook, and I miss it. Owning a couple of restaurants has improved my skills in the kitchen, and I go to work pulling out pots and pans and making myself busy until it's time to get in the shower.

My beef is cut, seared, and cooking in its stew on the old woodstove, and I leave it to simmer before stripping down and taking a quick shower.

This bathroom is probably the smallest one I've been in in a long time. Since the shower has more space inside it than the bathroom does, I get right in. When I glance over my shoulder to close the door, I catch my reflection in the mirror, and the sight startles me.

I make every effort not to look at myself from this angle until I'm prepared to face what I see, but I'm in unfamiliar surroundings, and the faded scar across my back catches me off guard.

We've all been through so much that seeing this painful reminder of my own past doesn't affect me like it once did. Watching Amara almost die twice and seeing my own brother take a leap toward his own possible death to save her has given me a different perspective on life and the bullshit we've all survived to get to where we are.

The warm water is limited here, and I don't waste any more time gawking at myself.

As the water sprays over me, I take a deep breath and force my muscles to relax on the exhale.

I needed this.

Ryder and Lennox are the ones who run the family business. They're hands-on. Sure, I check in when I'm in Portland, but it isn't my thing.

I'm more of a people person. I'm personable with the staff when I want to be, and I'm the family enforcer when I need to be.

Spinning to reach for a towel, I push my responsibilities out of my head. I came out here to check out for a while, and this is where my head goes?

No. I'm not thinking about some nice piece of ass, not the woman who is waiting for me, not a night out with the guys. It always goes back to my family and my work.

That's disappointing.

The heat from the fireplace is already warming the small cabin up nicely, and I decide to leave my shirt off.

The fire is starting to die down, and I add another log, choosing birch because it'll burn longer than the logs I started the fire with. The fire crackles back to life, and the smell of my dinner hits my nose.

I haven't had a decent meal since I was at Ryder's, and I'm

looking forward to this. I break apart a fresh loaf of bread and butter it before spooning some of my stew into a bowl and sitting down at the little table to eat.

Food always tastes better when you make it yourself—at least mine does. I eat in silence, checking my phone now and then for bars. There are none.

I'm finished with my last bite and about to go for seconds when a flash of light catches my attention. I don't remember seeing any other cabins up this road, and I move to the front window, blowing out candles and dimming the lantern to darken the room as I cross it.

It's too dark to grab a good description of anything outside, but I can tell from the shadows and headlights that a car has pulled in near my truck.

My first instinct should be to go for my gun, but no one knows I'm here except for the old guy I spoke to last minute, and I wonder if he's driven out to check on me.

That theory is dismissed when the person approaching drops something, and a woman mutters under her breath as she picks it up and stuffs it into her bag.

When she straightens, my dick decides to follow suit, twitching at the sight. The porch light illuminates her features, and she looks over her shoulder toward my truck parked right beside hers before she turns back to the cabin.

My attitude shifts to surly as I take her in.

What the hell is someone like her doing all the way out here, in the middle of the night, without cell service?

By the looks of her, she's contemplating her life choices and wondering the same thing as she shifts in her stance. She's unaware she is being watched.

Lowering the paper bag she's carrying to the ground, she drops her backpack off her shoulder and unzips it, pulling out a folded map. Carefully, she opens it, looking it over and I watch, amused, as she glances from the cabin to her car, then my truck, then back to the map. She trails her finger along the paper as though she's retracing her steps. Then she folds it up, places it in her backpack, and lifts the paper bag back into her arms.

This is the most fun I've had watching anything for a long time. Hiding in the shadows, watching her cautiously approach, is giving off some serious prey vibes, and my predator is eating them up.

She takes a step toward the door, and I move to my side of it when I hear her foot fall on the first step.

"Hello?" Her sweet voice stops me dead in my tracks.

How long has it been since—it's been a while.

I don't have trouble hooking up—I never have—but I've been distracted.

Watching this woman now, I realize how much I've neglected my own needs.

I don't want to scare her off, but at the same time I'm not ready for her to decide to leave, so I unlock the door.

She brushes her light blond hair off her face when she sees me, and her eyes round as she stumbles for something to say.

Her awkwardness lands deep inside my chest, and my mood shifts on a dime. Tonight is shaping up to be even better than I could have imagined. Unless, of course, she's the wife of the old man I spoke to on the phone.

I glance down.

No wedding ring.

Still promising.

I lean against the door frame. "And who might you be?"

3

HARLOW

Today was the day to run.

I've been lying low for a few days since Genie was murdered, and I'm starting to outstay my welcome. Making the last-minute decision to leave wasn't ideal, but if I stayed for one more day, I'm sure I'd be dead.

James heard through his connections that some crime family was looking for me, and it's only a matter of time before they ask the right person for a name that will match whatever photo they have of me or my sister.

There's only one person I trust, and I need to get myself out of the city and down to his place. The guys I'm staying with will eventually catch wind of why I'm there, and they would give me up if the price was right. That's just the way it goes.

The people I know don't come from money, and most benefit by using each other as currency.

I have no allies here.

Three minutes was all it took for me to pack up my most valued possessions. Then I was on the road and heading out of the city.

It absolutely sucked balls that I was driving out of town in a car with bright flowers painted all over it, but I had no other choice. James told me to stay away from buses and trains, and I don't have the proper ID to board a plane or cross the border into Canada.

When you witness the murder of your half sister and overhear gossip that some people are asking questions, you don't stick around to hem and haw over what kind of car you're driving.

The plan is to get to James, then give him the car to break down or sell.

I'm still nervous about going to my brother's place right away. I don't want to bring any of this to him, so I decide to pull over and see if there are any places I can stay overnight that are out of the city. This way, I can make sure no one is following me.

Now, driving down this dark road, I'm starting to think I should have stayed closer to town. An almost-deserted little town an hour and a half out of the city should be far enough away from curious eyes. Plus, it was the first house to respond with a vacancy on the rental site.

I sent an email through the website and heard back about ten minutes later. The woman told me her place is secluded and off the main road. She said it was rarely rented. She mentioned that she and her husband are separated, but she still knew the code and offered it to me at a discount price because I was so last minute. I kind of think she did it to piss the guy off, but beggars can't be choosers, so I jumped on it since my cash is running low.

As my vehicle bumps along the old dirt road, I'm wondering when the last time someone would have rented this place was. I don't imagine it has many amenities—like soap— but I only need it for the night, then I'll be gone for good.

As I pull into the parking spot, I reach for the map I picked up at my last stop and turn the dome light on to take a last look. It's less than a one-minute walk straight up the path, and the keys are in a lockbox near the door.

Sounds easy enough.

I hoist my backpack onto my shoulder and grab the few groceries I picked up at a gas station on the outskirts of the city before shoving my wallet and phone into the glove compartment. There's no internet up here anyway, and I don't need my ID any longer.

Harlow Stinton won't exist after tonight.

As soon as I get to James, I'll ask him to help me with a new identity. Then I can ditch this awful car and disappear for a while.

I turn to look around before I lock up the car. That's when I see it, and I'm not sure how I didn't notice it when I first pulled in.

There's a truck parked along the tree line.

When I spoke to the lady about the property today, she said it was isolated, and worry sets in. I'm twenty-five minutes past a little town in the middle of nowhere. Cell service depends on which way the wind blows, and there is no internet access for miles.

I slide my brother's old pocketknife out of the glove compartment, jam it into the front pocket of my jeans, then take one last look around.

I try to settle my thoughts; maybe the truck is broken down. No one knows I'm here, so it's not like anything could be planned.

My nerves tingle as I lock my car and follow the path toward the cabin, careful to step over the roots and rocks sticking out of the dirt.

A roll of toilet paper I lifted from the gas station bathroom drops out of my paper bag and rolls a few feet before I grab it and jam it in with my groceries. Then I keep walking toward my place for the night.

As the rickety little wood cottage comes into view, I stop dead in my tracks.

Someone is here.

Smoke billows slowly out of the chimney and lingers in the air against the still night.

Shit.

I pause in front of the little cabin and set my bag down to take out the map one last time. There is just enough light from the full moon to see that I must be at the right cabin. How many derelict old cabins could there be in this area?

Stuffing the map back in my backpack, I move to the front stairs. As I near the cabin, the ghost of a shadow in the dimly lit interior draws my attention. When I take the first step onto the porch, the cottage creaks its age and the shadow stops moving.

Clearly the person on the other side of the door wasn't expecting company.

Panic sets in, and I call out a quick hello. I'm in the mountains, hours from any town that is named on a map, and I don't want to risk being shot for trespassing.

A long pause, then the floor inside groans as the person moves to the door. With the click of the lock, light from the fireplace pours into the yard as a man fills the doorway, and I swallow hard.

Standing in front of me is a showered and stunningly muscular man. I know because he isn't wearing a shirt, and my brain temporarily stops working as I process what my mouth should be saying next.

Embarrassment flushes my cheeks as I listen to myself stutter out a few vowels, then his soft chuckle snaps me back to the present.

"And who might you be?" His voice is kind but firm.

His light hair is disheveled and a strand falls from his head to hang at his ear. His full lips smile at me through his beard, and I suppress the overwhelming desire to ramble.

I fail.

"I'm, uh—" Then, catching myself, I recover quickly. "Hi, sorry. I'm Nicole. My friends call me Nikki." Reaching out my hand, I smile, tamping the nerves rising in my gut. I hope I've covered well enough. There's no way I'm leaving a trail out of the city.

Standing his ground, he extends his hand and grasps mine, but he doesn't shake it. Instead, he holds it steady in his grip. His finger pushes against the inside of my wrist, drawing circles over my skin.

For such a slight gesture, it sure sends shockwaves to all the right places.

"Pleasure. What brings you out here tonight, Nicole?"

Looking into his eyes, I get the impression he's waiting for my answer before he decides what to do with me, and my stomach tightens at the thought of what I'd like him to do with me.

His question catches me off guard.

I hadn't anticipated talking to anyone until I reached James. I hadn't prepared any cover stories, and now I need to come up with something fast and stick with it.

"I emailed earlier. Spoke to the lady who owns this place. I'm on my way to a funeral—um—up in Canada. I've been on the road for eight hours already. It was a last-minute thing. I just couldn't make it the whole way." As I finish rambling, he stays still, watching me speak, but he isn't quite making eye contact. His eyes drift a little lower, to my lips maybe.

"Huh. Well, I think I know what happened then. I spoke to the owner today as well, probably your lady's husband, and he told me it was also available. I'm driving to Olympia to help my brother—move." As he finishes, he squeezes my hand once before letting it go, and I step back, unsure of what this means for my accommodations for the night.

"So, um, then..." I trail off as the light from the fireplace catches on a drop of water trailing over his hard abdomen.

It is suddenly warm out here.

I clutch my pathetic excuse for dinner close to my chest as the most delicious scent fills my nostrils. It smells like a damn restaurant in there.

I take an impulsive step toward the door.

He did get here first, and the road is fairly deserted. I should drive down the dirt road a bit and park for the night. It's not like I've never slept in my car before.

"I'm sorry, Nicole. You'll have to excuse me. I just got out of the shower. It was a little bit of a process heating the water and everything. Seems like you've been driving awhile. If you'd like a shower, I can heat up some more water. It'll just take a while to get it going." The man at the door takes a step backward into the room and raises his arm for me to enter, and I take a glance around him into the cabin.

It's really warm here.

I shudder as the cold refuses to let go of my limbs, but I don't step forward.

Sensing my apprehension, he continues to face me but walks backward into the room, then he lights two candles and a lantern before returning his attention to me. "I've forgotten my manners. I'm Cole."

I smile, and he grabs his shirt off the back of the couch and covers himself up. The cloth of his shirt clings to his damp body.

His body isn't the only moist thing in this room.

I push down my thoughts. Those are for another time.

Standing at the door, I take in the small space. There is only one door off of the living area, and the write-up online indicated it only had one bedroom and a bathroom.

So this is it.

A couch sits in the middle of the room, facing a beautiful stone fireplace. The little kitchen has a large wood-burning stove, a tiny sink, a fridge, and some cupboards. A small table with two chairs separates the area from the rest of the cabin.

As my eyes trail into the kitchen, I see a pot on the stove, and my stomach growls.

I haven't eaten all day.

"There's no point in you leaving now. It's too dark out there, and I'd never forgive myself if your car broke down in the middle of nowhere so late at night. There's a bed and a couch, and you look a little hungry." His voice drops at the end of his sentence.

I turn quickly to see his eyes have lowered as he scans the length of my body, sending goosebumps across my arms.

"I am—hungry, I mean." My face warms, and I'm sure it's flushed red in embarrassment. By the look on his face, it's noticeable. He licks his lips and walks past me, brushing gently against my arm.

This is a man who walks with the confidence of someone who knows what he's packing.

"Great. I have some stew left, and there are a couple of buns on the table. I'm just going to set the heater on that shower." He pulls out a chair at the table for me to sit, and it isn't lost on me how easily I am following along and doing as I'm told.

As I watch him leave the room, I take a moment to let my brain catch up to my situation.

It's now that I notice I've removed my shoes without realizing it. I'm more exhausted than I thought.

It's been a long day. I've been running on fumes for hours, and my adrenaline is still pumping furiously through my body. I'm anxious and high-strung. I just hope I don't look like a hot mess on the outside.

I straighten myself in my seat as his footsteps pad along the worn wood floors of the cabin.

"Where did you get this food? All I got was some cereal and those chips." I point at my paper bag now sitting on the counter. "May I have a glass?" I ask, glancing at the half-full bottle of wine on the table.

His small grin turns into a big smile as he hooks a finger along the side of the bag and looks inside. "I got my groceries from a store on the way and made this stew from scratch. I used the wine in it. Cooking is kind of a hobby of mine." He places a bowl in front of me when I realize the amazing smell isn't because I'm hungry. It looks like something I would order in a fancy restaurant—there are actual freshly chopped herbs floating in it.

"Wow. That looks amazing." I look up as he places a buttered bun beside my bowl, then turns to grab the bottle. He pours each of us a glass and takes the seat across from me, and I smile to myself.

I haven't sat down to a real meal in a while. The last time was over the holidays, when James and I went all out and bought the smallest turkey we could find.

It feels good to be taken care of.

The thought makes me sad.

It's been so long since I lost my mom. Now I'm twenty-six, and it is just me and my brother, and I'm about to leave him behind too. I'm exchanging a lonesome existence for complete seclusion, and this small kindness is not something I'm used to.

I take my first spoonful. I should have taught myself to cook, but buying the cheap, ready-made stuff was always easier.

This is the best meal I've had in a long time, and I groan between spoonfuls.

"You doing okay?" My eyes snap to his, and I realize I must have been stuffing my face in front of him.

I'm close to being out of breath.

"I—I'm sorry. I was hungrier than I thought," I stammer, reaching for my wine. Nervous, I take a bigger gulp than I probably should and finish my glass in three swallows. Taking a chance, I motion my glass to the almost empty bottle of red, and he straightens in his seat.

"I think that's enough wine for you tonight. You'll have water," he states as he slides a small bottle of water in my direction. I'm taken aback by his authority, by how I'm reacting on the inside.

I think I like it.

I swallow as I consider my words. Then I nod, crack open the water, and drink it down. "Thank you."

At my sheepish appreciation, he smiles, and a comfortable silence settles between us.

I use the seconds to take him in. His shirt still clings to his body, and his dark blond hair clumps in waves, as it is still drying from the shower. Dropping my eyes to his full lips, I lick my own as I imagine how soft they must feel.

What the hell is happening to me?

I'm fleeing for my life, and my hormones have decided to just—what—get some?

"You're welcome, Nikki. Can I call you that? We're friends now, right?" The seductive tone of his voice tells me there is something else, but I like hearing him call me by the fake name that only my pretend friends call me by.

"Yeah." I nod, unsure of what to say. Then my eyes drop back to his lips, and I watch them move.

"So, what do you think, Nikki?" I look back up to him, now

aware that I wasn't paying attention. I missed part of the conversation, and I don't know how to recover.

"Can you repeat that?" I offer a guilty shrug, and his smile widens even more. This guy must know what he's doing to me. I mean, he reeks of hotness, and he has to know it.

He's covered in assurance from head to toe, and his certainty in himself is giving me butterflies. I feel completely off my game right now, and it's been so long since I've been with anyone. I imagine my awkwardness is painted all over my face, and there isn't anything I can do to hide it.

"I was suggesting you stay. We both need a place to sleep. You can take the bed in there." He points to the only other door in the little cabin. "The couch is rather comfortable. I can sleep out here—if you choose." He lets his words linger, and I get the feeling there is another offer on the table besides separate sleeping arrangements.

COLE

I thought I wanted time alone and in my own head, but now I'm thinking about spending tonight buried deep between her legs.

The back and forth with Nikki is intoxicating, and I'm already addicted to her company.

This girl wears everything on her sleeve, and it's nice to be around someone who either isn't afraid of me or who doesn't know who I am.

I'm not a victim. I use others just the same as they use me, but this woman is—I don't know what she is yet, but I want to find out.

I wonder if she knows her cheek twitches up in a smile even though I can tell she's trying to hide her interest when I flirt with her.

She got the gist when I suggested she might have a second choice besides me sleeping on the couch, alone. I could tell by the subtle double take she did when I finished talking.

Her little twitch tells me she really wants to know what else

I have in mind, but I get the feeling she's too sweet to outright ask.

It's okay. I'm enjoying this little dance we're doing.

"Sure. That sounds good." She stands as she answers me and glances around the table, busying herself by clearing her bowl, and I rise to meet her and take the dishes from her.

"I'll get those. You've been driving all day. Let me take care of you." I make a point of covering her hands with my own for a second longer than is necessary. Not much fazes me, and I'll stand here holding this connection all night if it means I get to watch her squirm like this. I decide to offer her an out—this time. "Have a seat on the couch. I'll soak these, then I'll get the fireplace going again."

I turn around before she responds, letting her know my words aren't a suggestion, and she turns and obediently makes her way across the small area.

I wish I had more time here. Nikki doesn't seem like the kind of woman you just walk away from, and it's too bad we are both expected elsewhere in the morning.

By this time tomorrow, she'll be in a different country.

She seems like a sweet girl. Someone I would never meet in my line of work or with the company I keep, and I wonder for a moment if she's better off not knowing anything else about me.

This time tomorrow, I'll be back in my role as enforcer. I'll be hunting down some random woman, probably a junkie. I can't bring someone else into this life I've made for myself, not when everything is so volatile.

Watching Ryder risk his own life for Amara nearly broke me. Part of me thinks he should have stayed away a while longer. It would have kept her safe, but then we wouldn't be any closer to finding out who killed Grayson.

While Ryder and Grayson were the closest, he was my friend too.

"So, Nikki. I'm sorry to hear about your friend. How did they die?" Yeah, I'm using the nickname her friends use. I have a feeling, before the night is through, I'll be pushing for more.

I relax into the couch beside her, stretching one arm over the back and angling my body so I face her.

The expression on her face falters at the mention of her friend.

"Oh, um—it was a car accident. A drunk driver hit her. It was—unexpected." She combs a loose strand of hair off her face.

"Shit. I'm sorry." I feel like I want to give her a hug and comfort her, but I don't know her well enough to offer, so I sit and give her room to share what she wants.

"We grew apart over the years." She shifts in her seat. "What do you do, Cole?" She changes the subject.

Noted—she doesn't want to talk about it.

I prop my hand against my head and relax into the couch with her, lightening the mood with a smile. When I meet her eyes, something flashes between us. Maybe it's an attraction that only I feel, but I hope it isn't.

"I own a delivery company. Nothing extravagant, I know." I'm not sure when I decided to start lying. Maybe it was when I realized I shouldn't mess with Nikki after tonight.

She reminds me of a pretty flower, and I want to pick her. I want to pick her so bad, but as soon as you pick a flower and take it home—especially to my home—it starts to wither and die.

She's best left growing in the garden, so I take control of the conversation and lead her away.

"Do you have a boyfriend? Married?" Judging by the lack of a ring, I'm assuming no one has scooped her up yet.

"No, none of that. I'm single." She struggles to look me in

the eye, and I smile to hide all of the wicked thoughts going through my mind.

"Interesting. There's something we have in common. Between my business and helping my family, I've been too busy to devote a lot of time to—something else." When I answer, she clears her throat and takes a deep breath.

She doesn't exhale.

Instead, she attempts to busy herself in the silence. Looking around for something to occupy herself, she lifts her backpack up from the floor.

An old teddy bear falls out between us, and she gasps in embarrassment as she grabs him and attempts to stuff him away.

I don't allow it.

I slide closer and reach over her to get a better look at him.

"This yours?" I ask, scanning her face.

"Y-yes. It was from my mom. She isn't around anymore. I mean, she passed away when I was little."

"I'm sorry to hear that. He's cute. I like his blue ribbon." Her eyes snap up to mine, and she scans my features. I hold my grin tight to tell her I'm not making fun of her. I think it's sweet she has something like that to remind herself.

"The ribbon is purple." She draws her thumb along the thread around the bear's neck before straightening his tie.

I gloss over her response, not sharing that I'm color blind. I've never shared that with anyone.

Growing up, my father would have viewed this information as a weakness, and weaknesses are to be exploited.

I push the thoughts of my family away once more when she hugs the little toy to her chest before securing him into her backpack and setting it down.

A foreign feeling hits me when I think that I'd like to take the place of her bear for one night and comfort her.

I lean forward, and my finger trails the opening to her bag. "What else do you have in there?" I lift it, testing its weight without opening it. "It's heavy."

Her smile turns sly. "That's because of my personal bodyguard." Opening the bag once more, she digs in and pulls out what looks like—

"Is that a brick?"

She blushes, shoving it back inside. "Yeah. It turns my little bag into a flail, but it's heavy to carry around." She rubs her shoulders to indicate the pain, and my gaze falls to her slender neck.

She must sense the tension between us.

She shifts nervously away from me when her face contorts. Then she jerks back, bracing her hands against the couch with a pained look on her face. Her yelp makes my stomach lurch with worry.

"Are you okay?" My tone is commanding but controlled, and I shift away from her to find blood soaking through a cut in the thigh area of her jeans.

I follow her eyes, looking down to the couch. Lying open, a pocketknife sits on the cushion between us.

"My knife must have fallen out of my pants. I forgot I put it in my pocket. Um—do you have anything to stop this?" Her hand clasps around the growing crimson patch spreading through the fabric of her pant leg, and she looks up to me, her eyes set in panic.

I move to my own bag and grab my medical kit.

As I near her, she reaches out her hand to take my supplies, and I pull them into my chest. I don't know what she thinks she's going to do, but I'm the one who is going to take care of this.

"I'll help you. Undo your pants and slide them down to your knees. This might sting a bit." I open the little box in my hands and go back to my kit, looking for something to disinfect her wound.

"It's okay. I can do it myself. I'll just go to the bathroom." She keeps her hand outstretched, and I look at her like she's offering to curl my hair.

The need to take care of this for her is overwhelming, but that's something I'll have to revisit long after she's gone.

I shake my head. "Leave your underwear on. Pull your pants to your knees. I'm going to stop the bleeding." I break eye contact and end our discussion. It wasn't much of a discussion anyway. Not when she's hurt and I've decided I will take care of her.

She freezes for a moment, and I continue looking for everything I need.

A moment later, she shifts back on the cushion, unbuttons her jeans, and slides them down to her knees, just like I told her to. Her acceptance makes me happy, and I step toward her with a napkin to put some pressure on the cut.

I'm so close to her that I smell the wine on her breath as she winces. I consider warning her again about the pain that is heading her way then decide against it. Her body deflates, and she relaxes near me, and I wait for her to release a deep sigh before I dab the disinfectant on.

I know this shit stings; I've used it on myself before, and her face crumples in pain before she grabs my shirt and buries her face in my chest, screaming into the fabric.

Now I wrap my free arm around her, and she allows my embrace.

"Shh. It's okay. I've got you. That's just something to clean it out. It's not deep. I'll get this bandage on you, and you'll be fine."

She holds her head against my chest as I finish bandaging

her up. When she looks up again, her face is red and her eyes are glossy with tears, but she isn't crying.

This one is strong.

"Nikki, I gotta tell you, you are lucky I was here to help you. You came up here all by yourself, carrying nothing but a teddy bear and a pocketknife that you ended up stabbing yourself with, and you had no medical kit. And, to top that off, you only have stale cereal and chips to eat. I have never met anyone as—*intriguing* as you." I chuckle as I finish with her leg.

"You're right. I'm lucky I'm not dead." I pause at her admission as a chill runs through me and I don't know why. "How did I ever make it this far in life?"

The answer comes to me instantly, as though it was always sitting there, waiting for me to find it: "You need someone to take care of you."

I pause everything else I'm working on to look at her, and she grins before meeting my gaze. Then her smile fades. I'm no longer joking, and I enforce my initial statement. "You do."

The room around us fades out of focus as we sit in silence, staring at each other, and I swear I hear my heart beat in time to the heavy thudding in my chest.

This is a new feeling for me.

"Um—" Her eyes flit around the room. She looks like she's trying to find something to talk about when I stop her cold, placing my hand over hers.

"Did you like it when I fed you, Nikki?" I decide to go for the direct approach. It's getting late, and don't want to dance around anything else tonight.

"I—yes." Her confession is a whisper.

My thoughts go to a dark place.

We're adults, and we're alone, and there is nothing wrong with taking what we want from each other before we go our separate ways tomorrow.

"And did you enjoy having me dress your cut?" I already know the answer. Her breathing deepened as I worked on her leg, and it wasn't because she was in pain.

I feel her desire as though it's my own.

She nods.

I'm leading her along a path I'm pretty sure she wants to follow me down.

Tomorrow is another day, and I want this pretty thing in my bed tonight. I'll back off if it isn't what she wants, but the way she's looking at me is telling me to keep going.

So I do.

"I like taking care of you, Nikki." I wrap one hand around her wrist and turn her palm up. My fingers draw little circles over the soft flesh along the inside of her forearm, and she shudders in my grip. "Do you want me to take care of you tonight?"

5

HARLOW

Blinking quickly I try to clear my throat, but nothing happens. My mouth has gone dry.

The same vowels I started speaking in tongue when I first saw him in the doorway blubber out of my mouth.

Do I want him to take care of me tonight?

Hell yes! I do.

"I. Uh—"

I do want to let him.

Just once.

One night.

My whole life has been me taking care of myself.

I want to feel something other than fear and loneliness.

"I really do."

Did that sound desperate? It probably did.

"Good." His eyes stay on mine, and it's now I realize I'm sitting beside him with my pants around my knees. Before I fix my situation, he's off the couch and moving toward the only door in the cabin aside from the one that leads outside. "I'll be one minute. I'm going to check on the shower; I need to wash that blood off you. Remove your pants."

As soon as he's gone, I do a quick check around the room as though I'm searching for something—probably my common sense, or my shame. Nope, apparently I've lost them both.

I stand and push my pants down the rest of the way, then I step out of them and rest them over the couch. I lift my backpack in front of me, hiding my bare legs.

The smile growing across Cole's lips as he enters the room tells me my attempt at modesty is amusing to him, but I feel secure right now, so I decide to stay still.

"You're not going to hit me with that weapon of yours?" He points to my bag, and I shake my head. His gaze travels farther down my legs. "Cute socks." His grin turns mischievous.

I step on one of them to pull my feet out when his smile falls from his face.

"Leave them on—Socks."

I'm pretty sure my nipples just pebbled under my shirt at my new nickname.

He moves to the window, blows out the stub of a candle, and then does the same to a second one that's sitting on a bookshelf. Then he turns to walk toward me. Stopping a few feet away, he lifts the lantern off the table then reaches out his free hand toward me.

"Come."

I take a quick moment to examine him. We are obviously attracted to each other, and tomorrow morning we are heading in opposite directions. He knows this as well as I do, but I can't help the gnawing feeling that I'm not being completely honest. I feel like I'm the one taking advantage of him, but I want tonight desperately.

He's better off not knowing me anyway.

Genie died, and soon whoever killed her will be looking for

me because I saw something I shouldn't have. They've probably already been to our apartment.

I can't bring Cole into this no matter how lonely I am.

But as long as he believes he's with Nicole who is heading up to Canada, nothing will happen to him, so one night before I disappear won't hurt anyone.

I want to know what it feels like to be taken care of in this way. It's been so long, and there isn't one good person in the world right now who wants to be with me like this.

Reaching out my hand, a firm tug sets me in line behind him as he leads me into the bedroom.

Cole sets the lantern on a dresser before turning silently toward me. He takes my pack from me and places it on the floor beside the bed, then focuses his attention back on me as he moves his hands to his shirt, pulling it off over his head and exposing his chest to me again. It is even more impressive this time around because now I know it's mine for tonight.

"You can touch me." His voice is soft, almost comforting, and I trail my fingers over the ink on his hard chest then down to his rigid abdomen, stopping just shy of his jeans. His body feels hot to the touch, but I can't tell if it's from the shower or something else.

As I pull my hand back, his hands move to the buttons on my shirt. Undoing them one by one, he takes his time, stopping in between as I watch his eyes drop down my body as each new button is opened.

When the last button is free, he glides his hand up my body and over my shoulders, releasing me from my shirt, and I sigh involuntarily as his eyes roam over me.

He turns me so my back is to him, and his hands tug at the hook on my bra. After one soft pull, I spill out as his hands cover my shoulders and turn me back to face him.

As though they were always his, he cups the heaviness of

my breasts, caressing one, then the other, before pinching my nipple and drawing a moan from my mouth.

This makes him smile.

"You're very beautiful, Socks." His eyes stare into mine as his fingers move over my skin, and my nipples peak, sending a tingling sensation further down into my body.

I rub my feet together.

I like his nickname for me.

Speechless, I watch him dip his head over my left breast, and the warmth of his tongue over my areola causes me to reach out for him to hold my balance.

"Do you like it when I take care of you, Nikki?" His voice is low, and I need to focus to hear his words.

In my head, I imagine what he would sound like saying my real name. Just once, asking me, *Do you like it when I take care of you, Harlow?*

Standing back up, he watches my face as he continues to pinch my nipple between his thumb and forefinger.

I forgot to answer him.

"Yes."

"I want to hear you say you need me. Say, *I need you to take care of me, Cole.*" His voice is soft, coaxing, and I want more than anything to please him.

"I need you to take care of me, Cole," I repeat obediently and finish with a soft gasp as his fingers pinch my sensitive nipples again.

The pressure building under his touch drives me into a space I've never visited before, and the outside world slips away.

As far as I'm concerned, it can stay away.

"Hmm." He doesn't share the rest of his thought as he takes my hand and leads me toward the bathroom.

As he walks in front of me, the ridges of his muscles catch

my eye. Then I pause without thinking as my gaze settles on an old scar across his back.

Turning to face me, he doesn't give any impression he's surprised at my reaction. His calm voice soothes me. "Are you okay?"

"Um, yes. Your b-back," I stammer, feeling superficial. His scar doesn't bother me, but I imagine he experienced a lot of pain.

"Long time ago. All healed." Then he pauses, and his eyes roam across my face as he continues, "You know, we all have scars. Mine are just out in the open." Then, stepping into me and gripping my upper arms so I can't back away, he says, "I'd like you to show me your scars, Nikki."

My breath catches in my throat. He would run for the hills if he saw my scars right now, and I don't know how to answer him when he turns and pulls me into the bathroom.

The room is clean, but it was clearly made for one person at a time. We squeeze around each other, and he places me where he wants me.

"You're probably not used to showers like this, so I'm going to clean your leg and wash your hair first in case we run out of hot water." I grin like a little girl in front of him as my mind wanders to what we're going to do if there is still hot water left after he's cleaned me up.

And just as quickly as my smile came, it leaves in a wave of heady lust as my mouth drops open at the same time he drops his pants, exposing himself to me.

His reality pushes my fantasy of him down the stairs as his cock bobs up in front of him, and I feel awkwardly inexperienced as he casually steps to me and kneels to pull my underwear down, carefully avoiding my self-inflicted stab wound.

"Does it hurt?" His eyes meet mine, and I huff out a sigh.

Of course it doesn't hurt.

This is the best thing that's happened to me in as long as I can remember and—

"Your cut. Does it hurt?" Clearly, I was supposed to know what he was talking about and answer him the first time.

"Oh. Not really."

Smiling to himself, he taps my ankle with his finger. I brace myself on his broad shoulders while I step out of my panties for him. I lift my eyes to look straight ahead while I wait for him to stand, but he doesn't.

I'm almost too nervous to look back down.

Almost.

Dropping my eyes, I only see the top of his head. His face is a foot away from my center, and he's paused. His delay is draining my confidence, and I take a half step back toward the shower.

"Don't move. Not until I tell you to. Do you understand?" His low voice sends a shiver through my body.

"Yes." I swallow hard and will myself to stay still. I'm in only my fuzzy socks; the rest of my naked self is on full display.

"You're so good," he murmurs to himself as his fingers graze along my calf.

His attention on my body grants me some time to take him in.

As his hands move over my skin, goosebumps grow under his touch, and my nipples strain in anticipation. His shoulders are solid and muscular, matching the rest of his upper body, and I want to run my fingers through his hair, but I've been told not to move so I don't know if that would count as—

"Ungh. Oh, mmmm—" My train of thought leaves as quickly as my senses do when his finger gently parts my folds and slides toward my clit.

I move my gaze to him. He's shifted his focus, and he's

watching my face as I begin to fall apart around him. His lips are parted in concentration, and a dizzy rush hits me. My equilibrium shifts, and I worry I might fall over when he gently pushes me back a step until I am resting against the shower door.

Placing one strong hand on my stomach, he holds me still as he continues sliding his fingers along my sensitive areas. I'm sure my face no longer holds any composure as my hips wriggle with him.

The silence around us anchors me. I have nothing else to pay attention to. I have no questions to answer. I am only watching and feeling him take command of my body.

Slowly, he drops his head to one side, his eyes still on mine when his finger circles my opening, and I know I'm already wet.

As he drops his eyes down, he groans to himself as he pushes one finger inside me, and my legs relax, further opening my body to him.

Dropping my head back against the shower door with a thud, I no longer have control over my unnecessary appendages as all of my senses swirl around the rhythm of his finger gliding in and out of me.

"So good." He's become a man of few words now, and it doesn't matter. Who needs words when he's got all of the right actions? "I want you really dirty before you get in the shower, Nikki. I want you to come for me. Keep your eyes on me the whole time." His commanding tone sends a tingle into my core, and my stomach pulls tight as my hips jerk with the thrust of his finger.

He slides a second finger in and continues to push deep inside of me. My body twitches each time he hits my sensitive areas, and he commits each of them to memory, hitting them over and over.

His eyes move between mine and his hands, and I don't look away. Each time he glances up, his stare is more primal than the last, further driving me toward the end that's rushing toward me as I whimper uncontrollably.

"Y-you're gonna make me—n-no—yup—I'm coming." There's no stopping what's about to hit me. When he raises his eyes to look at me one last time, I swear I see a fire burning behind them.

He licks his lips hungrily, and a carnal sneer grows across his face as he pushes his head between my legs, wrapping his lips around my swollen clit and sucking hard.

Fireworks zap across my vision, and the room around me blurs as I choke out my orgasm and boldly clench my fingers into his damp hair to hold him to me.

My entire body shakes around him as the most powerful orgasm I've ever experienced continues its attack in waves.

"I told you to keep your eyes open." His words, muffled from between my legs, startle me as I come down from my release, and I shoot my eyes open in shock. There are soft chuckles against my clit that send an aftershock rippling through my body. "You'll do better next time."

6

HARLOW

I've only ever had one orgasm at a time, and this one sent me spiraling. I'm surprised I'm still standing on my own.

Then I notice I'm not.

Strong arms are holding me in place at my hips, and Cole slowly releases his grip as he tests the sturdiness of my legs.

He stands, sliding his body flush against mine and pinning me to the flimsy door behind me.

Our height difference is evident. Cole towers at least a half a foot taller than my five-and-a-half-foot frame, and his body could easily wrap around mine.

I allow myself to wish, only for a moment, that this was the life I had instead of the one I'm running from.

Wrapping one hand around me and pulling my body into him without a word, he opens the door and leans into the shower to turn it on. Drops rain out of the showerhead, but there is no real pressure.

Testing the water once with his own hands, he lifts me into

the shower then fills the doorframe with his body. Turning briefly to pick up some soap, he begins to lather his hands up. Then he trails his fingers around my body, washing away my sins—and hopefully clearing the path for some more.

My breath catches once as his fingers remind me of the cut on my leg, then I settle as the pain dulls.

"Thank you for taking care of me, Cole." I speak into the water pouring around me, and his hands temporarily freeze in place before continuing on their path.

"I take very good care of my things, Socks." He leaves his words to linger around me.

He's figuratively testing the water by taking another step, and I don't want this to end.

I want to be his, even if it's only for tonight.

I relax my shoulders and push my body back into him.

His nearness comforts me.

Taking my movement as a sign to continue, he brushes his fingers under my chin, lifting my face up and out of the water.

The scent of citrus fills my nose as he works up a lather on my head. First he combs the shampoo into my hair, then he massages my scalp as I lean my back against his chest and lull into his control.

My head nods and bobs gently as he washes my hair. Then, turning me to face him, he lifts my chin again to angle my head under the water and washes the suds away.

His face has softened from before; he's become more of my keeper now, and his smile is soft as his eyes scan my head, probably looking for places he's missed.

I brazenly reach out for him and pull him into the shower with me. I'm pretty sure I'm clean now. We still have hot water left, and I'm not going to waste another drop. I want to feel his skin on mine.

His hand juts out to brace himself in the shower as he

settles against my body. I rise onto the tips of my toes and open my legs, shifting my hips so the apex of my thighs is wrapped gently around his thick cock.

I slowly rock my hips back then forth, and his tip glides between my thighs, followed by his hard shaft. A determination builds inside of me as I watch his eyes gloss over and his face drop.

I love that I have this effect on him.

Cole doesn't strike me as the type to relinquish control for long, so I make my move, stepping back and dropping to my knees in front of him.

His eyes widen as he follows me down. One of his hands picks up a strand of my hair and begins to wrap it around his finger as he watches me hungrily.

He isn't the only one who's hungry.

Running my hand up his thigh, I glide my fingertips over his balls, drawing a gasp from him before continuing up his length to the tip of his fully erect cock.

Swirling my finger over a drop of precum, I meet his eyes. His back is blocking most of the water falling from the shower, and his attention is focused on me.

I lift my finger off of his swollen length, and he watches as I lead a string of fluid from him to my lips. I bring my hand up to my mouth, slowly parting my lips to take my first taste of him.

"Oh, fuck." His fingers slide into my hair and tighten as he hisses, no doubt trying to maintain his control over himself. I'm determined to see where his restraint ends, and I tighten my other hand around him and begin to stroke his length as I watch his eyes focus on my hands.

His taste lingers on my tongue, only slightly salty. I want more of him, and I lick my lips then lean in to take his wet tip into my mouth.

He fists my hair tight but doesn't guide or push me. Instead, he allows me to lead, and I push myself further around him, driven by a new need to take everything I want from him.

My fingers wrap around the base of his cock and don't meet my thumb as my free hand cups his balls, and his hips jerk forward as I push my tongue along the underside of his length, taking him in as deeply as I can.

Intoxicated by the sounds of his moans and the thrust of his hips in response to my efforts, I increase my pace, drawing more of his control into my hands.

A swirl of cold water hits my knees. He shifts above me, turns off the water, then returns to watch me, and I'm not ready to stop.

But he has other plans.

"Stand," he commands as he loosens his grip in my hair, and I brace myself against the wall of the shower as he catches my hand in his and helps me up.

"Nikki." He waits for my response as he pushes some of my wet hair off my face.

"Yes, Cole?" I try to stifle a smile from getting too out of control. I'm rather full of myself right now.

Taking a deep breath, he reaches around my waist and pushes the door to the shower open, flooding our little area with cool air.

"I like when you take care of me too." His sly smile dances across his lips, and he winks as he guides me into the chilly room and grabs a towel off a hook.

Wrapping it tight around me, he takes a second for himself, then he moves us into the bedroom. Habit leads me toward my backpack, and I'm looking for my clothes when his words stop me.

"Leave your bag. You don't need anything from there right now. Come with me." Without waiting for my response, Cole turns on the spot and walks back into the main area, leaving a trail of water on the floor as he goes.

As I enter the room behind him, Cole is already unzipping a sleeping bag and spreading it out on the floor in front of the stone fireplace.

"Get comfortable. I'll get the fire going again." He smiles at me as he stands to grab some wood from beside the fireplace.

I step onto the sleeping bag and lower myself as he turns his back to me. As if he has eyes in the back of his head, he continues, "You don't need your towel. Take it off."

The dominance in his voice catches me off guard, and I'm thankful I'm not under his watchful eye as I try to calm myself. Everything inside of me is turned on by how he speaks to me, and I pull my towel off, tossing it aside a little more enthusiastically than I intend to.

The fire takes on a second life as flames blanket the room in a soft glow.

Cole removes his own towel from around his waist. My mind temporarily glitches at the thought of my hands digging deep into his meaty ass cheeks as we fuck, and I choke on air like the awkward dork I am.

The sound catches his attention. As he faces me, I struggle to maintain a small fraction of the normalcy I now feel slipping away.

He holds my gaze as he opens one of his bags and unzips a side compartment, pulling out a foil wrap.

He lies down beside me and shifts his body so he is partially on top of me, pinning me in place and commanding all of my attention. As he lowers more of his weight onto me, his heartbeat pounds against my chest—or is that my own heart pounding against his?

"I knew you needed me to take care of you the moment I

saw you standing on the steps. There's just something about you that makes me want to—protect you." His words rattle around in my head as he slides my thigh to the side for him, and I open eagerly. "I need to take care of you, Nikki."

Harlow. Please say Harlow—just once.

Not wasting his time on pleasantries, Cole pushes his fingers inside of me. I arch my back, and my head lowers to the floor. His hair tickles along my sensitive skin as he drops his mouth to playfully bite my nipples, and my sanity leaves the room. His warm tongue gently glides over my areola, soothing the pinch as he moves to the other side and continues.

He lifts his head to watch me as he rubs inside of me in an agonizingly slow rhythm. "You're going to show me how you take care of yourself, Socks."

"Huh?" His statement throws me a little. I think I know what he's asking, but I've never done anything like that in front of someone else.

His smile turns wicked as he lifts his hand between us, and I swallow hard as he takes the length of his two fingers into his mouth and sucks my taste off of him.

Lifting himself just enough to grant me access, he continues in a low, seductive whisper. "I want to watch you play with your pussy."

"I—" My inexperience is about to show, and I lift my hand between us and settle it on my stomach.

I do get myself off, but I'm always alone, with nothing but my vibrator to help me out—my vibrator that I left in my bedside table in an apartment that is probably being ransacked, now that I think about it.

A calloused hand wraps around my fingers. Cole lifts my hand to his lips, and I straighten my digits to feel if they are as soft as they look.

They are.

His tongue glides across my fingers, and I watch in a trance as he sucks two of them into the warmth of his mouth, moistening them for me before guiding my hand down between us and settling my fingers over my clit.

"Touch yourself," he orders as his head drops and his lips trail kisses down my neck.

The need to feel him inside of me is at a fever pitch, and I'm not going to get what I want until I do as I'm told.

Okay, so we're doing this then.

Closing my eyes, I soften my body into the arm he has wrapped around me. I delicately run my finger over my mound and into my slick center as I slip slowly in between my folds. They slide effortlessly along my clit. I'm wet and ready for him to have what he wants.

My wrist bends from side to side, moving my fingers in a circular motion and hitting all of the spots I love to touch when I'm by myself.

Then suddenly I feel like I'm dancing—to a slow, quiet song. My hips move, and my body stretches and bows as everything falls into place. Sensations tickle through me, and muted moans escape into the room, but I don't care.

I'm lost in pleasing myself because I know it is pleasing him.

A shift in his weight brings me back to the room, and I open my eyes to find him watching me. Opening my mouth to attempt to fill the silence, I let out a whimper at a dull pain. I started to bite my lip in my daze, and I'm ready for more.

At this point, I'll want everything, and I want to give him everything. I'm floating high on a wave I've never felt before, and I don't want any of it to end.

Then, just past my vision, something moves, drawing my

attention away from his eyes, which are burning right into me. Following his strong arm down, I fall mesmerized at the vision of him stroking his hard cock as he watches me fuck myself with my fingers.

"Please, Cole. I want you to—I want you." I'm past the point of sanity, driven completely by lust. This insatiable need has taken over, and the only way out is to give in.

Understanding registers in his eyes.

I'm naked underneath him, and I'm completely dependent on him right now.

He doesn't let me off the hook that easily.

Rolling onto his back, he lifts me, straddling my legs across his chest, and his hands go to work underneath me, tearing at the packet and sheathing a condom over his shaft. His cock stands straight in the air, and I shamelessly lick my lips at the sight of him.

"Show me how you take care of yourself. Take what you need." At his words, I don't hesitate.

Not this time.

Desire is in the driver's seat, and I'm gone in the morning.

I'll go back to being alone, and for once, for one night, I need this.

Climbing on top of his solid frame, I'm focused on his erection. I align myself over it and lower down. I move as measuredly as possible, but as soon as his tip breaches my entrance, I'm done.

I let my weight slide me all the way down, impaling myself on his length as we both groan in unison, and his hands shoot up to either side of my head.

"You'll look at me. I want you to know who is giving this to you. Don't take your eyes off me, Socks." His determined words rattle into me, and a giddy wave of euphoria washes over me as I begin to move my hips greedily on top of him.

"You're so—fuu—" I'm pretty sure my sentences are just coming out in grunts now.

The feeling of him stretching me out and gliding himself all the way in is the only thing that matters right now.

But it's not enough.

Shifting from my knees to my feet, I continue to ride him as I squat over him for better leverage, but I'm missing the force I want to feel.

Keeping both hands on my head, he's looking between my eyes and my hips, watching which way my hips move to get him deeper inside to the places I desperately want him to hit.

"Cole, it's not enough. I want more. Please. I need you to take care of me."

In one quick movement, he grabs my waist with one hand and the back of my head with another.

Spinning me around, he places my back on the sleeping bag and shifts to open my thighs wide for him.

"Jesus—fuck, Nikki. Hands on the floor beside your head." His composure falters as his hips begin to roll into me, and I drop my hands away for him, allowing him to take full control.

Using one hand, he wraps his fingers around my throat, closing them enough to tell me he is in charge without choking me out, and a suffocating pressure builds inside of my head.

My body rocks under his guidance; I move in reaction to him.

I want everything he's giving me, and I want to give him everything he's taking.

"Who do you belong to, Nikki?" His voice is strained as he continues to ride me to the end we both need tonight.

Harlow, I imagine. *Harlow.*

Without hesitation, I respond. "You, Cole."

"Whose is this?" Rubbing his free hand over my mound, he

slides in between my lips and gently pinches my clit, sending me into another dimension.

"Yours. It's all yours. Please, you're gonna make me come again." Tears fill my eyes as he relentlessly pounds into me, and I let go.

My arms relax; the muscles in my body go soft.

"Do you think you deserve to be fucked like a dirty little girl here on the floor?" His words shock me for a fraction of a second before my entire being switches on and responds to him.

"Yes. I want to be yours. Fuck me harder, Cole. I need to come." Unfiltered words pour out of my mouth as my body winds tight on itself, and my head swirls as I realize I've been holding my breath as my orgasm furiously closes in on me.

"Shit, Nikki. You are mine. You. Belong. To. Me." His final words match his thrusts, and the certainty in his claim pushes me over the edge.

In my mind he said *Harlow*.

I reach around me and clench the sleeping bag tight in my hands, pulling it off the floor as I scream out my release. His fingers tighten as he continues to fuck me hard through my orgasm. He's building up to his own end, and mine isn't stopping.

I gasp for air. The force of the waves hitting me throws me into a temporary limbo, and I feel nothing but intense jolts of electricity that seem to flow from him deep into my bones.

From just beyond my consciousness, he growls his release as he follows me into the abyss I'm now floating in. Moments later, the weight of his body settles on me, pinning me in place under him.

My mind reconnects with my body back in the little cabin as my situation begins to sober me out of my daze. As the last shocks flutter out of me, his steady breath on my forehead calms me.

Opening my eyes, I meet his gaze.

He studies me in silence.

I've never felt anything so intense with anyone before, and I wish this didn't have to end. I wish I could tell him everything. I wish he really could protect me.

But he can't.

No one can.

I'm sure it's now well after midnight.

I'll be gone in less than eight hours, and I'll never see this man again.

For his own safety, I can't.

"You know, I'm only going to help my brother for a couple of days. My company operates in a number of cities. I'd like to see you again, Nikki." His voice is gentle. It matches the soft circles he's drawing around my nipple with his finger.

"I'd like that," I answer.

And it's the truth.

I would like that, but it won't happen.

"We should get some sleep. We both have a drive ahead of us in the morning. We can talk more when we wake up." Lifting himself off of me, Cole stands, extending his hand to help me up.

The last of the dwindling flames flicker around the room, barely lighting our path into the bedroom. I follow behind him, grabbing my backpack off the floor and pulling out a pair of soft pants and a little tank top to sleep in.

Cole removes the condom, tosses it into a bin, then joins me at the bed.

Sliding under the covers, he keeps the sheets lifted, motioning for me to join him, and I obey, pulling them over me and laying my head on the pillow facing him.

"Good night, Socks." He leans into me, places a soft kiss on my forehead, and wraps an arm around me, pulling me close.

I'm happy he used my nickname.

That name isn't a lie.

"Good night, Cole." I take in his scent with a deep breath before closing my eyes.

I want to tell him I'll see him in the morning, but I don't want to lie to him anymore tonight.

7

COLE

When I fell asleep last night, I didn't think I'd be waking up alone this morning.

Nikki's scent is all over the room, yet she isn't here to greet my morning hard-on, and I'm both disappointed and impressed that she was stealthy enough to have left without waking me.

The sound of an engine sputtering spurs me out of bed, and I run to the front window in time to see her reverse out of her spot and turn around.

In the morning light, and thanks to winter, I can easily see through the leafless trees.

Are those fucking flowers all over her car?

And why does that not surprise me?

I chuckle as I release the curtains and they shut out the rest of the morning.

Scanning the cabin, I find nothing left of her except the stale junk food she left behind. Her scent, her smile, her perky tits, and her beautiful wheat-blond hair all linger in my thoughts.

I forgot to get her contact information.

Dammit. That one did a number on me.

My survival instinct left the moment I saw her standing on the porch last night, looking all confused and vulnerable.

But that's fine.

I love a challenge, and as soon as I finish this job, I'll track her down.

I'm good at tracking things. It runs in the family.

Especially things that belong to me, and I recall her claiming she did somewhere between her first and last orgasm.

As I pack up my clothes, I make a mental note to contact the cabin's owners with some excuse that she left something valuable behind and get her forwarding information.

I know quick hookups usually come with no strings attached, but I've woken up wanting another taste. Nikki doesn't strike me as someone I'll be able to fuck once and get out of my system.

But I've got things to take care of, so I decide to put a pin in my girl for now. I turn my attention to packing my things when I see something staring at me from under the bed.

In her haste to leave our darkened room this morning, she must have missed her teddy bear.

I pick up the old thing. Holding it to my nose, I take a deep breath, and her scent fills my head, sending me back to her arms last night.

Fuck, I need another go at her.

Holding her memory in my head a while longer, I gently lay it across the top of my open bag like it's my prized possession.

It is my prized possession. Because it belongs to her, and she belongs to me.

I finally pull into the driveway of our family home, and my phone pings with notifications as soon as I turn it on. Most of them don't make sense.

I leave everything I drove up with in the car and head toward the front door, which is oddly open.

"Dagen, your autocorrect is lit. I think you meant to type 'witness,' but it came through as 'wedding' on my text. It still doesn't make sense though." I wave my phone at my brother when an older man I've never seen before turns around to face me.

I shift my glance from this guy back to my older brother in confusion. Then shit gets really weird: our youngest brother, Ryder, joins us, and he's wearing a tux.

For a brief moment, I wonder if Nikki fucked me so hard that we woke up in an alternate reality. Then Sloane runs by going on about flowers, and Ryder tells her to ask Amara about a song I've only heard at weddings, and my grin takes over my face.

"You're fucking doing it."

Ryder's tying Amara down. I mean, I knew he wouldn't wait. The fucker couldn't wait to drag her ass back here as soon as he had the chance.

"Yeah. I'm fucking doing it, and I have an important question I need to ask you." Ryder's not one for showing emotion, and the look on his face tells me he's trying to get over himself.

I offer him an out and answer for him: "You want me to be the best man?" I'm all on board and ready to accept when Dagen steps in.

"Fuck that shit. I'm the best man. He already asked me."

Fucker.

"You both are the best men I know, but, Cole, this is really important to me." Ryder's impatience shows in deep lines along his forehead. "Amara has asked that you give her away."

I'm stunned into momentary silence. Amara asked me to—

This day is full of surprises.

I choke up and mumble something about how honored I am. And I am.

Amara lost her father four years ago, then she lost her brother—our friend—and she's asking me to give her away.

I push Dagen out of the way.

He can have his best-man bullshit.

"Does this mean she has to call me daddy?" I can't help myself.

Getting a reaction like this out of my little brother is what gets me out of bed some mornings.

Sloane calls down from the top of the stairs, and Ryder ushers us up with the man I haven't met yet in the lead.

I follow in behind everyone else and finally lay eyes on Amara.

My soon-to-be first sister.

Everyone shuffles around the room, settling into place. I wait until they stop moving to circle the bed and place my hand over Amara's cast.

She has a dress lying on top of her, and it looks like Sloane played makeover on her face and hair. She looks happier than I've seen her in a long time.

The man who I now know is the officiant starts talking, and I miss a beat when they ask who's giving Amara away.

Speaking for someone and taking the responsibility of giving them away chokes me up, and I lean into her.

"There is no one better suited for my brother than you, Sunshine." I kiss her forehead, and she smiles back at me, her eyes glassy with unshed tears.

This is a woman who has been to hell and back, and she knows what she wants. She's fought for all of us with everything she has, and I'm so proud of her. I'm equally happy my brother locked her in before he fucked up and sent her away again.

We Saint boys don't have the best track record with keeping women.

We can all get them easy enough. It's finding the right ones, then holding on to them, that seems to elude us.

My mind drifts to Nikki, and I wonder what she's doing. She must be across the border into Canada by now.

The ceremony continues, but I don't listen to the guy talking. Instead, I watch Ryder and Amara steal glances at each other. I've never seen my brother so happy.

I wish our mom could be here to see this, but I know why it is only us.

This secret won't leave this room once the ceremony is over.

No one can know for now. Not until we know what is going on.

When Ryder starts saying his vows, I come back to the conversation. His words are all from the heart and off the top of his head.

They are words Amara deserves to hear.

When it's her time to respond with vows of her own, she starts to cry. Then she tells us her painkillers are kicking in, and I can't help but laugh.

Amara's words are equally beautiful—they're just laced with some good drugs—and my heart feels full knowing Amara is now my little sister.

The officiant pronounces them husband and wife, and Ryder leans over and kisses his new bride before the guy is even done talking.

Sloane clears us out of the room, reminding us that no one says anything around Henry.

Henry.

Even though I know he's not my nephew, I still enjoy my time with him. He'll always be family as far as I'm concerned—so will Sloane.

I trail down the stairs behind Dagen and listen as he finishes up with the officiant. The guy tells us that under Amara's special circumstances, they can sign the paperwork as soon as she's feeling better, and he'll drop by to pick it up. It's a little unorthodox and not technically allowed, but, as a favor to the family, he'll overlook it. He hands the papers to Dagen, who thanks him for his time and sees him out.

When we turn into the house, Ryder is already behind us, motioning toward the office.

I go straight for the bar.

After my night with Nikki and now the wedding, I need a drink, and there is no way I'm drinking alone.

I pour one for each of us.

"I leave you assholes alone for a few days, and you go and get married." I raise my glass to Ryder. That's my toast to the groom; he can accept it or shut up. "I'm really happy for you, bro. I mean—shit—you got your girl."

Dagen joins me. "I'll drink to that. Congrats, Ryder."

Ryder downs it in one gulp.

My little brother is married.

"Amara will sleep for a few hours, so we have a little time, then I'm all hers." Ryder sets his glass down on the desk then looks at Dagen, who grabs a blue file folder. He sets it on the desk but leaves it closed while he shares what he knows.

"Our body is still a Jane Doe, but we were able to capture some clear video footage from a nearby business. It shows the dead girl approaching with another woman, then the other woman running away around the time of the shooting, and we have a still photo of the car she was driving."

Dagen stops to chuckle, shaking his head, and his reaction seems out of place.

"What's so funny?" I smile as I join them.

"Well, it's just that this should be the easiest person in the world for you to find. I mean, she drives a car with big flowers painted all over it."

"What?" My stomach drops, and the room goes dark.

Both of them stop laughing and stare at me. Judging by their faces, I must look like I feel.

Dagen starts to repeat his words, looking a little less sure of himself. "She drives a—"

I don't wait for him to finish.

I zero in on the file and walk toward it, setting my cup on the desk so hard some of my drink sloshes up and over the rim.

The cover of the folder rips as I open it with more force than necessary.

My ears start ringing as my eyes meet the beautiful eyes of the woman I'm about to hunt down. The same woman I buried myself deep inside of last night.

I blink once. Twice. Then one more time, as though the action will change the photo.

It doesn't.

She looks absolutely terrified.

My Socks was with the girl who was murdered a few nights ago, and if she was fleeing and I ran into her south of Seattle, there is no way she's heading north to fucking Canada like she told me she was.

"SON OF A BITCH!"

As if I'll find anything in the file that will contradict her photo, I flip through the pages, and, sure enough, there's a grainy photo of the same damn car I watched her drive away in this morning.

"What's wrong?" Dagen's voice sounds far away, and my brothers exchange a glance with each other before settling back on me.

I throw the file away, not because I don't need it. I'll commit every word of it to memory in a moment. I toss it because I'm angry, but I won't throw the photo of her.

Because she's mine.

Stepping away from the desk, I take a deep breath to rein in my anger before answering Dagen's question.

It's not going to happen.

I'm pissed. May as well get this over with now.

I wave the photo by my head. "What's wrong is I fucking know her!"

Ryder and Dagen both square themselves on me, and the questions start flying, but I tune them out.

Lifting the image of Nikki, I scan every detail.

What the hell are you up to, and where are you going?

She lied to me.

I lied to her.

It looks like my little angel has some secrets, and she isn't as innocent as she looks.

None of it matters now because I will find her.

And when I do, I will take care of what's mine.

8

HARLOW

y heart skips a beat then hammers into my chest when someone idling in their car outside of the bar leans into their horn. I settle my hand over my sternum, as though my own touch will calm my nerves.

It takes a minute for my breathing to even out before I lean over in the booth and slide the thin curtain back to scan the street.

Everything looks normal, like it always does. It's felt eerily like the calm before the storm since I made my way back here about seven weeks ago.

When I first left Seattle, I was a walking time bomb. I made my way to James, and I couldn't bring myself to step one foot outside his apartment for the first week. Even within the safety of his locked apartment, I kept to the walls while I moved around, and I avoided all windows.

Eventually, my brother convinced me to sit on a bench and watch the traffic go by. Then he took me with him to run an errand. Slowly, I've assimilated back into the life I once had, but it isn't exactly the same.

It's been two months since I left Genie, and I'm still jumpy.

I look over my shoulder and take odd detours wherever I go to see if I'm being followed. I wonder if the feeling I'm being watched will ever go away.

When I first arrived in Portland, I had plans to run, but I never did. James is all I have left, and I'm his last family. I can't bring myself to leave him.

Then, as the days went by and no one came looking for me, I didn't see a point in running from nothing.

It's only been the last few days that James says something feels off, and we've started talking about possible places where I can lay low for a while.

As for my sorrow, it's there, but it is tempered by the numbness still working its way through me.

I'm in shock, and I'm not sure if I truly understand that Genie is gone. James and I were never given a chance to lay her to rest. We can't claim her, because then we would have to answer questions. James says it isn't the cops he's worried about. So we had to leave her, and she's all alone.

I don't allow my brain to travel too far on that train of thought.

The events of that night are still raw in my mind.

I remember everything in segments.

Every day, I want to call to find out what will happen to my sister's body, but James keeps reminding me that they track those kinds of calls, and our secrecy might be what is keeping us both alive.

Our mother was no angel, and we all have different last names to prove it. Since the three of us were separated when we went into the system, it's difficult to connect us to each other, especially now that our mother is gone.

For once, our screwed-up childhood is keeping my brother and me safe.

I've been stalking Seattle news stations and websites, looking for any news on Genie's murder or a call for tips, but I haven't found a thing.

It's almost as if it never happened, and I wonder if this is why I've been unable to properly grieve losing her.

I've been having nightmares about finding her lying on that cold floor. Then I wake in a cold sweat with the thought that maybe she's alive. Maybe that's why there is no news. I know it isn't true. I know what I saw, but not having her is messing with my head.

"Afternoon, Levi." Two men and a woman greet my brother from the door, catching my attention, and I look over my shoulder before returning to the bowl of soup in front of me.

I'm facing the wall, blocking out the world around me so I don't draw attention.

Genie's death may not be on the evening news, but it doesn't mean someone isn't looking for me right now.

At least my eyesore of a car is gone.

James helped me sell it the day after I arrived, and I put the money away for a rainy day. It seems like that day has come, and I need to figure out where I'm going to go.

Voices get louder as the three people approach the table I'm sitting at, and my brother joins them. He's holding out his hand, cutting them off and rerouting them away from me.

"This table over here just opened up. I'll wipe it down for you."

I don't look at them directly, but I glance back as he leads them away from my seat.

"Thanks, Levi." The woman answers this time, and I notice her smile for him.

My brother goes by Levi here. It's part of his last name. I

think I might be the only one who calls him James—at least, the only one still alive who does.

James looks back at me with a hard glare as he seats them and drops some menus on the table before excusing himself.

I watch out of the corner of my eye as he turns and makes his way over to me instead of back to the bar.

My brother has been on edge ever since I returned from Seattle, but his furrowed brows and thin lips twist my stomach in a knot.

"What's wrong?" I ask as he slides into the seat across from me, leaning to one side before pulling his phone out of his back pocket.

"A buddy of mine just texted. We need to get you out of here sooner than we planned. People are looking for you, and it's bad—like, crime family bad."

Now I know why he seated those three away from me. This isn't the kind of conversation you want someone to listen in on.

"Who's looking for me?"

James has his phone open, and he's already swiping at his screen before I finish my question.

"I don't know what Genie was wrapped up in, but it sounds like it's two groups. The first is a family out of Seattle—they own most of the west side up there. The second is local. They run a lot of...shady stuff here in Portland. You might have heard of the Luccianos?" His wide eyes look at me like I'm already dead, and a cold chill travels up my spine. "This isn't good. I'm going to get someone to come in and cover for me, and I'm getting you out of here today."

My brother knows he isn't in a place to judge our sister. He's wrapped up in his own group of guys, but the look on his face tells me this is way out of his league.

"Should I go now?" I look down to my half-eaten soup.

"No. Wait for me. I'll be right back. Here." He slides his

phone across the table. "These are some photos of the Saint brothers from Seattle. There are four of them. They're looking for you too. I'll grab some of the Lucciano family when I get back. Just look through them, and commit them to memory so you know who to look out for."

James stands and makes his way to the kitchen, and I turn my attention to his phone.

The first photo is of a man in a suit. I've never seen him before. He looks younger than me, but looks can be deceiving.

Since he hasn't crossed my path yet, this is promising.

When I swipe to the next photo, my world crashes down. The image pulls me back to the night my sister was killed.

This one was there.

I saw those dark eyes staring into the room I stood in, and my body shuts down with the same fear I felt that night.

I stood there, in the darkness, afraid to move, while my sister was dead in the other room.

This one looks older than I am, or he's lived a life that makes him look more mature.

These men are now looking for me.

Reminding myself I still have two more brothers to look at, I swipe again, and my blood runs cold.

NO!

Those gorgeous, deep eyes.

It's Cole.

I steal a guilty glance to the closed kitchen door.

How could I have been so stupid?

Even though I lied through my teeth that night, it never occurred to me that he was lying too. Or maybe I just wanted to forget so badly that I put blinders on the moment he smiled at me.

He said he was traveling up to Olympia to help his brother move.

He must have been going up to Seattle to help them find me.

He obviously didn't know who I was then, or I wouldn't be here now.

My soup threatens to come back up at the thought of how lucky I was.

But my luck has run out, because he obviously knows who I am now, and he'll be coming for me. I'm in worse trouble than I ever could have imagined.

In hindsight, it was smart to tell him I was driving to Canada, but he must know it was a lie since he found me south of the city he now knows I was in.

Does he know my real name now? I wonder.

I wanted to hear him say it the night we were together.

Cole has consumed my thoughts every day since I left him. He'll continue to haunt me for a different reason now.

I can't pry my eyes off his photo.

He looks the same but different.

The person I was with that night was softer around the edges. The man in this photo looks cold, calculating, and hard.

Do you like it when I take care of you?

The hairs on the back of my neck prickle as they rise.

I did like it.

I loved it.

This man made me crave something I have no business wanting. It's a luxury I should have never entertained, because now I have to turn my back on it and run.

The man in this photo is the one I need to remember.

Cold eyes look off to the side, his expression stern.

He's the man I need to run from.

My older brother and sister always looked out for me. I couldn't look out for my sister, but now I have the chance to look out for James. He has done more to save me than anyone in this world, and I won't bring Cole and his brothers to his doorstep.

If I leave now and disappear, he can't be caught in a lie.

It seems excessive that Cole and his brothers—and a criminal organization—are looking for me though.

My brother's question floats to the surface.

What was Genie involved in?

I mean, the murder of a woman is one thing, but why look for me?

If it's to shut me up, then I get it. But sending this much manpower after me feels excessive.

I check the inside pocket of my jacket.

The few hundred dollars I got from the sale of my car is still there, and it's enough for a bus ticket far enough east that I'll be able to disappear again. I just need to get to James's apartment and grab my backpack.

My stomach growls, and I shovel in a few more spoonfuls of soup before lifting the bowl to my mouth and drinking the rest down.

I'll be hungry later if I don't finish this, and I need to make the money I have last for as long as it can.

I take one last look at Cole's face on my brother's phone before turning it off and leaving it on the table.

I wish I could say goodbye to James properly, but he'll just insist on coming with me, and it's my turn to protect him.

I slide out of the booth, zip up my jacket, and turn to leave behind the only family I have left.

I clutch my palm to my chest and startle, taking a step back when my safe haven collides with my worst nightmare.

"Hello, Socks."

Standing between me and the exit, and holding the teddy bear I thought I had lost, is Cole.

And he does not look happy to see me.

COLE

I've waited almost two painstakingly long months to see her again.

If I hadn't run into her on her way out of town, I'm not sure I would have found her first.

I've been in town for two days and sitting in my truck in front of this bar for a couple of hours.

Ryder has been staying close to Amara and Sloane, to keep up appearances, and since Dagen is the only one of us who works for himself, it wouldn't be suspicious if he left town for a bit, so he joined me when I decided to drive south to pick up her trail.

It took weeks to get a lead on the dead woman, and even longer to find the car my Socks was driving. By then, it had already been sold for cash at a junkyard.

And here we are.

I sent Dagen on a couple of errands to get him out of my hair. I don't want him with me when she first sees me. He'll meet me at my apartment later.

I didn't tell my brothers everything, and I'm not ready to

explain myself. I told them she and I accidentally shared a place while I was heading into town. That was it.

The looks they exchanged told me they didn't buy that nothing happened, but neither of them pushed it.

Sharing what happened between us didn't seem cool. I felt protective of our experience.

Nikki showed up to the bar an hour ago, and my throat tightened the moment I saw her.

Nikki.

It's not her real name, and it doesn't suit her.

I had to cash in a few favors I would have rather held on to in order to find out who my girl was, and even then the information was limited.

Harlow Stinton has a clean record. Released from foster care when she turned eighteen, she became a contributing member of society. As for her life in the system, those records have been a little harder to open.

Her last known address is this bar, which is owned by James Levine.

A boyfriend, maybe? The thought makes me angry.

The dead woman in Seattle is still a mystery to the cops, but we got a name.

Genevieve Landry.

After I told Ryder and Dagen as much as I was going to share about our ships literally passing each other in the night, we made sure the video footage was destroyed. But that doesn't mean something else out there isn't leading the woman's killer to this doorstep as well.

I need to make myself known and get her out of here today.

I already attempted to make my way into the bar when three people stumbled in before me, and I retreated to collect my thoughts before trying again.

James, the owner of this bar, does have a minor record, so I hang back and watch as he joins my girl at her table. The two are deep in conversation, and I push away the thought that they may be lovers.

After a few minutes, the guy stands and leaves her, and I decide to make my move.

Grabbing the stuffed bear from the passenger seat, I get out of the truck and cross the street. A few eyes meet mine when I enter, and I take a couple of steps toward the table she's at.

Her back is still turned to me, and the guy is nowhere to be seen.

Sliding out of the booth, she turns to walk my way when she freezes mid-step.

Our night together in the cabin hits me, those moments I can't get out of my skull, and I wish more than anything that neither of us left the morning after.

I wish we hadn't gone on with our lives. I wish I hadn't learned who she was. Instead, I'd stay out there, hidden away from the world and buried deep inside of her, still believing she was this innocent little thing.

The color drains from her face. It isn't the look someone would give a guy they shared an intense night with upon being reunited.

It's the look of someone who thinks they are about to die.

She knows who I am.

"Hello, Socks."

Her eyes lower to my hands. I'm probably clutching her teddy bear harder than I'd like to. It's only when I follow her line of sight down that I notice I'm strangling him, and I ease my grip.

I guess we have a couple of issues to resolve.

Forcing an odd smile across her lips, her eyes dart toward the kitchen before returning to me. Her lips stretch further into an awkward grin. It isn't the same way she smiled at me when we were alone in that cabin, and it doesn't sit well with me.

She opens her mouth to say something but is cut off when James returns from the kitchen. The expression on his face falls fast when he notices her forced smile, then he looks my way.

"Can I help you?" His tone contradicts his question. The only thing this guy wants to help me with is finding the exit.

"No. I've got what I came here for." I take a step toward Harlow, and this guy takes a step toward me. I stop.

"I think you should go." A combination of worry and panic fills his eyes.

This guy is smaller than I am, but I don't think his concern is for himself. He's worried about Harlow, and the thought grates into my head like fingernails on a chalkboard.

She's not his to worry about.

I sent Dagen on his way so I could approach Harlow while showing her I'm not a threat. It's clear: this decision isn't going to work in my favor today.

"I'm not going anywhere." I turn my attention to Harlow. "I need to talk to you, Socks."

James recoils at the nickname I'm using for her, and his head snaps accusingly in her direction.

All this time, Harlow stands staring between us, eyes wide and mouth contorted into a panicked grin. When her eyes meet his, she shrugs.

"I'm not asking. Get out!" James raises his voice, and with that, two men from a table and another two near the bar stand up.

When I turn my attention to James, he opens his fleece shirt, showing me his gun. I'm sure all of his buddies are packing too.

James waves his hand, and a guy from the bar approaches

me with a quick pat-down before shaking his head and stepping away.

This isn't how I wanted to approach her today. I left my gun in the truck on purpose. I had wanted to put her at ease, but this guy is going to force my hand, and I won't back down until I get what I walked in here for.

I hold my hands away from my body to show I'm not armed.

"I can't do that." I lower my voice. My eyes land on Harlow, and she takes a deep breath.

The fear from the photograph Dagen showed me matches the current look on her face.

"You need to go now." This time, James turns his attention to Harlow, and she startles in place before attempting to walk around me.

I take a step to block her path, slowly shaking my head in warning.

She's not fucking going anywhere.

She freezes in place, her attention bouncing between me and him.

"Listen. I'm not the only one looking for you. You need to come with me." Then I turn to address James. "I can keep her safe."

He considers my words while he shakes his head.

I already know he's going to turn me down.

"We're leaving." His answer is final, and the two men at his back take a step toward us with their hands ready for their guns. "Keep him here for an hour, then let him go." James talks to them without taking his eyes off me.

Harlow takes a step toward him, then turns her attention back to me and slowly closes the distance between us. James mutters his disapproval, but she doesn't back down.

I breathe her in as she approaches. I still believe she's too good to be mixed up with these people.

Her wide eyes scan my face. They're filled with everything she's not saying to me.

I jolt when her fingers skim the skin on my hands, and she takes the bear I'm holding back before mouthing the words *I'm sorry*.

Dropping her head, she steps around me and allows James to lead her toward the exit.

"We are not done." I don't hide the threat in my tone, and she turns to take me in, the color draining from her face.

I'm not a man who allows disobedience, but I know when I'm outnumbered.

James nods to his guys and opens the door.

"Grab a seat at the bar." One of the guys points to an empty section near the end, and I walk toward the stool while looking outside. Random guy keeps talking. "Give me your phone."

I chuckle at that. "No."

On the street, James is pulling Harlow away from his bar when she stops abruptly and takes her arm back. It looks like they are in a disagreement over something. Her face isn't turned to me, so I can't make out any words she's mouthing, but she points at the building across the street.

The guy behind the bar tells me to give up my phone again, and I'm not having it.

Without taking my eyes off the two in the street, I lay out my terms so everyone understands where we're at. "My courtesy of not killing them"—I lift my chin toward the street— "doesn't extend to anyone here. I'll keep my phone."

"Fine. But it's on the counter where I can see it."

I slide the barstool out and take a seat, then I set my phone on the bar. My gaze is still locked on my girl in the street. I'm thinking now would be a great time for Dagen to decide to drop in.

Harlow and James are still standing in front of the bar. Whatever they are arguing about, she's holding firm, and he waves his hands in the air before pulling her across the street toward the building.

That must be where they're staying.

When the door closes behind them, I turn my attention back to the ones left in the bar.

"A new bottle." I lift my chin to the liquor lining the wall behind him. There's no way I'm taking a drink from something already open.

The one standing behind the bar turns and takes stock of what he has, then grabs one, breaks the seal, and pours.

I need to come up with a plan before they leave that building.

The two guys who stood from the table have returned to their seats to eat, but their eyes remain on me. There's one seated a few stools down from me, and there's the bartender.

What keeps me seated isn't any of them. It's the group of three seated in between us, who seem oblivious to everything going on around them.

Some people have no survival instinct.

I'm about to take a drink when the screech of tires catches my attention. A car stops abruptly in front of the building across the street. No one else seems to notice how out of place it looks parked at an angle and facing the wrong direction.

Three men get out.

"Your friend is about to be in a world of trouble." Holding my drink, I point to the car on the street, and the two guys at the table stand and look out the front window.

It's obvious the guys approaching the building Harlow just went into don't think they are being watched, as the one in the rear pulls his gun out early.

"Shit," one of the men at the window mutters, and they look at each other.

I quickly learn the second in command is the one seated at the bar beside me when they all look to him for orders.

"You two, help Levi." The two guys at the window leave and run across the street. He levels his eyes on me, his voice lowered. "You, stay seated." Then he looks at the remaining bar patrons. "All tabs are covered. GET OUT!"

No one argues.

The numbers inside the bar just became more manageable.

As soon as James's two guys enter the building across the street, I lift my phone to text Dagen.

This sets the second in charge off, and he approaches me. "I said leave your phone on—"

I don't give him a chance to finish. I grab him by the scruff of his neck and slam his head into the bar as hard as I can to knock him out.

The bartender jumps back with a mixture of shock and fear. He must realize it's just him and me now.

I pour the rest of my drink across the top of the bar and pull my lighter from my pocket, setting the counter ablaze.

The last man standing gapes at me and reaches for his gun.

"You have a friend out cold and a bar on fire." I talk to him like I'm the new one in charge, and his eyes lower to the man unconscious at my feet. I point over his shoulder. "Extinguisher."

As he turns to unhook the fire extinguisher, I get up and walk out of the bar like it's a normal fucking Tuesday afternoon.

I've waited almost two months to see my little angel again, and she doesn't disappoint.

Adrenaline seeps into my veins as I hurry across the street.

It's time to crack some skulls and take what's mine.

HARLOW

We're halfway to my brother's car when I stop in my tracks and reach for James's arm to get his attention.

"I need my backpack." I tilt my head to the building across the street.

His place is on the third floor.

"No. They're already here." He points toward his bar, indicating Cole, and a fresh wave of hell washes over me.

I still haven't gotten over him being who he is and seeing him again.

No part of me wanted to leave him in the bar, but I can't afford to trust anyone other than my brother right now. I remind myself the Cole I spent a night with didn't know who I was at the time.

Everything has changed.

We're no longer strangers who shared a night. We're on opposite sides of whatever this is.

Clutching my teddy bear to my heart, I shake my head. "I'm not leaving without it."

The familiarity and comfort of holding my stuffed animal again is a reminder: I can't lose anything else.

"Harlow. They're going to kill you." His forehead wrinkles, and he steps toward me, reaching for my arm, but I pull away and point at his apartment.

"I'll be quick. Please. I can't go without it. Maybe you should come with me too. Pack some things. I have enough money for two tickets."

James looks toward his bar for a minute then shakes his head. I'm not sure if that means he's coming with me.

I hope he is.

I'm not ready to do this on my own.

"Fine. But be quick." He closes the distance between us and lifts his hand to my back, ushering me across the street to his apartment.

The blare of a horn startles him, and he moves his hand to my upper arm, gripping me tightly.

We both turn, ready for a fight, when the car that honked continues on, turning the corner, and James mutters profanities to himself.

I know he's worried and upset that I won't leave without my backpack, but he doesn't understand. To him, it's just stuff.

To me, it's irreplaceable, and it's all I have left.

Clutching the teddy bear my mom got me when I was little, I let him drag me through the front door and toward the stairs.

He doesn't have anything from when we were kids. If he ever did, he got rid of it long ago. I still don't know if it's better to have left everything or to still hold on to what little we had.

James doesn't like to talk about when we were younger. I imagine it's because he's a little older than I am, and he remembers things differently than I do.

I remember smiles, ice cream, and teddy bears, but I know it wasn't as happy as my childish mind made it out to be.

While we were still together, James and Genie made everything into a game for me. They would always smile at me, then turn and lower their voices when they spoke to each other. They taught me how to hide so I wouldn't be found when we played hide-and-seek. James taught me how to run really fast so kids couldn't catch me when we played tag.

My favorite game was Simon Says. I learned later that we often played those games so they could keep me out of trouble. Genie would say things like, "Simon says close your eyes and pretend you are asleep no matter what" when our foster dad would come into our room late at night.

My version of my childhood was different than theirs, and I wish I knew then what I found out too late.

"It's risky, but I'm putting you on a bus. I have a friend in Nebraska who'll help hide you for a while. You can work on his family farm. I don't even know what they farm out there...." James murmurs the last part to himself.

"I'm scared, James."

My confession makes him pause, and he finally looks at me.

Worry has carved its way into every feature on his face. The sober realization of the deep level of shit we are in settles around us.

"Get your bag." He unlocks the door, and I race through the living room into the spare bedroom where I've been sleeping.

Zipping my teddy into his place, I sling the backpack over my shoulder and join James just as the door bursts open and a stranger lunges toward him, catching him off guard, and they go down together when a gunshot rings into the room.

Clutching my hand over my heart, I jump back into the wall behind me, jarring my neck and shoulder.

I think I scream.

"RUN!" James yells at me as he stands, holding his gun.

He's the only one getting back up.

I take two steps toward the front door when James reaches me first and pulls me farther into our apartment.

"Not that way. The fire escape." He points toward his bedroom, and I do as he says, barreling down the short hall toward his room.

I know there is a staircase just outside his bedroom window.

A shuffle and another two shots ring out behind me, one after the other, just as I enter his bedroom.

I push with all of my strength to open the window, thinking once I have it open, I'll return and get James.

The window doesn't budge.

I try two more times. All I need to feel is the smallest give, but there is nothing, and I check for nails in the window when I realize this exit has long since been painted shut.

A sound at the door catches my attention, and I turn as James walks in.

"I can't—"

My words fade when James trips and stumbles into the room. His bloody free hand reaches out to brace his fall, and when I run to catch him we both go down. His gun clatters to the floor.

"NO! No, no, no. James, I'm so sorry." The rest of my words are apologies and pleas, and everything runs into itself as I turn him over and help him into the room. I shut the door behind us, as though that will keep him safe from the people on the other side.

How could I have been so selfish? I thought I had time to get my things.

Now, seeing James like this, I should have listened. There is nothing more important than my brother.

Cole was right; he isn't the only one here looking for me.

Cole.

I shouldn't have left him in the bar.

Another shot, farther away, echoes into the old building, and the sound of yelling and fighting goes on for a few minutes before everything quiets.

I pull James along the floor to the back wall, leaving a trail of blood behind us.

If he loses consciousness now, I'll never be able to get him out of here.

I can't lose him too.

Panic sets in, and tears pour down my face as he struggles to get up, but I keep him down to try to slow the blood he's losing.

I find the wound and grab a shirt off the bed, stuffing it onto his side before setting his own hand over top and telling him to hold it tight. Then footsteps in the apartment make me still.

My eyes settle on the gun just out of my reach.

Propping James against the wall, I turn to crawl across the floor to reach it when the floorboards in the hall creak. Abandoning the gun, I scurry back to my brother. Then everything goes quiet for an eerie second before the door bursts open, splintering the frame around it.

A man zeros in on the both of us huddled against the wall. He doesn't speak; there's nothing to be said. He reaches to his side, unsheathes a large hunting knife, and takes a step toward us.

"We've been looking for you."

James reaches his blood-soaked hand across my midsection, trying to pull me out of the way, but there is nowhere to go.

Then I catch movement from over the man's shoulder.

My reaction draws his attention, and he steps to the side to follow my gaze. Cole comes into view, but it isn't the Cole I know.

Hard, cold eyes target the stranger holding the knife, and Cole steps into him with rage wrapped around his entire being.

The lips I kissed are pulled back into a snarl, exposing teeth. Cole grabs two fists of the guy's jacket and rips him off his feet, pulling him back into the hall. The door is on its last legs, but it closes enough to shield us from what is happening.

The walls shake, and heavy steps move out of the hall and back into the living room when wood cracks apart. I imagine they've broken James's coffee table. The sound of glass shattering has me confused, and I wonder if my brother's friends have come to help him. Then, worry that they might kill Cole sends a shiver through me.

I crawl forward as fast as I can and lift the gun before sliding myself back beside James. I've never fired one of these in my life.

Nausea rolls over me, and my arms feel like they weigh fifty pounds each.

"You need to get out of here." James's tone holds a combination of exhaustion and fear, and I set the gun on the floor beside us to pull him into me.

"I'm not leaving without you. I can't—I won't lose you too." I hug him desperately.

I know he doesn't like "mushy shit," as he calls it, but I don't care.

When James looks at me, the weight of my guilt is too much to carry.

"I couldn't save her, James. Genie died, and it was my fault." I lower my head and cry into his chest.

If I'm going to die now, I want someone to know how sorry I am.

"No. Genie died because of the choices she made. She knew it. None of this is on you." His shaky hand wraps around my head to hug me back, and I sob into his chest.

He may be right, but if he dies here today, it is on me.

I should have listened to him and left with nothing.

No guns have gone off in the last minute. Whoever is still standing out there is using his fists—or that knife. Violent grunts and items smashing riddle my body with fear.

Whoever is winning that fight is coming for us next, and I won't be able to hold my own. I'm not strong enough.

"I love you, Harlow. You deserve better than you got with all of us."

My world falls out from underneath me.

James never says the L word.

He knows this is the end.

When I listen for the sounds of fighting, there are none. Instead, one set of footsteps measuredly thuds down the hall toward our room.

The floorboards creaking is the only sound loud enough to drown out the rushing of blood in my ears.

I release my hold on James and dry my tears with my blood-soaked sleeve, then I lift the gun into my lap.

"I love you too, James."

I don't understand why anyone would want to go through this much trouble to kill me, but it isn't for me to understand.

My time has run out. This is ending today, one way or another.

I lift the gun, careful not to put my finger on the trigger until I'm ready to fire it.

My heart hammers into my chest as I lean forward and reach my body across my brother's to protect him.

Then I point the gun at the door and wait.

The shaking in my hand increases as the seconds tick by, and my tears roll down my cheeks.

The person stops on the other side of the door, and I brace for it to be kicked down once again.

Instead, it is simply pushed open. It groans on its hinges as it slowly swings into the room.

COLE

I'm in the stairwell leading up from the first floor when the unmistakable blast from a gun points me in the direction I'm headed. I slam through the second-floor stairwell door to—nothing much.

A woman runs into her apartment, slamming the door behind her and leaving me standing alone in the hall.

The residents are either all out or too smart to leave the safety of their own homes to actively seek out where the gunshots are coming from.

Footsteps and the sound of something heavy hitting the floor above me pull me back into the stairwell. The urgency of getting to Harlow before anyone hurts her acts as my fuel, and I take the stairs two at a time to the third and top floor.

There are no floors above us, and if they make me go to the roof, there's a good chance I'm throwing one of these assholes off of it, just because I can.

When I step into the hallway this time, I know I'm in the right place. There's one body lying facedown in the hall, and one of the guys disappears through an apartment door.

That's my guy, and this is my fight.

Tilting my head to the side, I crack my neck as I quickly and silently make my own way into the apartment.

The doorframe is busted, it looks like a bomb went off, and three bodies are scattered around the room.

There's no sign of Harlow or James.

A creak in the old wood floors catches my attention, and I glance down the hall in time to see one of the guys from the street kicking a door in before he steps into the room.

I don't see red, as they always say. I see crimson. Blood blurs my vision, boiling in my veins, and my heart hammers into my chest at the thought that Harlow is behind that door.

I don't remember the steps I took down the hall; I don't remember entering the room. The next thing I see is the look of horror on Harlow's beautiful face as she sits, clutching the man I know as James, and my heart sinks into territory it's never been in before.

The guy between us is holding a hunting knife. He turns, squaring himself on me in surprise, and I recognize the look in his eyes. I've seen it before. It's the glazed look of someone who is here for a paycheck. It's the look of a hired killer.

I grab the first piece of his clothing I can reach and pull us both out of the room. We crash into the wall in a heap, and I tumble on top of him, swinging my fists into his face as we go down.

By the time we stand, his knife is nowhere to be seen. I hope he dropped it to protect himself, because he could gut me with it if it's still on him.

This guy is the same size as I am, but I'll bet he has nowhere near the amount of rage I feel in my bones.

I tear him off the floor and drag his ass back into the living room to give myself the space I need to take him down.

When he gets to his feet, he wastes no time rounding on

me. I expect him to go for a punch, so I'm already lifting my arms to block him when he lowers his upper body and runs at me in a tackle instead. The wind is pushed out of my lungs when we both crash through a coffee table in the middle of the room.

As much as I've been craving a release from my built-up adrenaline, I don't want to give Harlow the chance to run from me a second time, so I make this quick.

When we stand, he pulls his arm back and lunges for a punch. I block it, then shoot my free arm across his throat and wrap my hand around the back of his neck, pulling his face forward and down to meet my knee.

The bones in his nose crack on impact. The full weight of his body takes his unconscious ass all the way down to the floor, and I make my way toward the room this guy was going in before I interrupted him.

As I near the room, Harlow's muffled words through the closed door punch me in the gut.

"I love you too, James."

I barely know the girl.

This shouldn't affect me.

But it does.

I give a light push, and the door swings in on its own, revealing James lying on the floor. Blood seeps through his shirt, and a terrified Harlow has draped herself across his front like a shield.

Her hand shakes under the weight of the gun she's pointing at me, and tears stream down her face.

"Don't!" She sobs, refusing to lower her arm, and I lift my hands so she can see I'm still not carrying anything.

She lowers her gun with a pained look in her eyes.

I lean my head to the side to get a look at the man behind

her. The guy is down, but there isn't enough blood to make it fatal.

Unless it is something internal. The memory of rushing Amara to the hospital flashes through my head.

He's of no use to me, and I won't be able to get both of them out of here in time. If this guy could walk, he'd be standing by now.

"I need to get you out of here." I speak to Harlow, taking a step toward her and James, and she pulls the gun onto her lap, shaking her head.

She isn't going to make this easy.

I change my approach.

"There are at least four guns in the other room. If I wanted to kill you, I would have come in here with one of them." I point to James. "He's hurt. Let me take a look." I take another step toward Harlow, and she shifts her attention to him just as I kneel at her side.

It's a shit move, but I grab the gun and disarm her first. I'd bet my bike that she has no idea how to use one of these, and I don't trust her not to accidentally shoot herself.

Not after I've already witnessed the amount of damage she can do to her own leg with a pocketknife.

Startled, she pushes herself between me and James as I set the gun on the bed, just out of her reach.

"Please don't kill him," she pleads, and I'm not sure what makes me more angry: the fact that she thinks I would or the fact that she's protecting *him.*

I give him a once-over and watch as he struggles to get her behind him. He's trying to protect her with the strength he has left.

He cares for her just as much as—

I don't finish the thought. "I told you I'm not here to hurt you." My words are meant for Harlow, but my attention is focused on James's wound.

I meet his eyes. "You'll be okay. I need to get her out of here." I lower my voice, trying to get this guy on my side. If he cares for Harlow as much as I think he does, he'll realize I'm their only hope in hell.

His gaze flashes to Harlow. He knows I'm right.

I try to offer the guy some help. "Listen, I'll call some people I know. Have you heard of the Lucciano—"

"No." He suddenly tenses, grabbing her wrist and trying to tug her back to him.

I try to reason. "I don't know who else is after her. I need to get her out of here."

"That's who's looking for her." James winces as he speaks.

I sit back on my heels, staring at him in shock.

Either I'm missing something, or this is incredibly bad.

I pry James's fingers off of Harlow's wrist and stand with her.

"We're leaving. Now."

Creed is someone I never would have crossed. If it's his group tracking her, none of us is getting out of this without one hell of a fight.

James leans forward, reaching for Harlow before grabbing at his stomach and hissing in pain.

She tries to get to him, but I hold her back. Then she turns to me and places her free hand on my chest.

I flinch. The reminder of her touch erases the last two months and sends me back to the little cabin where I had her.

"I'll go with you." Harlow's voice is a whisper, and we both turn our attention to her. "Please. Just help my brother."

Brother.

Shit.

This changes a lot of things.

I glance from her face to his. I don't see any relation, but how they protect and care for each other now makes sense.

I pull my phone out of my pocket and use my free hand to dial Dagen. Then I hold it to my ear, waiting, while Harlow and her brother watch me and what I'm about to do.

The other line picks up.

"Hey."

"Where are you?"

"I'm at your place. Your security system needs an upgrade. I'm sitting on your couch, and I found your candy stash—and I'm still wearing my shoes. What's up?" Dagen chuckles.

Fucker.

"Plans have changed. Get home to Seattle now, and stay off Creed's radar. Something isn't right. I have the girl. I'm taking her somewhere safe. I'll check in when we're settled."

I disconnect with Dagen and glance at Harlow's brother.

"Look, you don't know me, but I'm her only shot at getting out of here alive. You're two hundred pounds of dead weight." I point at the bedroom door. "Someone else comes through that door, and you're both done."

Harlow stills in my hold while her head swivels toward her brother for his response.

His shoulders slump.

He knows I'm right.

If I wanted to kill her, I'd have done it the moment the gun was in my hands.

Harlow tries to answer for her brother. "I'm not leaving without him." Her wide eyes glare at me, then she turns to him. "I won't go," she pleads. The glint of hope that he'll back her up is written all over her face.

"You will," James orders her.

She tugs at her arm in my hold and begs him to change his mind.

He glares at me, teeth clenched together. "Don't let anyone hurt her." His eyes gloss over. "She's—all I have—fuck!" He winces in pain and fumbles to pull out his phone, checking the screen. "My guys will be here in five minutes. Go." His head turns to Harlow, who's now trying desperately to release herself from my grip. "You contact me when you're safe. Got it?"

She opens her mouth to argue, but he cuts her off. His voice is stern—angry.

"FOR FUCK'S SAKE, DO AS YOU'RE TOLD!"

Harlow freezes.

Chastised, she drops her head and submits, allowing me to turn her and lead her out of the room.

I glance back at her brother over my shoulder.

He doesn't watch us leave. There's a mask in place, but I still see the unmistakable mixture of guilt and regret etched into his features.

This was the only way she would leave with me.

I glance out the front door and down the hall. We're still alone, but I'm sure we won't be for long. One of the residents must have called the cops, so taking the main stairs is out of the question, and I search the far end of the hall for another way out. I turn my attention to the end of the hall closest to us, and my prayers are answered when I see a door that I'm pretty sure leads to a fire escape.

It's locked with an alarm, but I kick it open. The cops are probably already on their way, so one more alarm isn't going to change anything.

As we hurry down the steel stairs, Harlow stops, pulling her arm sharply out of my grasp. I allow it, releasing her.

"I can do it on my own." She lifts her chin at me.

Defiance. I like it, but now is not the time, and I glare at her.

She recovers quickly.

"I-I'm going with you. I won't run. Just—you don't need to drag me out of here." She adjusts the backpack on her shoulders and straightens herself.

Fine, I get it. She doesn't want to be treated like a child. Her brother putting her in her place in front of me probably did a number on her.

I won't deny I have my own need to put her in her place, but now isn't the time.

"Stay close. You run, and we have a problem."

She nods once, and I turn to descend the last three stairs before I get to the lower ladder. I release it and climb down first, holding it steady for her as I glance up and down the alley.

I hurry to the street with Harlow close behind, and I stop at the corner as a few men run into the front of the building. Momentary worry sets in as I wonder if these are James's friends, but I recognize his second in command, now conscious. I turn my attention back to the street and head to my truck, thankful I just happened to park in a close spot, considering the party moved across the street.

I jump in, start up the engine, and Harlow joins me on the passenger side without a word.

Pointing to her feet, I tell her to stay down. She lowers herself to the floor and wedges herself in the footwell. I take a deep breath then pull slowly into traffic.

Once we're a few blocks away, I give her the all clear.

I keep one eye on the road ahead and one on her as she pulls herself into the seat, glancing out the rear window.

I know that look.

I felt it when Ryder jumped off the bridge after Amara.

She's worried for her brother.

We settle into a comfortable silence as I drive north out of town, and she shifts her attention from me to the landscape out the window.

We all have our secrets.

I'm driving toward one of mine right now.

An odd feeling settles into my bones. For the first time in weeks, I'm not agitated. Harlow's sweet scent fills my nose, and I know my new calm is because of her. It's because I have her with me and, for now, I know she's safe.

"Why did you keep my stuffed bear?" Her soft voice pulls me from my thoughts.

I want to tell her it's because I knew it was important to her.

I want to tell her it's because I knew I would be looking for her.

I want to tell her it's because I felt things with her that I can't shake, and I've become obsessed with feeling them again.

I keep my eyes on the road ahead, but out of my peripheral vision I can see she's frozen in her seat, waiting for my answer.

I have her full attention.

"I told you, I take care of what's mine."

12

HARLOW

We haven't spoken a word to each other since we passed Portland city limits and Cole announced I was his.

I didn't know how to respond. Partly because I'm not sure if he is referring to what happened between us at the cabin, or if he means I'm his problem and he needs to *take care of me* as in deal with me.

I only like one of those scenarios.

We stopped once for gas, and I considered running when Cole slipped inside to grab some things, but going it alone isn't as appealing as having someone who has, so far, looked out for me. Especially not now that I've seen what he is capable of.

Cole also took my phone and backpack from me, so I'm here for a while longer, because James's number is saved in my contacts, and I have no other way of checking in with him for now.

If he's alive, there's no way he's at his place, and I'm sure he won't be back to his bar for a while.

Following the highway signs, I know we drove north when

we left, and we were driving for close to an hour in silence before my eyes started getting heavy.

We were still heading north when I fell asleep. I know because the sunset to my left was beautiful.

When I open my eyes, the road is quiet, and the sky is a midnight blue. I'm shocked I was able to drift off in the first place.

Instinctively, I move my hand to my pocket and still, remembering I don't have my phone anymore. Cole had said something about tracking our location when he took it from me.

I wonder where James is now, but I won't ask for my phone back. Not so soon after I screwed up, got yelled at by my brother, and had to be rescued by Cole after ditching him in a bar. None of that fuels my confidence right now.

Cole's masculine scent fills my head. His jacket slips off my shoulders as I adjust in my seat. I didn't have this on me when I closed my eyes, and I glance at the only person who could have covered me with it.

I like taking care of you. The memory of his words gives me goosebumps.

My gaze immediately goes to the tattoos covering his biceps. His muscles flex as he tightens his grip around the wheel, and I draw in a deep breath to drive oxygen to my brain before I pass out.

It's getting warm in here.

I tell myself it's his jacket that is heating me up as I slip my arms out from underneath the heavy fabric.

He hasn't called me by my real name yet. I examine his face when I realize I still want to hear him say it, and I catch him stealing a look back out of the corner of his eye.

"How long have I been asleep?"

"About an hour. Maybe a little more."

I simmer in awkward silence for a few minutes with only

the sound of the pavement under our tires, before asking my next question: "Who are you taking me to?"

This gets his full attention, and his head turns to look at me. His features are unreadable before he looks away and out the front windshield. Maybe he feels my question doesn't warrant an answer, so I ramble, "I mean, it's obvious we're going back to Seattle."

"I'm not taking you there, but we'll be close."

I'm still not sure how to read his response, so I turn my attention out the passenger window. The trees hurry by like giant shadow monsters, and I wish I could go back in time to earlier today.

I would have told James to come with me as soon as I saw Cole's picture. I would have made him drop everything. I would have left my backpack, and we would have just run away. We could have disappeared, and he wouldn't have been shot.

As if sensing my hurting heart, Cole fills the void. "No one will know where you are until I can figure out who is after you."

"James said you and this Lucciano group are." I stop short of telling him I recognized one of his brothers from the photos James showed me earlier, but I steer the conversation in that direction. "How close are you with your brothers?"

The muscles in Cole's jaw clench tight. He doesn't look over to me. "They're my family. It's—complicated."

I turn my attention to the center line, which is coming at us in rhythmic beats under the truck's headlights as we put more distance between us and Portland.

Eventually, I lift Cole's jacket to offer it back to him.

His gaze lands on the heavy leather before traveling up my arm and across my own body. "You use it. I'm—"

In the space of time before he answers, I put my own response in: *hot*. Because, damn, he is.

"—good."

I pull his jacket up my arms, trying to get it as close to my nose as possible without looking like a stalker. The fabric's deep scent swirls around in my nose with reminders of our night together.

His heady gaze warms me better than this jacket does, and I wonder if he still feels some of the things I felt when I was with him.

In a different life, he would be mine, and I imagine what it would feel like to blindly trust him.

He clears his throat, drawing my gaze to him just as he turns his attention out the front window once more.

I know I wear my thoughts all over my face. I was never good at lying to my brother, and I wonder if Cole caught me lost in the memory of us.

It isn't just a memory; it is an all-consuming thought.

I've thought about him since I drove away from him that morning.

Showers aren't the same. Falling asleep isn't the same, and food doesn't taste as good as it did that night. I haven't been able to get myself off as easily as I could before. The fantasy of him is nothing compared to the intense reality sitting beside me.

His presence does something to my brain. It's like a short circuit that goes on as long as he's near me.

Cole didn't just rock my world—he owned it. He carved out a place for himself, and he's been a permanent fixture ever since.

"Tell me about your brother." Cole's low tone startles me. He keeps his eyes forward.

It's only now that I realize no one has ever asked me about

James. I'm not one for small talk, and no one has taken an interest beyond the stuff that floats around on my surface.

Where do I start?

"Um—what do you want to know?" I glance at his hands, my eyes refusing to travel the rest of the way up to look at him again.

"Anything. Just start talkin', Socks."

Still not my name, but I'll take it. "He's older than me."

He nods.

I'm going to assume that, since he found me, he knows my name, and mixed in with that information would be my age, but I tell him anyway. "I'm twenty-six."

A flash of something crosses his face, and his jaw clenches before he speaks. "I know."

Of course he does.

"You have different last names." His eyes remain on the road.

"We have different fathers. My mom—um—I was young when she passed away. She was all we had. We went into foster care after that."

"Do you have any other siblings?"

I draw a long, steady breath.

Cole obviously doesn't know everything.

I force my answer out on my exhale. "A sister."

"Where is she?"

I'm not ready to talk about Genie. Not here, in a car, late at night, after everything that happened today.

I shiver, then tuck his jacket around my sides.

"She—um—she passed away." Once again, I turn my attention out the passenger window. Everything is still so real and painful.

"I'm sorry."

His voice is low and clear, and I turn my head to him, confirming he is looking at me as he says his condolences.

I mutter a thanks, but inside I feel like I don't deserve his kindness.

Genie's death has been an open wound, bleeding out for the last couple of months, and I've only just been able to temporarily stop the flow. Now everything threatens to spill over once again.

I'm not ready to deal with my pain.

"Can I—um, message him?"

I don't get an immediate response. Instead, the features on his face relax the tension that held his brows in a furrow.

"As soon as I know you're safe." He glances at me, his features illuminated by the glow of a passing vehicle. "I promise."

Something settles between us.

There's a finality to his words and a potent weight in his stare that calms me.

"Were you together in foster care?"

"At the beginning. We were split up about a year after and sent to different places. I don't know why. James doesn't talk about it. He found me when he turned eighteen. He tried to apply to raise me, but he couldn't pass some of the requirements. By the time he got on his feet, I was almost ready to get out on my own, so it didn't matter anyway. Besides, my last foster parents were the best I'd had." I glance out the window for signs of our location. "It feels like we're going to Seattle."

"We're going to Bainbridge Island. I have a place no one knows about."

"To get there we have to go through Seattle." I hear the tremble in my own voice as I speak.

I don't want to go back there. I glance down at the door

handle, as though it is perfectly logical that I can open the door and jump out of the truck as we speed down the highway.

A strong arm reaches across my midsection, acting as a seat belt and securing me in my seat.

"Hey. You're okay. No one will find you." His deep tone is oddly soothing.

I pause, wondering if I spoke my concerns out loud. His eyes widen when he meets my stare. The look of shock on my face must spur him to continue. "I'm taking a different route. We left Tacoma almost an hour ago. We're going the long way. Wow, you must be really tired to have slept through all of that." He attempts a smile, but his eyes still show his concern.

I try to calculate in my head.

The distance between buildings is becoming less and less; we should be in the heart of Bainbridge Island in about twenty minutes. From there, everything is a ten-minute drive, and I start to watch my surroundings.

"Do your brothers know about this place?" I attempt to make my question sound as nonchalant as possible.

"No one knows about it—but you." There's a deeper meaning in his words.

He's trusting me with his secret.

Maybe I should trust him with more of mine.

We turn off the main road, and less than a minute later, Cole pulls into a driveway. It's lined with evergreens, which hide our destination from view until we are almost at the front of the home.

I stare stupidly at the building as it comes into view.

The homes out here start in the millions, and this one is no different.

I didn't grow up around the rich, so I know extravagance when I see it, because it makes me feel like I don't belong.

Who buys a place like this and uses it as a secret safe house?

The silence is my first sign I'm being watched; the fact that the car is no longer running is my second.

I pull my eyes off the property and turn to face Cole, trying to hide my thoughts as I hand him his jacket.

"This is your place?"

This earns a smile like the one I saw when we first met.

"I come out here when I want to be alone." Guilt washes over me. I'm intruding on something that was only ever his. "Come on. I can't wait to show it to you." Cole reaches his hand out and jostles my arm, snapping me out of my thoughts.

The chilly night air rushes in when he opens the door to his truck, and I leave the comfort of the front seat to meet up with him at the back.

"We have enough to make it through tonight. I'll head into town to grab more supplies in the morning." Cole lifts two bags, then settles his eyes on my backpack slung over my shoulder.

Yep, this is literally everything I have, I think.

"I can carry something." I stretch my arms out and take the paper bags, allowing him to turn and grab some more items before I follow him to the front door.

Although I can tell the heat isn't on inside, the house feels warm in the way it is decorated, with oversized furniture, knit blankets, and plush area rugs.

Cole shuts and locks the front door before walking past me, and I follow him through the house into a large sitting area off of an open kitchen.

He drops his bags on the counter that separates the kitchen from a sitting room. While he sets the thermostat, I place my bags down beside his and turn my attention to the large windows on the far side of the room.

With the light on inside, the night blankets everything in a cloak of darkness, and I wonder how close we are to a view of the water.

Cole makes himself busy behind me, and I spin to ask him what I can do when he plugs in a kettle and starts opening some containers. My stomach grumbles at the sight of the snacks he brought with him.

His phone on the counter beside him dings and lights up, and Cole stiffens as he looks at the screen before looking up and taking me in.

Our conversation isn't particularly forced, nor is it nonexistent. I get the feeling we are both trying to find a place to start, and he takes a step back, brushing his fingers through his hair before crossing his arms and staring me down.

I'm out of place. Both in this beautiful home and in this element. I cross my own arms to match his stance, but I'm nowhere near as intimidating as he is, so I abandon my false bravado and drop my arms. Instead, I clutch my backpack.

His expression softens. "Let's have a seat. We need to talk."

I suddenly realize why I don't feel right.

There's something missing.

He still hasn't called me by my real name.

He flicks a switch on the wall, and fire instantly surrounds the logs in the fireplace as he points to the couch ten feet away from the hearth. Dropping my backpack, I circle the sofa and join him there. The fire immediately warms my skin.

"I need to know what you were doing with that woman the night she was shot."

Panic roils in my stomach, and my eyes sting with the threat of tears, but my cheeks stretch into a grin.

Just smile, I tell myself.

Genie used to tell me that all the time. She's the one who taught me to smile to hide my pain. *People ask you what's wrong when you frown,* she would say. She was always so much better at faking it than I was. James only had to look my way to tell if we were really happy or if something was wrong.

When I look up at Cole again, his eyes are still on me, but I see them bounce slightly from my eyes to my mouth and back again.

My smile isn't fooling him, but he doesn't call me on it.

Instead, he waits in silence for my answer.

13

COLE

Harlow's expression isn't genuine, and the energy between us is stifling when she smiles at me.

Her smile is nothing like it was the night I first had her.

Now, it's fixed and vacant.

For a moment, it feels like she isn't here with me. It's like she's hiding somewhere in a dark corner behind those stretched lips and wide eyes.

I don't feel good when she looks at me like this, and the forced grin makes me angry. It takes concentration to sit in silence and wait for her to open up to me.

I don't deserve a mask.

I put my life on the line for her today. As far as I'm concerned, I've earned her honesty and trust.

I lean forward, opening my knees and clasping my hands together to keep myself from reaching out and shaking her into compliance.

When I pull myself out of my thoughts and look at her once more, I wonder if I've allowed my own mask to slip.

Her distressed smile isn't there anymore.

Instead, her eyes glisten as tears threaten to spill from her lids.

"Her name was Genevieve." I start by sharing what I know, hoping Harlow will fill in the blanks.

Sad eyes meet my stare before Harlow lowers her gaze to her lap.

"I called her Genie." Her voice is rough. When she blinks, her tears roll over her cheek and down her neck. "She was my sister."

Holy fuck.

I open my mouth to say something—anything—but nothing comes out.

The night I almost lost my brother was the same night she did lose her sister, and if only we could have gotten there—

That train of thought crashes off the rails when a darker one barrels toward me.

Her sister is dead because of me.

I am the one who set everything in motion.

I'm the one who told that asshole he had to get me the video. I'm the one who threatened him to deliver it or else. I'm the one who scared him enough that he sent Harlow's sister to be murdered in his place.

Harlow is halfway through her sentence before I realize she started talking. "—get away from the guy she was with." She sniffles. "Genie wanted to come home. She said if she did this one thing, the guy wouldn't bother her anymore."

I listen in silence as she tells me about the man I know as Steevers and what happened from the moment they showed up that night until she found her sister dead on the floor.

"Um." Her round eyes lower to my hands, which are still fisted in my lap. I know my limbs are shaking without looking at them.

I'm really going to murder that weasel when I find him.

"Did you see anyone else there?" I clasp my hands together, rubbing my fingers against each other to soothe the ache in my knuckles.

Harlow fidgets with her own fingers before lowering her eyes to her knees.

Her brows pinch together when she responds. "It was dark —and I was in a different room—" She slips away from our conversation for a moment, not looking at me, but not looking away either. It's almost as though she's looking inside of herself.

Then she drops her head into her hands and sobs. Her body heaves as she sucks in deep breaths of air. I slide closer to her on the couch and reach my hand out, gently skimming her arm to test the water.

She melts into me, allowing me to comfort her. The warmth of her body heats me better than the fire in front of us ever could, and I can't escape the nagging voice that tells me I don't deserve her.

I own my shit.

I always have, but I freeze, the confession stuck in my throat.

"It's my fault."

For an awful second, I'm crushed by the fear that those words were mine, that I've just said my thoughts out loud.

Panic chills my bones. This feeling is foreign to me.

For the longest time, I've felt untouchable, invincible, but these last few months have changed everything. Almost losing my brother, helping him save Amara, and gaining a sister have made me feel beyond myself.

I haven't known Harlow long enough to make any decisions about how I feel for her, but this uncertain feeling in the pit of my stomach is definitely an indicator, and now I fear I've confessed to something that isn't even mine out loud.

But when I see her face, I realize I'm wrong.

Those words didn't come from me.

She's expressing her own guilt.

I don't know how to answer her, but I won't let her take the burden of blame. It's not hers to carry.

Harlow looks at me with the weight of the world on her shoulders.

"I knew—there was a moment before we went into the building where I knew we shouldn't be there. I didn't say anything, and I let her hide me away in a room. I heard the gunshot, and I did nothing. I froze. I did everything wrong, and she's gone. I should have—"

"No!"

She snaps out of her downward spiral when I interrupt her.

"There is a long list of people who are responsible for your sister's death." I leave off *me included*. "You aren't on it."

The shrill whistle startles both of us. I forgot about the water I was boiling.

Bracing my palms against my thighs, I push up and circle around the couch into the kitchen, grabbing a bottle of whiskey from the cupboard, along with a jar of honey.

I'll never admit to my brothers that I not only know how to make a hot toddy, but I actually enjoy them. I drink them all the time once the winter sets in.

"Do you know what your sister was handing over?" Reaching for the lemon, I ask the question without looking up.

I have an idea of what it is. If it's the video footage, then there are only so many devices it could be stored on.

"She had a flash drive thingy with her when we were in the car. It was light blue. I didn't see it after we got out. Do you know what it was? What they killed my sister for?"

"I think I do. My brothers and I have been looking for video footage of a crime that happened a few years ago—a murder.

We think it might have been the evidence we need. If we're right, it is definitely evidence her killer would be after too."

Harlow hugs her arms around herself, and I get the feeling I've overstayed my welcome on questions for the evening.

"Eat something." I look at her and point to the little ledge behind the couch. I grabbed the best food I could at the gas station on our way here, and Harlow looks over the snacks before taking a handful of crackers.

A welcome surge snicks through me. I like it when she listens to me. It's damn irritating when she doesn't.

"Can I call my brother?"

I glance at my phone. It's later than I thought, and I open her phone.

Harlow once mentioned in passing that she doesn't know how she's still alive, and I have to agree with her.

Her phone is unlocked, and I easily pull up her contacts.

There aren't many.

The first thing I do is send a text to myself, so I have her information.

The second thing I do is pull up James's number and send him a short message.

Harlow: This is Cole. She's safe. Talk soon.

Three dots are already bouncing on my screen before I read over my own message.

James: OK

His response is anticlimactic and expected. At least I know he survived.

He won't say anything more until he knows it's Harlow he's

talking to, and I don't blame him. I'd do the same in his position.

James doesn't want to give me too much information, nor does he want to piss me off—not now that I'm the one in charge of his little sister. I wonder exactly what he's heard about me, what he's learned since I took Harlow away from him earlier today.

The thought of being *in charge* of Harlow sends a depraved chill through me.

Should he be scared of me?

If it was anyone but Harlow, probably.

"Your brother is okay." I lift her phone off the counter so she knows I'm using it to text, then I pocket it in my shirt so she knows she's not getting it back right now. She doesn't fight me on it.

Lifting the hot drink to my nose, I inhale the spicy citrus scent, then bring both mugs back to the couch and hand her one. She takes it from me and mirrors my move, taking a deep inhale.

The soft whimper she makes on her exhale hits me hard. She catches herself and coughs to clear her throat.

I smile into my drink.

She doesn't mask her feelings well, and I like that.

Harlow pinches her lips together as though going in for a chaste kiss, and I watch, mesmerized, as she brings the cup to her mouth and blows on the liquid before closing her eyes and taking a sip.

The toddy warms me from the inside out on my first sip.

"It's called a hot toddy. The bartender at one of our restaurants showed me how to make one a few years ago. It'll help you sleep." A slice of lemon floats on the top of my cup, and I watch it for a few seconds before asking, "Why didn't you run when I went into the gas station?"

When I look up to meet her eyes, I already know the answer.

On some level, she knows I'm telling her the truth, and she knows I won't hurt her. The connection we made on our first night together changed everything, including her fate.

"I—I didn't have a choice."

I smirk at her answer, wondering if she's lying to me or to herself. "We always have a choice, Socks."

A muscle in her cheek twitches.

She both likes and hates that I call her that now —interesting.

When Harlow blinks this time, her lids open lazily.

"We need to get some sleep." I reach for her cup, and she leans back, taking one last gulp before handing it over.

A surge of pride forms in my chest at how she likes the drink I made for her. I felt the same way when she ate my stew in the cabin like she hadn't eaten in days.

Maybe she hadn't. The thought makes me mad.

I clear our drinks and turn to gather the snacks from the table when I catch Harlow out of the corner of my eye.

She doesn't ask about sleeping in one of the many rooms this place has; she doesn't look around. She simply lifts her backpack onto the couch and sets it down, patting it as though she's going to use it as a pillow. Leaning over the rest of the couch, she reaches her palms out and pushes the cushions down, as though testing them for firmness.

Fuck that shit.

I turn and set the dishes on the counter, speaking over my shoulder. "You'll sleep with me."

I catch the outline of her reflection in one of the windows. There's no mistaking how fast her body goes rigid, and she shoots up straight when she thinks I can't see her.

"Wh—it's no problem. I can crash here." She points to the couch. "Or if there's a spare room..."

I shake my head then walk to a panel on the wall and key in a passcode. "The alarm is set. You'll sleep in my room."

It's getting late, and I don't have the mental capacity to have it out with her. If it were a normal day, I'd probably prod her a bit, to see if she was really willing to be punished on this hill, but I'm tired. "I can't protect you if I'm not near you."

I turn the fireplace off and grab my bag, making my way down the hall to the stairs. When I turn to start the climb, she's behind me with her backpack in hand.

The top floor has heated nicely, and I open the door at the end of the hall.

Harlow will love the view from the window wall in the morning light.

I give her a quick tour, and she goes straight for the washroom, hauling her backpack in with her. I busy myself with unpacking my stuff and getting into the sweatpants I left behind the last time I was here. This room heats up really well, and I go shirtless. I always end up pulling my shirt off in the middle of the night anyway.

The faucet turns on and off as Harlow gets ready in the other room, and I go over my plans for tomorrow as I lie on the bed. I messaged Dagen to let my brothers know we were safe. He got home without a problem.

Then I sent a text to Creed, telling him we needed to talk. His response simply said he's ready for my call. There was no indication if we are still allies or not. I'm curious to find out which, but I won't call while I'm here. I'll get in touch with him in the morning when I go into town for more food.

The subtle click of the door draws my eyes to the curves in Harlow's body, and I rub my thumbs against my fingers as I remember what it felt like to touch every inch of her.

I don't like what she's wearing—not because I can see all of her. That part, I do thoroughly enjoy. What bothers me is this is what she sleeps in both when I'm not around and in the cool late spring months.

Then my gaze falls to her feet.

Those fucking fuzzy socks.

You know what I see when I see those socks: I see her legs spread wide as I pound into her, making her moan. That tight pussy wrapped around my cock, milking everything out of me.

Sweet Jesus.

I might have mumbled that last part out loud. It's too late for this.

I tilt my head to the other side of the king-size bed, and she drops her bag at the foot before rounding the mattress and pulling back the layers of sheets to crawl under.

She's cold in those flimsy pajamas.

Pulling the covers up to her chin, she looks at the ceiling as she settles into her spot, and I'm not having it.

I slide under the same sheets and push my pillow into the center of the bed.

When I said she'd sleep with me, I meant it.

Wrapping an arm around her midsection, I pull her, pillow and all, into my space and fold my body around hers. When she squeaks at our contact, I hide my smirk in her blond locks.

She doesn't pull away. Instead, she wriggles her body, carving out a place for herself.

Then she does it.

She tests me.

Meekly, she slides her hips around as though she's getting comfortable, but there's no mistaking her ass grinding against my cock.

When I said she'd sleep with me, I meant it, but that's all we're going to do tonight.

"Go to sleep, Socks." She freezes, her hips pulling away just enough to ease the pressure. After a minute, her body deflates then settles, accepting its place.

The tension is thick, and that's because we haven't dealt with the main thing hanging between us.

I sense it's coming, and when it hits, I'll be ready for it. But right now, the thing she needs most is sleep.

14

COLE

Last night was the best and worst sleep I've ever had. It was right up there with the night I fell asleep beside Harlow in the little cabin after fucking us both into a near comatose state.

She stirred a lot throughout the night, often waking with a jump only to turn over, look at me, and fall back asleep, tucked safely at my side.

The thought that she must be used to sleeping alone, too, is comforting.

After what happened yesterday, the long drive and her restless sleep, I woke up this morning to find Harlow out like a light. Her body had finally had enough, and she was in a deep sleep.

My morning wood, however, was wide awake and ready to go. Her little snores against my chest almost did me in, and it took everything in me to finally remove myself from her side and wrangle my needs.

I wrote her a note to let her know I was going into town to

grab some groceries, then I left it beside the bed along with instructions not to go outside until I returned.

Keeping Harlow hidden will keep her safe, but we needed food, so I hit the grocery store five minutes after it opened. Most of the people who would recognize me would still be asleep at this early hour.

My attention returns to my finger, which is thumbing across the locked screen of my phone as I sit in my truck in front of the store. My gut knots with tension, but I've put this call off long enough.

The phone picks up on the third ring.

"Cole."

"Creed. Thanks for taking my call."

There's no response on the other end. Creed only makes small talk when we are scheduled to meet under more pleasurable circumstances.

He's scarier than I am when it's business.

My text last night and my calling him so early is unusual, and he knows it.

"I need to know who Genevieve Landry is to you."

We sit in silence for half a minute before he takes a deep breath. Then he muffles the phone while he talks to someone else.

My mind drifts to the worst-case scenario: he's sitting in a room with his men, and they are talking about me and what I know about the girl they are after.

When he comes back to the phone, a woman's voice says something to him in the background, and his tone is clipped when he tells her to get her things and get going.

He isn't talking about Harlow's sister with his men. He's with someone; they're probably just waking up.

I listen as he closes a door, takes a few steps, and opens

another door. The sound of papers shuffling fills the silence until—

"She's no one to me. Why?"

Now it's my turn to quietly ponder things, but I don't take too long. Creed isn't known for his patience.

"Last one. What about Mick Steevers?"

"Cole." There's no mistaking the warning in Creed's tone.

"I'll owe you one."

Another long silence.

Creed knows I don't offer that lightly. I don't owe anyone anything—ever.

Except now.

A low chuckle comes through my phone. "It's your lucky day, kid. It just so happens I might need something from you soon, and I'm not stupid enough to allow myself to go into debt like this."

I must reek of desperation, but I can't afford to be on the wrong side of the Lucciano crime family, and information is power. At least this way, I know what I'm up against.

"I don't know either of those names." Creed breathes a frustrated, gruff sigh. "Should I?"

He waits for me to answer, and when I wait too long, he adds, "It's better if I hear this from you."

He's right. We've never had bad business between us. Out of all of our allies, we trust and respect Creed and his group the most.

Elia Lucciano is a different story. That working relationship was between him and our father. They are the founders of their respective empires, and both men did everything under an old-school mindset.

It wasn't until Creed took over as Elia's second that my brothers and I found more common ground, and I don't want to cross any lines we all worked hard to draw.

"Genevieve Landry was found dead in Seattle two months ago. She was sent by her boyfriend, Steevers, to deliver a package to one of ours, and we never got it. Now there are some people looking for—an acquaintance of hers." I leave Harlow's name out of it. Her, I'm willing to keep a secret. "Word is it's the Luccianos who are looking for her."

I flinch the moment my last word leaves my mouth. I shouldn't have given away that the target is a woman.

I watch as an older lady pushes her cart across the parking lot. The rattling of its wheels on the rough pavement causes a package of toilet paper to bounce out and onto the ground.

"I want to talk to Ghost. Now."

At first, I think Creed is talking to me, and I have no idea what he's saying, but his voice is distant. Then he says goodbye, and I know I'm not the only one he's talking to.

"Listen, Cole. These names mean nothing to me, and we're not looking for any—acquaintances. But that doesn't mean Ratchet's group isn't. If it turns out they're hot for her, then we may want her too. Just telling it like it is."

We're still being honest with each other, and that is a good sign. So far, we are on the same side.

"Is it getting bad? You've been quiet."

Creed swears under his breath. "Yeah. War's coming." For a guy who just woke up, he sounds tired.

There's another pause before he speaks again.

"I'll call when I hear anything—as a courtesy, and out of respect for our ongoing business."

"Appreciate it."

I don't get the chance to say anything else. The line goes dead.

Knowing Creed isn't the one looking for Harlow settles my nerves only a fraction, because the one who is is still out there.

I don't like that I had to put Harlow and myself on Creed's

radar, but he's right. It is better coming from me. It shows trust in our association, and it strengthens ties—if it doesn't kill us first.

My phone buzzes, pulling me out of my thoughts. It's a notification that the alarm at my place has gone off.

Someone opened a door.

I didn't think this through.

I have Harlow's phone with me and no landline, so I have no way of checking on her.

There's no such thing as rush hour here so there's no traffic as I race away from the little shops and back to our place.

Our. Dammit. What is she doing to me?

I manage to make an eight-minute drive in four. Then I pull up to the cottage and run in through the front door and up the stairs.

Her backpack sits by the foot of the bed, but she's not here.

I return to the main floor to check the alarm, not allowing my mind to sink to the worst-case scenario.

As soon as I enter the kitchen, the temperature drops, and my gaze stops at the cracked door leading out to the backyard and down to the water.

The alarm panel is open, and the disarm light is flashing as though someone thought simply pressing that button would turn everything off. I can't tell what triggered the alarm to go off first: the panel or the back door.

A bunch of birds startle out of a tree near the water, catching my attention, and a shadow moves along the edge of the trees. Someone's down on the bank near the water.

This time, I have my gun. I pull it out as I step onto the back deck and make my way down to the shore as quickly as I can without being heard.

Even though I just came in from outside, the chilled

morning air fills my lungs. My senses are heightened, and I'm primed for a fight.

A dark, oversized parka hunches over something near some bushes, and I jump around the last set of trees and right into Harlow's unsuspecting path.

I know she didn't hear me coming because she looks like she's going to stroke out when I yell. She spins around and throws her hands up in the air. With them goes everything she was holding, and my face is pelted with what feels like sand.

"What the hell are you doing out here?" I bark.

Clutching her heart, she tries to calm herself before she speaks, and I recognize the large parka she has on as one of my own.

She's swimming in it.

"I—saw the view. It's so pretty. I wanted to see it. And this was here." She points to a covered bin where the previous owner had kept their birdseed.

She was trying to feed the birds.

If someone wasn't trying to kill her, this would be fucking cute.

I tuck my gun into my jacket.

"I told you to wait for me. Didn't you get my note?"

"I read it, but—"

My demeanor changes at her admission.

When I take a step toward her, she takes one step back.

I lower my voice. "Good. I want to make it very clear that you knew you were not to come out here, but you did it anyway." My tone is steady, deliberate. As I chastise her, I stare her down, and my message settles.

She doesn't like it. She straightens her stance and crosses her little arms in my big jacket across her chest, jutting her chin up at me in pure defiance.

Again, I like it, but now isn't the time.

"I wasn't running away. I just wanted to—"

"No." I hold my hand up to silence her. "I want you to confirm that you read my note telling you not to come outside. Yet you did it anyway." There's no denying the threat in my tone.

She stares me down with all hell in her eyes. She holds her pose, so I stand to my full height, crossing my own arms across my chest and daring her to challenge me.

She pinches her lips together, weighing the situation.

"Fine." She speaks slowly. The taunt in her tone is crystal clear. "I read it—and I did it anyway."

There it is.

I swallow up the distance between us in three steps. Harlow struggles to get away, but she gets wrapped up in my parka, and her limbs flail under the heavy fabric. Grabbing her upper arms, I walk her backward until her back is pushed up against the large tree trunk behind her.

Moving one hand to her throat, I grip her just enough to show her that I'm now in charge of her airflow, and her eyes widen.

"When I tell you to do something—you do it. Do you understand?"

Dominance is something I enjoy immensely. I'm naturally an enforcer, and I thrive when I'm in charge of people and situations. But this is different. Harlow is different, and the gratification that surges through me, demanding I work for her submission, is overwhelming.

I'm consumed by my need to rule her and earn her obedience when she surprises me.

She's searching for her place just as much as I'm dying to stick her in it.

Her hips push forward, searching for friction against my cock, and my restraint breaks. Harlow's lips part with a lusty whimper, and I follow that beautiful sound deep inside of her, smashing my mouth onto hers and taking everything I've wanted since the first night we met.

Releasing her arm, I slide my hand into the front of her jacket and under her ass. She kisses me back, her soft lips opening to allow me to explore her further.

With my fingers still tight around her neck, I guide her and press her up against the tree at her back. Her legs open, wrapping around my midsection as she holds on to me for dear life. As if my cock has a mission of its own, I grind myself into the center of her spread legs, and she groans into my mouth.

This isn't how it's supposed to go, the irritating voice in the back of my head reminds me. I wish it would shut the fuck up, but it's getting louder because it's right.

I peel myself away from her, and we both work for our next breaths as I slowly lower her onto her feet. Her round eyes search mine in confusion.

"Socks, I—"

Her lips twist into a snarl.

Her bitter expression renders me speechless.

"Why won't you say my name?" She raises her voice. "I know you know it, but you won't say it."

Finally.

I smile.

This is what I've been waiting for.

"You're cold. Why don't you go inside and take a hot shower. We can talk when you get out." I give both of us a chance to calm down, and I turn to walk her back to the house.

"IT'S HARLOW!" I stop in my tracks and face her at her outburst. She stomps toward me, drowning in my jacket. "My name is Harlow. I'm sorry I lied to you. I didn't want you to have to deal with"—she waves her arms around her head—

"this." One last step brings her in front of me, and she pushes three fingers into my chest. "Say it. Say my name."

I'm about to smile again, but the look on her face tells me none of this is fun for her. She's really wanted to hear me say it all this time. I think of how sinful my name sounds when it comes out of her mouth, how much I need it—crave it.

There's still some air left in the space between us, and I close it out. Stepping flush against her front, I comb my fingers into her hair before fisting them at the base of her skull and holding her face up, inches away from my own.

I lower my voice. "I didn't say your name because you never gave it to me, *Nikki.* Are you sure you want me to have it? Because once you give this last little piece to me, there is no going back." We stand in silence, searching each other's eyes for understanding before I lean in, brush my lips against hers, and feel her heavy breath on my face.

My own heart thuds into my chest so hard, I wonder if she feels it too.

I thought her name many times, but I refused to voice it until it was mine to own.

"My—my name is Harlow. I want you to have it." Her lip trembles as tears well in her eyes.

She knows what this means.

Harlow is mine.

It's like that.

"Good. Now go take a shower. I'll be in to deal with you shortly."

15

HARLOW

I'm all the way up the stairs and in the bathroom behind a closed door, but I can't shake his presence. I feel him on me as though he's standing right here in the room. His smell hovers around me, and I can't stop wanting him like I did when we first met.

Last night stung. We were lying in bed, and I tried to shoot my shot and make a move, only to be told to go to sleep.

It was embarrassing, and it made me mad.

Then I woke up alone with a stupid note.

He still hasn't said my name, I thought.

That hurt most of all.

I had walked down to the shoreline to clear my head. I was feeling better once I found the seed container, and the birds came in close, looking for food.

Then Cole shocked the ever-loving shit out of me, and everything came barreling right back, and I snapped.

Then he kissed me like—

Looking in the mirror at my reflection, brushing my fingers along my lower lip, I attempt to re-create the intoxicating rush I felt when his lips touched mine, but I fall short.

What the hell am I doing?

People are trying to kill me, and I'm out here rubbing myself up against Cole like some horny, rabid wildebeest.

Do wildebeests even get horny? I ponder the thought as I remove my clothing and drop it in a pile until I'm left standing in my underwear and socks.

I used to look stupid stuff like that up all the time when I had my phone with me. James would roll his eyes as soon as I said the words, *Hey, did you know that (insert random fact here)?*

I hope he's okay. I make a mental note to ask Cole if I can talk to James later. I'll be able to tell by the sound of his voice if I need to get back to him.

I turn my attention to the large shower. It's big enough to fit a party of five in there. Actually, now that I look around, this bathroom is larger than a normal-sized living room. There's even a fancy couch in here, the kind that is missing the back and only has one arm. I forget what those are called.

I'll have to look that up too.

My hand is on the shower door when the bathroom door flies open, and a disheveled looking Cole stalks into the room.

The dark expression from ten minutes ago is back, and he zeroes in on me like I'm his next meal. My stomach flutters. I really hope I am, and the thought makes me clench my thighs together in search of the pressure I've wanted to feel from him again.

He lowers his eyes, consuming my body on the way down. He pauses as his attention falls between my legs before dropping even further.

"Those socks," he murmurs to himself, biting his lower lip.

Glancing down, I realize I still have my fuzzies on, and I

step one foot over the other to pull my foot out when he stops me.

"Keep them on. I've fantasized about fucking you in them for weeks. There's something that needs to be settled between us."

My eyes instantly go to the bulge in his pants.

I know what I want to settle between us right now.

"Not yet, Socks." As though he is reading my mind, Cole tsks me, shaking his head from side to side as he slowly steps toward me.

I'm standing in front of him, nearly naked, and he lifts his hand to my face, drawing his fingers over my cheek and down my neck before tickling along my collarbone.

I shiver with the flush of goosebumps pushing their way across my chest.

The room spins when his large hands wrap around my upper arms and he pulls me toward that odd looking chair.

"You know, I never did see the appeal of chaise lounges"—that's what they're called!—"until right now." He stands the front of my thighs up against the arm.

There's no mistaking his hard cock pushing through his pants into my ass over my panties as he leans into me, pinning the front of my legs to the chair before bending me at the hips. Then he lowers me over the arm with a one-word command:

"Stay."

I watch at an angle as he steps in front of the mirror, reaches for a hand towel, and drops it into the sink before turning on the tap.

In the mirror, his eyes examine me through his reflection. The muscles that run along his forearms to his biceps flex as he wrings the water out of the towel. I bounce one foot on my toes in apprehension as he rounds me, stopping out of my line of sight behind me.

"Let's recap." I don't know Cole well enough to tell if there is a hint of amusement in his tone, and I swallow hard as I listen. "I told you not to leave the house, and you read my note." There's a pause as he shifts, then my hips jerk back toward him, and I gasp, realizing Cole just tore my panties off of me. "And you did it—anyway."

Before my apology leaves my lips, a white-hot sting snaps across my ass.

It's not amusement.

He's not amused.

The pain registers like an aftershock, and I yelp, flattening my palms against the chair and pushing myself up. But his body towers over my own, and he lowers himself onto me, holding me down with his own body weight.

"Take a deep breath. Is it the pain or the surprise?"

My knee-jerk reaction is to say it's the pain, but it's not. I mean, it didn't feel good, but this is my punishment for disobeying him. It's probably meant to be something I won't soon forget.

He answers for me. "That's what I thought. Did you or did you not give me your name?" Cole brushes my hair off of my face and neck, then kisses a patch of skin below my ear.

"My name is yours."

Against my back, his chest vibrates with a growl.

"You're damn right it is." Thrusting his hips forward against my beat ass, he pushes us into the chair. My nipples grind into the canvas underneath me.

His hand wraps around my neck once more as he lines his mouth up to my ear. His hand, still holding the towel, pushes between my legs. I spread myself open for him, and he rubs the terry cloth along my folds. The fibers feel too good not to chase with my hips.

He growls, "Harlow," and I shudder beneath him.

My name.

It sounds wickedly filthy coming from his mouth. This man has the power to make me tremble and surrender with one word, and that word is my name.

He releases my neck and lifts his weight off me, then he runs his fingers over my bottom before stepping back and striking again.

The towel hits with the same force, but, now that I anticipate it, it doesn't shock my system as much as it just stings.

I ball my hands into fists and remain as I am, exposed to him, as I wonder what the pale skin on my bottom must look like.

Three more strikes land before I find myself blinking rapidly to clear the tears from my eyes before they form into drops. I sniffle to stop the sting of emotions in my nose.

I gasp with the next connection because it isn't a wet snap of the towel. It's the claiming squeeze of a calloused hand on my raw flesh as Cole soothes the bite of the towel.

I groan without reservation when his lips kiss the spots he just spanked, and I shift higher onto my tiptoes to chase the feeling of his mouth on my core.

The sound of shuffling behind me makes me think he's dropped to his knees.

Using his flat palms against my ass, he pushes me up and off of my toes, spreading my thighs open for him and shoving me further off the ground, my ass arced high in the air.

When he groans against my pussy and chases it with his tongue, licking deep inside of me, I splay my fingers open to claw against the chair for something to hold on to.

Cole doesn't just fuck, he consumes—he owns. He creates this transcendent space where I can just disappear for a while, and I drift away to him, groaning into the chaise.

Bracing his hands on my ass, Cole pushes himself up behind me. The sound of his belt and zipper being undone sends a nervous excitement up my spine, and he leans forward, kissing my bottom one more time before standing me up and turning me to face him.

His eyes follow mine down, and I reach out to trail my fingers over his inked chest. He stays still, allowing me to explore at my pace. It isn't until I graze the defined V leading to his erection that he sucks in a deep breath, showing me the effect I have on him.

The little gasp draws my attention back to his eyes, and I hold his stare as my hand lands on the tip of his cock. Cole's jaw clenches tight as his breathing evens out, and I shudder as a rush of excitement charges through me.

Gripping the back of my head, Cole pulls me into him. His tongue pushes between my lips.

He breaks the kiss, turns to open a cabinet behind him, and pulls something out.

He leans me back against the arm of the chair, and the rough fabric rubs against my ass, reminding me of who is in control.

"I want more."

I reach my arms out to brace myself as Cole leans me backward. Now it's my slick pussy on full display as my upper body lies helplessly upside down along the arm.

Just as I think I'm going to fall over, Cole wraps his arms around my hips and pulls my pussy up to his face, clamping his mouth around my clit.

His aggressive claiming overwhelms me in all of the right ways, and I buck in his hold as he devours me lick by lick.

I whimper and grind against him. I'm seconds away from coming when he breaks away and circles the chair to crouch in front of my face, his cock ready to be sucked.

Greedily, I reach my fingers out to him, pulling his hips closer and sliding his tip into my mouth.

"Atta girl, get me wet."

I rise to his challenge and open wider, allowing him to push in how he wants. His deep groan matches his long, slow thrust to the back of my throat.

The combination of my mouth being filled and my continued upside-down position makes my head spin.

Returning his mouth to my clit, he squeezes my cheeks while he eats me out, and I open myself wider for him when his finger goes to the rim of my ass.

Cole breaks away to murmur something about how I look with my socked feet spread high and wide in the air just for him before he slides his finger into my back hole. Then he swears under his breath, spurring me to suck him harder.

This time, when Cole breaks away, I almost fall off the chair, but he grabs me and helps me to right myself before pushing the chaise forward until one edge is flat against the shower stall, and I think for a moment he's going to fuck me on the floor.

That thought is dashed when he walks me to the arm of the chair and pushes me forward, saying, "Let's see if we can break this thing."

I'm not sure if he's talking about me or the chaise, and I'm fine with either.

The knowing tear of a condom wrapper behind me sends a wave of anticipation over me.

Cole slides into me in one easy thrust, and when I prop my hands against the chair this time, it's to push myself back into him.

My nipples brush against the rough fabric, adding to the sensations hitting me all at once, and I rub my chest down to add to the whirlwind of pleasure wrapping itself around me.

One strong hand grips my hip, shifting me higher and wider, while his free hand spanks my ass, reminding me of my punishment.

I'll take all of the pain as long as he doesn't stop pounding me into this chair, and I moan as I simply hang on and let him drive us both over the edge.

Strong fingers comb into my hair, and he lifts me off the arm of the chair and away from the friction of the fabric. I mourn the loss of contact.

But he spares me no time to wallow. Instead, he turns my head toward the sink and shows me our reflection in the mirror across the room.

I stare, dumbfounded, at the image as Cole fucks me like a beast from behind and I dangle in his hold.

Sliding me across the arm, he straddles me over the corner, spreading my legs wide and pushing my clit onto the rough fabric. My stomach twists tight.

His hand lands across my ass one last time, and the rubbing against my nub sends me soaring. He holds my head in his fist while I break apart, screaming at our reflection and shattering into space.

I'm coasting through my euphoria when he follows me over. With a rough growl and three final thrusts, he lifts me off the chaise and holds me, impaled on his cock, as he finishes along with me.

The next time I open my eyes, I'm seated in Cole's naked lap, wrapped in his arms. He's trailing gentle kisses across my forehead.

When I meet his gaze, he smirks.

"It's not broken. We'll have to try harder next time."

"Are you talking about me or the chair?"

He laughs at that, and it's the first time I've seen his unfettered smile since the night we met.

"Both. It's time for that shower. I want to take care of you, Harlow."

I melt at my name.

"I like it when you take care of me," I whisper, my own smile tugging at the corner of my lips.

He lifts me from his lap with a mischievous smirk on his face before seducing me with a wink. "I know. Come on. It's time to clean you up, dirty girl."

16

COLE

When we took a shower together on the first night we met, I was rushed. The water had to be heated manually, and it wasn't a large tank.

I've taken long showers here, so I know I have a generous amount of time to spend focused on Harlow.

After getting the water to the temperature I want, I lower myself until my face is even with her well-fucked pussy. I already want to go again.

Slipping my fingers along her ankles, I help her out of her soft socks, smiling to myself at how much of a turn-on they are for me.

They're everything I'm not: soft, warm, fuzzy.

Before I stand, I run my hand up her thigh and over her core, examining her closely.

Her fair hair is trimmed, and a strip of it covers her mound. It's just long enough that I can comb my fingers into it and clench my fist. The pull makes her suck a breath in with a hiss while her body bows. Her nipples pebble in reaction, and I watch her features for signs of pain.

A gentle tremor through her legs tells me it's affecting her, but it isn't hurting her. My dick threatens to rage into a standing ovation at the thought of bringing pain into play with her.

Harlow licks her lips and waits for my lead.

"I want to fuck you bare." Another tug on her pubes, and I slide one finger between her legs and into her pussy as I look up at her.

She whimpers.

"I—I'm clean. I mean, I haven't had—with anyone but you —since my last test. And I've never had unprotected—" She widens her feet, allowing me full access.

"Are you on birth control?"

She bites her lip before sheepishly shaking her head.

"I'll fix that," I murmur to myself before sliding my slick finger out and sucking her taste off of me while holding her gaze.

She bites her lip.

The list of all the dirty things I want to do to Harlow keeps getting longer and longer.

Testing the water once more, I step to the side, allowing her to enter in front of me, and she turns under the shower to wet her hair. When she raises her arms to the sides of her head, her breasts lift and round as the water cascades over her curves before disappearing down her body.

I love the sound she makes when she gasps in strained delight. To hear it once more, I run my fingers over her tits, chasing the droplets of water around before pinching her nipple between my fingers.

Crashing my mouth onto hers when she opens it in surprise, I wrap my hand around her head to pull her into me and move her as I want to enjoy her.

Turning us to the side, I lift Harlow just as I did against the tree, and she opens her legs for me, hooking them around my midsection and offering herself to me.

My kiss deepens as I push my length into her, painfully slowly, only to pull out and lazily push in again.

I want there to be nothing else between us, and the connection is electrifying. I've never wanted to be this close to anyone, ever. The thought of unprotected sex was unappealing, but I'm about to come from just the connection alone. I groan into her mouth as my tongue pushes its way into her, demanding more, more, more but unwilling to rush this moment and treat it like any other.

Harlow breaks the kiss. Her breathing is heavy, her eyes unfocused.

I capture her attention and watch her as her mouth drops open, and we fuck slowly, in unison with each other.

I hold back from drilling into her, but I push inside of her hard, bottoming out each time.

Her pussy grows tight around my cock, and her legs tremble as I watch a slight quiver in her lower lip.

Propping her up with one hand, I reach between us, tangle my fingers into her patch of pubic hair, and tighten my grip once again.

Dropping her head back against the wall, she moans as her fingers comb into my beard. She squeezes, matching the hold I have on the short strands between her legs.

Holding her hair, I slide my thumb over her clit, and she seizes, gripping me with her legs like a vise and screaming my fucking name. It almost undoes me, but I hold myself back. Riding out her orgasm, I slow my movements until I'm gliding languidly in and out of her, feeling the warmth of her channel spasm against my cock as her orgasm crests.

We still against the tiled wall before I slide myself out of her center and lower her legs to the ground, making sure she can stand on her own.

Harlow continues all of the way down, kneeling in front of me and opening her mouth.

I hold her head back.

"Watch."

Her forehead wrinkles in confusion, and I slide my hand into the back of her hair to keep her from leaning forward.

She fixes her eyes on my dick, and I stroke my length in front of her, showing her what she does to me.

I was close to the edge when she came all over my cock. Having her kneeling in front of me, ready to take anything I give her, pushes me the rest of the way, and I come in hot streams across her chest.

In my mind, I've marked her. It will be washed away when I clean her, but we'll both know it was there, and that is all that matters. Pushing my fingers into my cum on her chest, I rub it around her areola before pinching her nipples. They're sensitive. Harlow sucks air in with a hiss and smiles up at me, fluttering her eyelashes under the spray of the water.

A primal need to mark her even deeper pulls me under, and I lift my fingers to her lips.

"Open."

She obeys without hesitation, and I push my fingers over her tongue to the back of her throat. Her body stiffens as she tries to control a dry heave before settling to accommodate me, and she swallows me off my fingers. I remove my hand, help her to her feet, and kiss her hard.

I've never taken my time.

I've never fucked anyone slow like this, and I've never had unprotected sex. Most surprisingly, I've never felt the need to mark anything as mine so badly in my life. Not since Dagen and I fought over the last piece of pizza when we were kids and I licked it to stake my claim.

Yet here we are, I think as I look down into her glassy eyes.

I only have my shampoo here, so it'll have to do for now. Besides, I like the thought of Harlow walking around smelling like me.

I position her in front of me and work her hair into a lather. She stands still for me, waiting for me to move her as I need. Her head lulls in my hands, and she lets out the occasional sigh as I massage her head. Guiding her under the water, I rinse her off before reaching for the body wash and cleaning every inch of her.

As I finish, she turns to me and holds out her hand, palm facing up. "Let me take care of you?"

I relinquish the soap, and Harlow's smile lights up her eyes as she squeezes some into her palm before rubbing her hands together. The liquid turns to suds, and she lifts her hands, going straight for the tattoos on my chest and arms. Her fingers trail over the lines on each one, and she steals the occasional glance up to meet my eyes before returning to her task.

She nibbles on her bottom lip when she finds one she is particularly interested in, then she moves on to the next until I'm covered in bubbles.

I turn toward the shower, washing the soap off my front, when her fingers along my back send a shock through me.

I'm slowly starting to crave her touch, but no one has ever traced their fingers across that line on my back that I'm all too familiar with.

"Will you tell me what happened?" Harlow asks from behind me, and I push my face under the shower before turning to face her.

"Sure, Socks." Grabbing the bottle off the shelf, I squeeze some shampoo out and wash my own hair. "There's not much to tell. I was a teenager when it happened. Wrong place, wrong time, and I got jumped. The guy was twice my age and size at the time. I was just lucky my brother was there. If it wasn't for him—"

I wouldn't be here today is what I want to say, but the words hang back in my head.

I'm not prepared for the emotions to bubble up so fast, and I cut my sentence short, pushing my hair under the spray to avoid oversharing.

My scar is faint now, but it isn't the physical reminder that disturbs me.

The pain I felt as a kid when it happened is something I'll never be able to shake. Even now, looking back at myself, I still feel the raw emotion I felt then. As far as I've come, as strong as I am, I still know that level of terror and vulnerability.

I'll never be rid of it.

Some things always stay with you.

When I rub the water off my face, I'm met with silent understanding.

Harlow places her arms on my biceps and slowly turns me back to face the shower. Her fingers trace along my scar, and I don't freeze this time.

Then Harlow takes it one step further. She steps behind me so she's flush with my body. Her little fingers wrap around my front, and she hugs herself into me as she kisses a trail along my scar.

"You never wanted to cover it with ink?"

"It tells its own story."

I leave it at that for now.

I don't want to tell her it is a reminder of the bond I share with my brothers, even though sometimes it feels like it's fading. I don't want her to know it was the first time I saw my oldest brother kill someone right in front of me, and with his bare hands.

My older memories of my brothers are happy ones. We were close. Sometimes, when I think about them, I wonder if I remember them as they really were or as I wanted them to be.

We got kicked out of the house a lot as kids. My mother was always telling us to "take it outside." Our dad wasn't around much, unless they were having parties or friends over, and Lennox filled the fatherly role, always looking out for the rest of us.

Lennox grew distant as he got older, and he seemed to push Dagen, Ryder, and me away. I figured he was just growing up, that he'd grown out of the things we liked to do for fun.

Shortly after my attack, Lennox shut down. He became unapproachable. He didn't come around to visit as much, and things were always tense when we were in the same room. The tension is thickest between him and Ryder. I think it's because Ryder was younger when Lennox pulled away, so he doesn't remember how close we once were.

And now we've all sunk into some hell. I don't know if there is a way back for any of us this time.

I shut off the water and turn to Harlow, spinning her around and squeezing out her hair before opening the door, grabbing an oversized towel, and wrapping it around her.

Then I tie a towel around my waist and lift Harlow off her feet. She squeals then giggles as I walk her into our bedroom and toss her on the bed.

"Get under the covers and warm up. I have something for you." I dip my head toward the nightstand, and she follows my line of sight to her phone.

"Can I call him?"

I bow my head. "We missed lunch. I'm going to get an early

dinner started. Don't talk too long, and if anything is wrong, come and get me. Do you understand?"

Harlow's large, round eyes tell me she didn't think I would trust her to have her phone on her own. Maybe a small part of me still doesn't, but acting like a dictator won't earn her confidence.

She nods, reaching for her phone.

I drop my towel, giving her a good look as I pick out a pair of pants and a long sleeve shirt before leaving her to her phone call with her brother.

17

HARLOW

I have my phone in my hand, and I can call my brother, but I can't peel my eyes off of the man who just fucked me twice in the bathroom.

His muscles flex as he lifts his shirt over his head before working his beautiful body into it.

On his way out, he drops his gaze to the phone in my hand, and I wonder if he's second-guessing giving me this freedom. But he only winks at me with a knowing smile before sauntering out of the room and leaving me to my privacy.

James picks up on the first ring, but his voice sounds different.

"Hello?" It's more of a question than a greeting.

"Hey, it's me." I pull myself into a seated position, still naked under the covers.

"Is he listening in?"

Now I understand the hesitation in his tone. "No. He went downstairs to make dinner."

James sits in silence on the other end of the line for a few seconds. "What's going on, Harlow?"

"Well, we're hiding out. I don't know if I'm allowed to say where we are, but I'm okay. I wanted to see how you are, so Cole gave me my phone back. Did you go to the hospital?"

There's another pause before he answers, "I mean what's going on with you and him? I saw the way he looked at you, Ducky."

My nickname catches me off guard. I haven't heard that one in a long time. To Genie, I was her Little Harley, but to James, I was Ducky.

When I was little, Genie and James said "duck" instead of "fuck" around me, and I started saying it all the time. James has only ever called me Ducky when we were alone.

It was that one thing that was only ours, and I wonder if he's been taking a stroll down memory lane while he heals.

"It's—complicated." My answer is a cop-out, so I try again. James was shot trying to keep me safe; the least I can do is be completely honest with him. "No, wait, it isn't. I met him before. We kind of—had a one-night thing. It was supposed to be one night. I didn't know who he was, and—" I wince and stop talking. This sounds so irresponsible, and the silent pauses are painful.

"James, where are you? Are you okay?"

"I'm going to be fine. The guys got me out of there. I didn't exactly go to the hospital, but I got medical help. I'll heal. I'm worried about you."

"I know. I'm worried about you too. Are you laying low? Are you at the bar?"

"No. Pete is watching it for me. I'm staying away. I heard some people have been asking about the both of us. I'm not sure what I'll do yet."

My gaze falls on my backpack. "Maybe Cole can get you out of there."

"No." James is quick to cut me off. "I mean. I don't know. Do you trust him?"

I answer without thinking about it. "Yeah. I think I do. He got me out of Portland. I'm still alive. He hasn't locked me up. He gave my phone back and left so I could call you. Those aren't the actions of someone who wants to hurt me, right?"

I don't tell him about anything else that's happened between us, and I sit in silence, waiting for his answer. It's an awkward minute, followed by a deep sigh.

"Ducky, I—"

"I know. I love you too. I'm scared, but right now I'm safe, and it's thanks to you and Cole for fighting for me."

I hate that James doesn't have anyone other than me on his side. He has his friends, but it's not the same. He's spent his whole life looking out for me, and the best I can offer him is someone who stabbed herself with her own pocketknife and almost shot off her foot with a gun.

"So what now?" He changes the subject with a telling warble in his tone.

He doesn't like feeling helpless.

"Now we try to figure out why those people are still after me, and we get justice for Genie."

James clears his throat in response, and I tell him I need to get going, but not before I promise to check in again, soon.

I set my phone on the nightstand and tug the covers up to my chin. There's a chill in the air that seeps into my bones, and I'm not ready to jump out of bed yet.

My body is relaxed, and it's all thanks to Cole for taking care of me in more ways than one.

When I was little, I used to dream about places like this cottage. When I listened to stories about princes, I'm sure I imagined this is what their castles looked like. All of the sheets and towels feel extravagantly soft; everything looks new. There are no holes or stains anywhere in sight.

A little voice in the back of my head reminds me: this is not me. This is not a life I should get accustomed to, because it is not mine. Just because I'm here right now doesn't mean I belong here.

Just don't get attached.

"Did you fall asleep up there?" Cole's voice from the bottom of the stairs pulls me from my self-loathing, and the smell of cooking meat hits my nose.

"I'm not coming down until it's summer," I yell toward the hall, and his laughter carries up to my room.

"It's warm down here. I'll get the fire going. Join me."

Maybe I can enjoy this fairy tale awhile longer.

I tear off the figurative Band-Aid and go for my clothes, pulling them on before the cold gets into my skin. Lifting my backpack, I get out my travel-size antiperspirant and open it up. The smallest chunk of deodorant falls out, and I put it back then gingerly apply the little amount I have left, mentally telling myself to pick up a new one soon.

When I run my fingers through my hair, they get trapped in a tangle, and I reach into my bag for my comb. I don't find it on my first couple of dives, and I try to remember when I last had it.

When I stayed with James, he had a comb and brush in his bathroom, and I used those. Mine must have fallen to the bottom of my backpack.

I dig deeper, but I don't feel the teeth of my comb anywhere. It's been a long time since I've gone through my stuff.

Grabbing my backpack by the bottom, I pour its contents all over Cole's bed and search through my items for my comb.

There it is.

I don't usually go through my stuff unless I'm prepared to see the faces on the photos looking back at me.

I'm not ready to look at them today either, and I turn my body to face out the window, looking over the water while I comb the tangle out of my hair.

Cole turned some music on, and an upbeat jazzy tune makes its way up the stairs.

I don't know what I expected him to listen to, but this isn't it.

Cole is a man of many surprises.

I smile to myself, excited to know more about him, then I turn to quickly pack my stuff away.

I handle the photos with care, but I don't linger on them.

I know all of the faces by heart. I'm just not ready to see the smiles that are no longer here. My photos have become a reminder of everything I've lost.

I pack them away into a side pocket, and my eyes immediately zero in on something that's out of place among the rest of my things.

I stare at it for a few seconds before my stomach lurches into my throat.

Genie, what have you done?

I reach out to touch it to make sure I'm not seeing things, then I recoil, clutching my hand to my chest as though it could burn me.

Duck.

Duck. Duck. Double duck.

The last time I saw this memory stick, Genie was holding it in her hands in the car before we went into that building. But how did I end up with it?

I search my memories. I know I saw it on the table before we left. Genie was fidgeting with it as I drove. We talked in the car, then we got out, and she—

DUCK!

She went around to the trunk, and she must have had second thoughts. The only thing that makes sense is she slid it into my bag. Maybe she wanted to wait until that woman showed up before handing it over. I'll never know.

But what do I do now?

This is what everyone is looking for.

Will the other people just stop coming after James and me if I hand it over?

What will happen if I give it to Cole? He's looking for it too. Does this mean we both go our own way? I don't run in his circles—at all. I'm the help, not the one who lounges around in bed after being fucked twice and taking a luxurious shower in my million-dollar second home.

Insecurity sweeps over me, temporarily paralyzing me as I weigh my options.

Genie obviously felt the need to keep it close to her, but look where that got her.

I pack up everything else I dumped out, and I circle back to the memory stick over and over again.

What should I do?

Maybe I should call James back and ask him, but I know my brother and what he's going to say.

He'll tell me to run, and I'm not ready to leave Cole again. I've already left him twice, once the morning after and once in the bar, and it went destructively wrong both times.

I search the bathroom and find my warm socks, which I pull on before leaving his room and heading down the stairs to join him.

When I enter, his back is to me, but the little sway in his hips tells me he likes the tune that is playing.

His look of concentration brightens into a smile when he turns and notices me. He points to the counter between us. "I poured you a glass of red. It'll go with the seared steak." He nods at the meat in the cast iron skillet on the stove.

"Thank you." I step to my side of the counter to slide out a barstool, but decide against taking a seat. Instead I reach for the wine.

"So do you know who's looking for me?" I try to sound like I'm making small talk, but Cole freezes for a second, his eyes warily scanning my face.

"Not yet. But I'm working on it. What did you talk about with your brother?"

He's onto me, my inner voice warns.

"He's going to be okay. He's just worried about me. He said he heard some people have been by the bar asking about us."

Cole stops chopping vegetables. "Did he say who?"

"No. I don't think anyone knows. He's laying low."

"Good," Cole mutters to himself before he goes back to preparing dinner.

I take another gulp of the wine and look around the kitchen, trying to decide what to do.

Do you trust him? I think about James's question.

I do. Just like that, and this makes me not trust myself. But keeping things from Cole doesn't feel natural either.

I reach into my pocket. My fingers wrap around the little USB drive, and the hint of nausea rolls through me.

I realize I'm wearing my guilt all over my face when Cole looks up to meet my eyes.

"What aren't you telling me?" His face morphs into cautious concern.

We always have a choice, Socks. Cole's words from yesterday haunt me.

I have a choice

But the question is, which one is the right one?

18

COLE

I knew from the moment Harlow entered the kitchen that something was off.

I've either become a psychic in the last seventy-two hours, or she is incredibly easy to read.

When I turned to greet her, her eyes snapped to mine at record speed. With a forced smile on her face, she shuffled to the counter as though held back by an invisible barrier.

So while I know something is up, I don't know what it is. And until I do, I'll keep my own cards close to my chest with a smile. I'll wait for her to come to me.

Harlow strikes me as someone who is used to fending for herself. She's close with her brother, and I get the impression they grew up relying on each other.

Trust forged like that is unbreakable.

I know there isn't anything I wouldn't do for my family.

While I'm happy Harlow had her siblings in her corner, this makes it more difficult to work my way into her tight-knit group. In order to earn her trust, I'm going to have to start by showing her I trust her. That's why I left her alone to talk with her brother.

Do I want to know every single thing they said? Hell yes, but gaining her confidence is more important.

I take a sip of my wine while Harlow tells me what they talked about on the phone. I've returned to chopping vegetables when she tells me that James told her some people have been looking for her.

I really need to get a handle on who these *people* are.

As we drink and make small talk, Harlow begins to break down. Worry stresses its way across her face, and she glances around the room as though she's planning her escape.

When she looks like she's going to crawl out of her own skin and pushes her hands into her pockets, I snap.

I can't take the pained look on her face. Something is eating her alive from the inside out.

"What aren't you telling me?"

I don't ask the question in anger. I don't accuse her of anything. I just don't like to see her distressed like this.

It tugs at my heart, and I don't know why.

Pulling her hands out of her pockets, she clenches her fingers into fists and hugs herself.

We both know she's keeping something from me, and I wonder if she and James spoke about anything else.

Dropping her head, she takes a half step closer to the counter before looking at me as though she's trying to see into my soul.

"Um." She takes one deep breath before reaching her fist out and lowering her hand to rest on the counter.

When she opens her fingers and pulls her hand back, we both stare in silence at the USB stick.

Realization dawns on me, and I look up at her for confirmation.

"That's not mine."

"I don't understand." I brace my palms on the counter on either side of the stick.

When I level Harlow with a stare, her wide eyes tell me everything I need to know.

She's as confused as I am.

"I—I was looking for something in my backpack, and this was at the bottom of it. I just found it. I think—I think it's that thing you're looking for. The drive Genie was going to hand over. Only somehow it ended up in my backpack. Is that why people are after me? Is James still safe?" She looks at the little thing like it's about to come alive and attack her.

I know what she's thinking; I see it all over her face. I'll need to remember never to ask Harlow to lie on my behalf, because this one is no good at hiding her emotions and matching her face to her fibs.

Things felt different for her when it was just her running and she had nothing on her. Maybe she thought if she ran long enough, she would drop off everyone's radar. But now, she has something tangible. She has the files people have literally killed for.

Knowing all of this, Harlow trusted me. She gave me the files my family needs.

This is a big step forward from just yesterday. Twenty-four hours ago, I'm not sure she would have handed this over.

Harlow stares at the item between us, fussing her lower lip between her teeth. She's unsure if she made the right decision.

"Your brother is fine if he lays low. Help me with the plates. Food's getting cold." I top off our wine and check the steak.

"What? That's it? You don't want to..." She points at the memory stick.

"The only thing I want to do right now is enjoy a meal with you."

Harlow tilts her head to the side, like I'm some difficult puzzle she needs to figure out. Maybe I am, but I give her a little more to settle her nerves.

"Socks, neither of us knew that was in the bottom of your backpack until five minutes ago. I want to pretend it's still hidden, and I want to sit down and have a meal with the woman I just fucked silly in the shower. Please." I point to the counter. "It will still be there when we are done eating. I promise."

Her shoulders relax, and the worry slips from her face, replaced by a smile. I turn to grab her plate and serve her steak before opening the oven and pulling out a baked potato that I left in there to warm. Resting the plate on the counter, I point to the salad I just finished chopping. "Help yourself, but I want to see a lot of veggies on your plate."

I serve myself the exact same amount and follow her to the table to drop my food off before returning for the wine bottle.

Our dinner is relaxed as we slip away from all the bullshit we are dealing with and search for other things to talk about.

It turns out Harlow loves to hike. She doesn't like social media, and painting relaxes her, but she thinks she's horrible at it. James has never been able to guess what her pictures are supposed to be.

She has been watching my plate for the last five minutes. I'm swallowing my last bite and chasing it with a gulp of wine as I lean back in my chair when she finally speaks.

"There's one more thing I haven't told you. The day you showed up at the bar, my brother had just finished showing me pictures of your brothers so I would know who to avoid. Um— one of your brothers was there that night, when Genie was killed."

I pull my phone from my pocket and go to some of my favorite photos, pulling up a close-up of Dagen I took last year. He went to the address that night, but he said he got there too late.

I show her the photo, and she shakes her head. I swipe my finger across the screen, pulling up a photo of Lennox. He's a harder one to pin down for family pics, so I grabbed this one from Eros's social media a while ago to have on hand.

"That's him."

"Can you tell me more about that? Did you see him go in before she was killed?" My heart prepares for the worst.

"No. I didn't see him until after. It was someone else first. Maybe older. Your brother was the one I saw after I found Genie lying there and ran back to my hiding spot."

I huff in relief. I don't know what this means, but it does mean Lennox didn't pull the trigger. He was still there that night, so maybe he knows who did? Would he have hired a hit? Maybe he went back in because the killer wasn't able to find the memory stick. My gaze drifts to the counter where it still sits.

Just as one question is answered, three more pop up.

"I have dessert in the fridge, but before we get to it, I'm going to pop this into my laptop to see what's on it."

"Can it wait until after dessert?" Harlow licks her lips.

Maybe my little hellcat has a sweet tooth just like me.

"No. I plan on licking my dessert off your naked body. You'll be too sticky and exhausted to care about anything later." I rise, clearing our plates and winking at her.

Her lips twist into a mischievous smile, and she shudders in her seat.

I return to the table with my laptop and the USB and open it up in front of her. We're past the point of keeping secrets. I curl my fingers, inviting her to take the seat beside me.

She settles into my side when the link for the drive pops up on my screen.

I click to open it.

Nothing happens.

I try again before looking up the file information. In truth, it was stupid of me to just start randomly clicking away. For all I know, this could be loaded with viruses.

I'm anxious to find out what's on it, and it's clouding my judgment.

"It looks like it's encrypted," I murmur as I click to eject the stick.

"What does that mean?" Harlow's gaze meets mine, and I smile.

"It means there's nothing we can do about it tonight, and it's time for dessert."

Harlow returns to her seat, where she lifts her spoon, and I chuckle.

"I wasn't joking about you being naked, Socks. I need to make a call, and I'll be right up with some chocolate mousse and a ridiculous amount of whipped cream."

It takes her a few seconds to process what I'm insinuating before she fills our glasses with what is left of the wine and takes both as she leaves with a shy grin on her face.

Everything about this woman intrigues me.

She's nothing like the women I've gone for in the past; she makes the stark contrast crystal clear. I've always hooked up with the emotionally unavailable ones. The ones who were looking for a good time, because that was all I had the capacity to provide before.

But Harlow is different. She sucks me in like I'm drowning, and I don't want to save myself. Instead, I want to possess and protect.

The phone rings twice before Ryder answers.

"What the hell, man!"

"Sorry, I've been—" My mind wanders to the shower earlier today. "Busy. Listen, I can't go into it right now, but I think I'm holding the video Amara was supposed to get that night."

"WHAT?"

As soon as Ryder raises his tone, more voices join him in the background, and Ryder repeats what I just told him before he shushes everyone and returns to our conversation.

"How did you—I mean—WHAT?"

"Harlow found it in the bottom of her backpack and gave it to me."

Ryder is silent on the other end, but I hear Amara and Sloane, along with Dagen, asking for an update.

This information will hit Ryder the hardest. Grayson was his best friend, and he was close to our family. He was Amara's brother, and if this is the evidence we are looking for, then it's everything.

Every day that we can't let Grayson rest in peace is a day we've all failed him.

"There's a problem with the file. I think it's encrypted. We need to get it to our guy. I don't want to do anything stupid and damage it. Know what I mean?"

Ryder exhales a steady breath. This feels like we're trying to diffuse a bomb before it detonates.

I have a contact in Seattle who's done a lot of work for our family in the past, but he's a bit eccentric. He only deals with people who don't make him feel uncomfortable, and, for some reason, he and I get along really well, so I manage the jobs we do through him.

He's great, but he won't work with anyone but me.

"You're right. Where are you? Can you make it here?"

"I'm keeping Harlow out of Seattle for now. It's not safe for her there."

"Hmm."

I don't like Ryder's tone. "What?"

Ryder chuckles on the other end. "It's just that I don't ever remember you being this concerned about some random woman before."

I know he said it loud enough so everyone in the room heard him, and I hear Sloane and Amara talking back and forth in the background. I know I just heard the word "girlfriend."

Fucker.

They are going to be awful when I see them next.

"Shut up." That makes Ryder laugh out loud before he says something to Dagen I can't make out. "You're going to make me regret the plan I'm about to share with you."

"Hit me."

"I just might." I shake my head.

More chuckles from my younger brother.

I unlock one of the few small safes I keep around the place and set the memory stick inside before I tell him what I'm thinking. "Listen, I won't risk bringing Harlow into Seattle, and I won't leave her alone."

"So where does that leave us?"

I roll my eyes to the ceiling. I'm going to need to buy a new secret hideaway.

"How do you all feel about taking a road trip tomorrow?"

"Road trip?" Ryder repeats to make sure he understood me, and the two women squeal in the background.

Fuck me.

19

HARLOW

Cole waited until we woke up this morning to tell me some of his family would be driving out to stay with me for a couple of days, and I'm glad he did.

I probably wouldn't have slept a minute last night if I knew I'd be meeting his brothers.

I'm used to small, quiet gatherings, and I'm hit with anxiety every time I try to come up with topics for small talk.

I have to admit, lying in bed with him and watching his face light up as he told me about his family made me happy. He's assured me more than once that I won't be meeting his oldest brother anytime soon.

Now I'm covertly circling the house, trying to watch the driveway for signs of their arrival.

"You're going to wear the carpet out if you keep pacing, Socks." Cole chuckles into his coffee as I adjust the curtains for the tenth time.

I spin to look at him, then I take my empty mug off the shelf. "Maybe I'll get another cup." I take a few steps toward the kitchen when Cole stands up, blocking my path.

"If you drink another cup, I'll never get you off the ceiling." Wrapping his hands around my upper arms, he steadies me.

Right, that would make three cups, and I'm already feeling the effects of going over my one a day.

Cole holds his hands out, silently negotiating with me to hand over the mug, and I comply with a sheepish smile.

He combs my hair out of my face then rests his hand at the back of my head. "Relax. They are going to love you."

Am I that obvious?

"But—with everything—"

After breakfast, Cole and I talked about the night Genie died. He told me what had happened to them and how one of the women coming today almost died trying to get to Genie. He told me how they rushed her to the hospital and then how his other brother found my sister too late.

By proxy, how could these people like me so easily?

They don't even know me.

"Your sister died trying to hand over those files. You lost more than any of us did that night. We all know that, Harlow." Setting the cup aside, he pulls me in for a hug. He smells like sex—and bacon. "Besides, I have a feeling about you and the girls. You're right up their alley."

As if on cue, the crushing of rocks under tires announces the arrival of a vehicle.

"They're here." Cole tenses in my hands. "Damn, girl. Watch the nails."

"Oh. Sorry. I'm nervous." I loosen my fingers from his back.

"Well, save that business for the next time I get you alone." He meets my eyes and winks, licking his lower lip, and the gesture warms my cheeks.

Looking down, I fidget with my top, flattening it out and making sure it's presentable before gliding my fingers through my hair.

After a moment of watching me, Cole wraps his big hand around my own and tugs me toward the door.

He passes me the same oversized coat I wore yesterday, then he opens the door and steps outside as he slides his arms into his jacket.

Part of me wants to run out to join him, but I hang back, fastening the zipper before leaving the warm house. I keep my body behind him to slowly ease myself in, and from there I listen to the banter.

"I wasn't sure if you'd be coming here, or if I'd just drive in to meet you." Cole talks to the guy who gets out of the front passenger side.

"Please. Do you think I'd let Amara and Sloane come all the way out here without checking this place out myself? Besides, you've always been there to back me up. I'm not letting you do this alone. We go in together."

Cole steps to the side, pulling me into his side and pointing to the man he just spoke to. "This is my younger brother, Ryder. Ryder, this is Harlow."

Everyone stops what they were doing and looks at us for a hushed second before the two women step forward. One practically moves Ryder out of her way before he shakes my hand, and he rolls his eyes, saying "Here we go" to himself as she reaches her hand out to introduce herself.

"I'm Sloane. It's nice to meet you, Harlow."

I shake her hand. "And you are?" I point to both brothers, silently asking her who she is with.

Sloane points to Ryder. "I'm his fiancée."

Ryder rolls his eyes again.

"And I'm his wife," the other woman says from beside the car before stepping up to join us. "I'm Amara."

My hand is almost in Amara's when her words hit me, and I look at her in confusion.

They both laugh, and the man at the driver's side shakes his head before looking at Cole.

"Finally. Now we can all stop hearing about this. These two"—he points between Amara and Sloane—"have been dying to say that. For an hour-long road trip, it was the longest car ride of my life."

Cole laughs, and I look up at him with a smile. "I don't understand."

"They'll explain it later. I wanted to leave you with some things to talk about while I was gone." Cole kisses the top of my head and squeezes me against his body.

The women smile and look at each other, and both men straighten, zeroing in on Cole before exchanging a glance.

I grasp Amara's hand and shake it when I notice her other arm outside the sleeve of her jacket. It's set in a brace of sorts.

She's the one who almost died the night I lost my sister.

My eyes snap to hers.

Just smile, I tell myself.

"Hey. It's okay." Cole rubs my arm, pulling me out of my thoughts.

Amara lifts her arm, tapping it with her good hand. "It's healing fine." She smiles. "Besides, I can throw a better punch with this one anyway." She holds her good hand up, wiggling her fingers, and I laugh to release my tension when Sloane speaks.

"She's serious."

Amara closes her jacket over her wrapped wrist and takes a step closer, smiling. "We'll talk about it over wine later—lots of wine, and I'll get you to drunk-sign this stupid thing."

"No getting drunk, Blossom." Ryder raises his voice from behind her.

"You're no fun." Amara pretends to pout then shoots me a sly smirk out of her husband's line of sight.

"Just wait until I get you home. I'll remind you how much fun I can be." Ryder's threat is met with a blush from Amara.

Ryder and Sloane start taking things out of the trunk when the other brother joins Cole and me. I recognize him from the photos Cole showed me last night.

"And which brother are you?" I ask.

His smile turns mischievous as he levels me with a sly wink. "I thought it was obvious; I'm the good-looking brother."

"This is Dagen."

I shake his hand as well, but before I pull away, he turns my hand, lifts it to his lips, and kisses the back of it. When he looks up, his eyes aren't on mine. They're watching Cole, and Cole hugs me into him.

Dagen smirks. "That's what I thought," he mutters to himself, but we both hear him.

Cole clears his throat, changing the subject. "Where's Henry?" Cole asks Dagen specifically, and I get the feeling he is trying to pull the attention away from me.

"We dropped him off with Sloane's parents on our way out of town. Probably for the best since everyone will want to catch up, and he's not supposed to know about some things."

I smile between the two brothers even though the answer makes no sense to me.

"Let's get inside, and we'll talk before we head back to Seattle." Cole indicates himself and Ryder.

We all line up at the trunk and carry bags and suitcases into the house, where I crawl out of the oversized parka while everyone looks around the place.

"I can't believe you never told us about this place. Henry would love it out here." Sloane walks over to the fireplace and turns it on.

"What part of 'secret hideout' did you not understand?"

Cole asks incredulously before turning his attention to me. "Help me with the coffee?"

I follow him into the kitchen and to the cupboard where his cups are. He steps close to me, blocking me from the open room behind him.

"You doing okay?" Cole stands over me as though shielding me from life's disappointments, and I like being under his care in this way.

"I am. I like your family." I step into him, slipping my fingers into his shirt on the sides of his midsection.

He cups my chin with his fingers and lifts my head, capturing my stare. "Good. They like you."

"How do you know?"

"Because I like you, Socks. And they'd be stupid not to."

I can't label what is happening between us, but I want it to continue. I don't want him to leave.

As if reading my thoughts, he says, "It's only for a day. You'll be safe here—with them. They won't let anything happen to you."

I nod.

I'm humbled that Cole would pull his family out here for me.

Whatever is passing between us is overwhelming at times.

I step away and reach for mugs to set on the counter, and Cole pours four cups before announcing there is coffee ready for anyone who wants it.

Dagen and Ryder immediately take him up on his offer. They pass us on their way into the kitchen as we join Amara and Sloane near the couch.

Amara pulls a light jacket out of a bag as I take my seat. "Cole mentioned you didn't have enough time to grab many clothes or a warm jacket. I hope you don't mind, but Sloane and

I brought out some things for you." She holds the jacket up toward me, sizing it with her eyes.

"You didn't have to—"

Sloane cuts in. "We wanted to. Trust me, we both have way too many clothes. Besides, thrifting is kind of an obsession of mine, and now I have room to buy more." Excitedly, she opens a second bag and pulls out some more clothes.

"I love thrifting." Both women smile at my confession.

I like them.

Dagen and Ryder join us, handing Amara and Sloane a cup of coffee, and we settle in as they go over their plans.

Ryder and Cole are taking his truck into Seattle to see if they can get the files off of the stick. With the timing of the ferry, Cole will try to get back tonight, but that is a best-case scenario, and no one else seems confident it will happen.

Everyone else will stay here, so we'll get the place to ourselves. Amara and Sloane are already planning a dinner party followed by drinks and a movie.

To be totally honest, this sounds like an amazing night. These two are reminding me what it was like hanging out with my own sister before everything went bad. It's a bittersweet feeling.

After an hour, Cole grabs his bag and the memory stick, and we say goodbye.

I watch Amara and Ryder out of the corner of my eye. He's a different person when he focuses his attention on her. It reminds me of Cole.

Ryder lifts Amara's wrist and kisses it before kissing her and whispering something in her ear that makes her blush as she bows her head into him.

When I look at Cole, I find him staring at me from across the room. He looks like he's deep in thought.

If we were alone, I know I would walk across the room and

kiss him, but everything is new between us, and it is still early, so maybe we could—what? Fist-bump? High-five?

I'm so lost listing the different friendly ways we could say goodbye that I don't notice Cole has walked the few steps across the room and is standing in my space.

"Oh, hey. I—" That's the end of my thought when Cole pulls me tight against his body and crashes his lips onto mine. Everything tilts and swirls. He tastes so damn good.

When he breaks the kiss, the room is silent.

At least I think it is—I can't hear anything, but I might have blocked everyone out.

I smile up at him, and I'm sure it's a goofy one.

He just kissed me in front of his family.

"I'll see you soon, Socks." Cole takes one long look at me before stepping away. His tone changes when he levels his brothers with a death stare. "Not a word."

We walk them to the door, and I watch as the truck pulls out of the driveway and through the trees.

It's only a day, I tell myself.

What's the worst that could happen?

20

COLE

I didn't want to leave Harlow this morning. It's not because I don't trust my brothers; I would put my own life in their hands. It's because I knew the moment I walked out the door I would miss her, and I don't know how I feel about that.

On the drive to the ferry, Ryder didn't mention anything about the way I said goodbye. I would have deserved every little bit of ribbing from the way I teased him when Amara came back.

Instead, he waited until we were out in the middle of the bay before asking me about her. He probably wanted to make sure I had nowhere to run away to, although I considered jumping ship and swimming the rest of the way in.

There wasn't much to say.

It's still new.

We don't know each other well enough yet.

Blah, blah, blah.

It was all bullshit, and we both knew it. Those are the things you say when someone hits you the right way and you're too afraid to own it for fear you'll lose it the next time you turn around.

I've never been afraid of losing someone who wasn't family before.

I drove through Seattle with new eyes. There's something here that is a threat to Harlow, and I need to find out what it is.

As much as I didn't want to leave her, I have to admit: I thoroughly enjoy coming to see the guy we are about to meet up with.

The walking poster child for delusional paranoia, he calls himself Dark Webb because his last name is Webb. For someone who is so worried that the government is trying to take him down, I don't know why he would make his literal last name part of his secret code name.

I think if I had a code name, it would be something like Dirty Nutsack. That way, when I was taken down, the media would have to print that and say it on the six o'clock news, but I digress.

I like this guy, I think as we wait in silence to be buzzed into his lair. I don't dare say it out loud. He's probably got everything bugged, and I don't want to risk our good standing with him. We need his help, and he's the best at what he does.

Ryder stands behind me in a huff. My brother has been trying to get on Dark Webb's good side for years, but he's not having any of it.

The door buzzes and opens on its own. Webb isn't there to meet us. We still have some screening to get through, and I step inside in silence and walk down the hall toward a modified body scanner. It's homemade with wires and lights. I'm half convinced it doesn't actually work.

A voice comes through an intercom. "Do you have any guns?"

Ryder mutters a curse under his breath. His voice is laced

with frustration as he points to the metal contraption we just walked through. "Isn't that what your little x-ray time machine here is supposed to pick up?"

I turn and smack him in the chest and try real hard not to laugh.

"They're locked in the truck. I followed protocol, Dark Webb." I manage to respond with absolute sincerity.

There's a moment of silence where I glare at Ryder. This fucker's impatience is going to get our asses tossed out of here. Then I'll have to go in by force, and Webb and I won't be friends anymore.

Ryder lifts his hands in supplication. He knows what's on the line.

A second door in front of us buzzes, and I reach out to grab it before it locks again.

Leonard Webb is an eccentric man. He's harmless until you need something digital—then he's lethal.

"Hey, Cole. It's nice to see you." He stands up from his security station, which consists of eight computer screens that shuffle through different camera angles of the property. My truck flashes on one monitor, and the live feed of the room we are in remains on another.

"It's nice to see you too, Dark Webb."

I made the mistake of calling him Leo once when I tried to be friendly, and it took me a few months to come back from it.

Lesson learned.

"You have something for me?" Leonard walks away from his normal computer equipment and pulls out a souped-up laptop, which he sets on a table before sitting down.

I join him with Ryder at my back and set the memory stick beside his computer.

Picking it up, he examines the casing before inserting it into a port. Then he loses me when he starts typing away. Black windows with code pop up on the screen, and he types in a foreign language.

This is why we have him on speed dial.

"Pull up a couple of chairs. This is going to take some time." Leonard's eyes stay focused on his task, but Ryder and I exchange a glance.

Inviting both of us to join him is an olive branch, and Ryder knows it. My brother's scowl morphs into a smug grin as we grab our seats.

Almost an hour passes as Leonard taps away at his keyboard. Neither of us says a thing. Ryder has his foot in the door, and he's determined not to get kicked out this time.

I'm half tempted to taunt him into screwing up, but he was good enough not to push me about Harlow, so I decide to let him have this small victory.

"I have it. You're looking for a video file, right?" Leonard looks up from his screen, and we both nod.

He turns the screen toward us, taps a key, and the file loads.

"Gray," Ryder whispers, his face falling.

This is it.

There is no mistaking the warehouse where we found Grayson's body.

Both of us lean forward when he walks into camera range. It happened at night, so the video is dark, but it's clearly our friend.

Grayson takes a few steps, then he stops suddenly and turns around, as if startled by a sound. Ryder and I look at each other in confusion.

"Volume?" I ask Leonard.

He shakes his head. "There's no sound. If I had more time, I could tell you if the file is corrupt, or if the security camera lacked audio capabilities."

We look back to the screen, and only Grayson is in view from the camera angle, but he is clearly talking to someone.

Out of nowhere, his arms go up, and he falls back and down to the ground.

I feel sick all over again. I feel the same pain I felt when I heard someone found his body. Placing a hand on Ryder's shoulder, I give him a squeeze to let him know I'm here.

He fists his hand on the table, and I hear the swallow he forces down his throat at the sight.

We wait for someone to approach the body. I want to see a fucking face so we can end this, so I can give Sloane, Amara and Ryder—and Grayson—the peace they deserve.

A full minute passes, then another, and no one enters the video.

Ryder's impatience manifests into frustration as he leans back in his seat, crossing his arms, and I look at Leonard.

"Can you fast-forward this until we see someone else? Or the end of the video?" I don't want to watch Grayson lying dead and alone for much longer, and I sure as hell don't want Ryder to have to.

Leonard nods solemnly and turns the screen back to face him. Then he turns it back, pointing at the time stamp. "Here. Just over half an hour later."

When he presses play, it is still just Grayson on the screen, but I'm invested in what is coming.

Grayson was officially found over six hours later, the next morning, by some dock workers, so whoever this is didn't report anything.

A shadow in the upper left section of the screen sucks the air out of the room.

There's no mistaking who it is when they step into view.

"Lennox." Ryder says the name I'm thinking in my head.

Lennox walks into the frame a few steps before stopping suddenly as he finds Grayson's body.

I have no words. He knew Grayson had been shot hours before any of us did, and he said nothing. He knew Grayson. He knows Sloane.

Yet—

My thoughts are pushed out of my head when Lennox surprises both of us with what he does next.

He jumps toward the body, his hand going to Grayson's neck.

Is he checking for a pulse?

"What the—" Ryder sounds as confused as I feel.

Then we gasp in unison as Lennox goes into full CPR.

Is he trying to save him?

I know our oldest brother enough to tell when he is in crisis mode, and this is it. He jumps between mouth-to-mouth, chest compressions, and trying for a pulse before his body sags, his forehead lying on Grayson's chest as though—as though he feels the loss too.

After two minutes, he sits himself up but stays beside Grayson as he lies lifeless on the screen.

Then he does something he's only reserved for his brothers.

Lennox sets his hand on Grayson's chest and says something to him before standing.

When we were little, Lennox would tuck us in at night. Dad was married to the company, and we didn't see much of him. Lennox would wander into our room, pick out a book, and start reading.

When he was done, he'd put his hand on our chest or arm and say goodnight.

Before Lennox turns to leave the crime scene, he takes one look around. His body freezes when he squares himself on the camera. Then he leaves Grayson there to be found the next morning.

"Is there any more movement?" My voice hitches in my throat as I ask Leonard, and he turns the screen back to him.

Ryder wears all of his questions in his expression, but he stays silent. The pain we experienced when we found out Grayson was murdered is now raw and festering once again.

Those were his last moments.

"The video stops almost an hour after that."

The cameras were turned off well before Grayson was found. Now we know it wasn't done after the fact.

"Can I get a copy of the video that will play without doing all of"—I point to his fancy equipment—"this?"

"Sure thing. I'll have it in a minute." Leonard opens a drawer and pulls out a second memory stick.

Ryder is disturbingly quiet.

When Leonard hands over both sticks, I tell him he'll get his payment through our regular channels, and we leave quickly.

I start up my truck and turn to my brother. I hate what he saw, and he's hurting. We sit for a few minutes while the truck heats up, and eventually Ryder breaks the silence.

"Amara can't see that. Not—not until we figure this out."

He looks conflicted. I know he said Amara should be included in everything, and it pains him to keep this from her. But he isn't doing it out of secrecy. He's doing it because he knows this will crush her, and he wants to be able to fix it before she needs to see it.

"You don't think it was him?" We both know I mean Lennox.

The lines on Ryder's forehead become prominent as he considers my question. "He didn't shoot Grayson, but I don't know where that leaves us. We can't just ask him. What if he hired the person who did? Or what if he didn't, and he's in trouble?"

I share all of Ryder's thoughts on this, and I stew for a while before I pull out my phone.

"I'm going to follow up with Creed. He's assured me they aren't looking for Harlow, but that isn't what her brother heard. Maybe they have something." I hit send. "There. He'll respond when he can."

I glance at the time.

Shit.

"What is it?" Ryder looks at my phone.

"We might just make the last ferry." I put the truck in drive, but Ryder stops me.

"Let's go back in the morning. Stay at the house tonight." I must be showing my hesitation because Ryder continues, "Give them time to get to know Harlow. Amara and Sloane both need this. Besides, Dad's been bugging us to see Mom. Why don't I tell them we're dropping by on our own for once? We'll catch a ferry out after breakfast tomorrow."

This isn't the only reason Ryder is hesitant to make a run for the last ferry—he isn't ready to see Amara yet. She'll know something is off if he doesn't take some time to compose himself before he sees her again.

"Fine. But we don't share any of this with Dad. We don't know what's going on yet, and I don't want him involved until we do."

"Agreed." Ryder fastens his seat belt before pulling out his phone and texting our father.

Maybe he's right. I need to give everyone else a chance to get to know Harlow too.

While I'd rather go to our family house than visit our father, I do miss my mom. She has moments when she's confused, but she's doing well, and I don't see her much since they downsized and moved out.

"This is fucked up," Ryder mutters under his breath, and I have to agree with him.

We're treading a slippery slope, and one wrong step could seal our fate.

21

HARLOW

I can't help but steal another glance at the kissy-face emoji Cole used in his text message tonight.

While I'm disappointed I won't see him until tomorrow, I have to admit, I'm having fun and forgetting about things with Amara and Sloane here.

For one night, I can pretend that nothing is wrong. I'm not on the run, and everything is—normal. Even the word "normal" sounds—odd.

"I found the blender. We officially have everything we need to make frozen margaritas. Where are the glasses?" Sloane looks over her shoulder as she hauls the heavy appliance up from the bottom shelf.

I point to the cupboard behind Amara, and she turns, pulling the glasses out one at a time with her good hand.

"Aren't those a little cold for the season? I could make you both a hot toddy…" Then I mumble to myself, "If I remembered how Cole made them."

They both stop what they're doing and turn their attention to me.

"I'm sorry." Amara abandons the glasses and joins us at the counter. "Did you just say Cole made you a—hot toddy?"

"Yes." Judging by the sneaky smirk Amara and Sloane exchange with each other, I'm not sure I was supposed to share this information. "Um, I'm not sure I was supposed to say anything." My cheeks warm as they laugh.

The front door opens, and Dagen yells to tell us he's back from checking the yard. My eyes bulge. I shouldn't have said anything. "Hey." I look over my shoulder to make sure Dagen can't hear us. "Maybe don't say anything about that. I shouldn't have—"

Sloane covers one of my hands with her own. "Your secret's safe with us." She plugs the blender in and reviews the ingredients on the counter before meeting my eyes. "I do reserve the right to use it against Cole when he least expects it though."

"Deal."

Dagen catches the tail end of our conversation. "I don't like this one bit."

"What's not to like?" Amara asks, feigning an innocence I'm not sure she possesses.

"Well, for starters, this"—he points around the area between us—"feels a bit like a mutiny. Second, and most importantly: there are only three glasses on the counter. Somebody better be making me one of whatever you're having."

Amara looks at the four of us and then the three glasses before apologizing and grabbing another glass.

Dagen tells us that everything looks fine outside and we are all inside for the night, then he steps over to set the alarm.

I startle when the blender cuts to life beside me, and Sloane mouths the word *sorry* over the grating ice.

"I'm still a little jumpy, I guess." I look down to the counter in embarrassment.

"Hey." Amara leans in, setting her brace on the counter and supporting her weight on her forearms. "I get it." She looks at Sloane. "We get it."

"So you keep these coming, and I'll leave you alone until it's time for a movie, and no one says anything about this fruity drink to my brothers." Dagen takes the first margarita and lifts it to us in a cheers motion before walking out. He's one step from turning the corner when he looks back. "We won't be watching anything *romantic*, so don't even put it in your top three choices, because it's an automatic rejection." He shudders and sticks out his tongue in fake nausea before he leaves.

I watch him go, then I turn back to our group. "So I'm guessing he's single then."

They burst out laughing.

"That's an understatement." Sloane slides the drinks toward us on the counter, and Amara and I follow her to the couch in front of the fireplace.

"I don't know his story, actually." Amara takes a sip of her drink before humming her appreciation. Then she lowers her voice and continues, "Sloane, what's Dagen's history? Just, like, an eternal bachelor, or what?"

Sloane glances toward the stairs. "I think someone did a real number on him, but I don't know everything. I catch bits and pieces here and there, when Cole and Ryder bug him about things, but I never ask." Sloane looks at Amara. "You know how it was. Ryder and Cole were the closest, and since I was Ryder's friend..." She lets the insinuation that she wouldn't have been close enough to Dagen to know his personal business linger. "Anyway, he laughs along with them, but I get the sense it bugs him."

"What about the rest of your family? You have a brother.

What about your parents?" Amara prompts, turning her attention to me.

We had a short talk about Genie earlier, and she doesn't bring her up again.

At this point, I might prefer to talk about Genie rather than my mom.

"Um, I never knew who my father was. My mother, she—we all had different fathers. She passed away a long time ago." My stomach twists, and I take a big gulp of my drink to avoid saying more.

The sharp pain of a brain freeze explodes behind my eyes, and I lift my hand to my forehead.

"Ugh. Ice cream headache. Try swallowing."

I'm not sure which one of them said that, and I swallow a few times, pinching my eyes shut as hard as I can until the pain passes. Once it does, I blink, only to find them both looking at me in silence.

"Hey. You're okay," Amara says as she takes another gulp. "We don't choose our family. We choose who we love, and we make those people our family." I lift my cup to drink to that, and she keeps going. "If it'll make you feel better, my parents literally sold me—twice." She lifts her own glass to toast the air.

I choke on the crushed ice and splutter margarita into my hands as they both laugh.

Then I do the most normal thing I know:

I laugh with them.

What else can I do? Let my past define me? Let it dictate how I live the rest of my life?

Sloane grabs a towel from the counter and brings it to me to wipe up my spill.

"I never thought I'd say this, but I'm happy my parents are boring." She shakes her head as she returns to her seat.

We laugh some more, then they fill me in on why everyone

thinks Sloane is engaged to Ryder, and I listen with a combination of shock and awe.

There are only six of us who know about this, and Cole took a big chance trusting me with their secret. I think this is his way of showing me he trusts me.

I hope I deserve it.

By the time Dagen rejoins our tipsy group to watch a movie, I'm pretty sure I'm out of the running for the most dysfunctional family award.

Everyone went to sleep a few hours ago, and the place is quiet.

I slid under the covers of the bed I shared with Cole, then stared at the ceiling for a couple of hours before I gave up and made my way back to the main room, turning on the fireplace.

The lights are out, and the muted orange glow on the walls is calming.

It isn't the same being in that big bed all by myself. After only two nights of sleeping next to Cole, I miss the way he pulled me into him and combed his fingers through my hair until I drifted off.

My eyes are heavy, and I'm trying to choose between dragging my ass upstairs or falling asleep right here when Dagen startles me.

"Can't sleep?"

The shock wakes me up, and he apologizes as he makes his way to the couch. I move my feet for him, and he joins me, staring at the fire.

"Just thinking." I'm not in a sharing mood, and I haven't spoken to Dagen one-on-one yet.

"There's a lot of that going around."

I take the pause in conversation to look at Cole's brother.

The tension in his measured movements hangs around him like a cloud. He's attractive, like his brothers, but not as domineering. Maybe it's because I've only witnessed Ryder and Cole with the women in their lives, and I have yet to watch Dagen interact with a significant other.

Dagen jokes easily with everyone, but there is something about him I can't place.

Maybe it's the way he assesses everything. There is a familiarity about him. It's as if he looks at everything from the outside in, and I know firsthand what it feels like to be an outsider. Cole mentioned that Dagen is the only brother who chose to leave the family business and went to work for himself. I wonder if this gave him the benefit of a different perspective.

"Have you heard from your brother?" Dagen taps his fingers on the arm of the couch as he asks.

"I texted him a couple of hours ago, but he hasn't answered. He's probably sleeping."

Dagen nods, then shifts in his seat and runs his hand through his hair.

"Was Cole able to get anything off of the memory stick?"

My question intrigues him, and he looks at me. "When did you hear from Cole last?" He asks his own question without responding to mine.

"When he texted to say they wouldn't be back tonight." Dagen still doesn't answer my question, so I try a different approach. "Cole mentioned you work for yourself. What do you do?"

Dagen reclines into the couch, sprawling his arms along the back. "I find things."

I nod my head as though I completely understand what he's saying, but I don't have a clue. Leaning in, I ask, "Did you find me?"

He nods. "But you were a challenge."

I lift my eyebrows and smirk, feeling proud of myself at the compliment.

"And you certainly seem to be challenging my brother."

His comment is meant to pique my curiosity, and it does. "What do you mean?"

Dagen looks at me for a long time. "Nothing. Trust me. It's a compliment. "

I sit in silence with that information.

Cole and I connected quickly.

We were not meant to know each other beyond our one-night stand. I took for granted I would never see him again, and I poured myself into our connection.

I wonder if he did the same.

"What else do you *find?*"

"Whatever is missing. People hire me to retrieve what they lost or are owed. I collect to settle debts. I've found missing people."

"Really? That must feel pretty awesome."

He shrugs. "Only if those people want to be found." He winks at me with humor in his eyes.

A thud outside the patio door startles both of us, and we stand at the same time. Without thinking, I walk toward the door, reaching out for the light switch, when Dagen wraps his fingers around my wrist and pulls me back.

"Stay behind me." He steps in front of me and lifts the poker that I'm sure is there just for show from beside the gas fireplace.

I suddenly feel stupid. How did I slip into complacency so easily? I'm not cut out for any of this, and I can't believe I've made it this far.

I do as I'm told and crouch down to hide behind his back. I don't know why I'm hunched over; I can stand up straight and still be completely hidden by Dagen's frame.

Clutching his shirt in my hands, I peek around his bicep for a better look.

Dagen's body is stiff. He takes two hesitant steps to the patio and peers out the full-length window into the night before audibly exhaling and relaxing his arms.

"Look who's trying to break in."

This time, I use caution and crane my neck toward the window, only seeing my own reflection until the rest of the yard finally comes into view.

"Awwwww."

Three deer are in the yard. One made it all the way up to the back deck, while the other two linger by the tree line.

"They must be hungry. I wonder if we have anything here." I look toward the kitchen.

"Not tonight. We are locked up. I'm not turning off the alarm and freaking Cole out at three o'clock in the morning—as appealing as that sounds. You can put some food out in the morning."

I agree with him and turn to look at the couch. I'm already standing, so getting my butt upstairs to bed is a good idea. "I think I'm going to get some sleep."

Dagen takes a seat on the sofa as I leave. "I'll be up in a few."

"Good night."

I'm almost out of the room when he catches my attention.

"Hey, Harlow?"

"Yes?"

"For what it's worth, I think my brother needs a challenge."

22

COLE

I like to think I'm a patient man, but waiting to board the ferry back to Bainbridge Island is testing my limits.

Ryder and I sit in my truck and watch in silence as the boat docks. The gate finally opens, and the Seattle-bound vehicles drive off at an excruciatingly slow pace.

"Mom looked happy to see us." Ryder stares out the windshield at a couple in the vehicle in front of us who look like they are knee-deep in an argument.

I mutter my agreement.

She was happy and talkative. I wish I had more time to visit with her. It was easier when they still lived at the house since that is our home base when we are all in town.

They have their own, smaller team of security and a place in a gated community that gives Mom the chance to get out with some of her friends for coffee and cards. Ryder and I spent the night talking about his upcoming fake marriage to Sloane, which soured my mood.

None of us enjoy lying to our parents, but Sloane and

Henry are counting on us to protect them. Now we can add Amara and Harlow to our list of people we need to keep safe.

After my parents moved out, Ryder was the one who stayed, then Sloane moved in after Grayson was found murdered. The place is huge, and I still don't understand why my father needed to downsize, but I have a feeling it's because he wanted a clean break from running the family business, and being around our talk all the time wouldn't have helped.

As for Lennox, I know my brother well enough to tell when he is uncomfortable. He moved out as soon as Ryder turned eighteen and rarely drops in. Our house is a source of pain for him, and I'm not entirely sure why.

My phone rings from its spot on the dashboard, and I look over.

"Switch with me. It's Creed." I open the driver's door and walk to the passenger side as Ryder takes my spot.

"It's Cole."

The vehicles at the front of the line start moving.

Creed skips the formalities. "I have some information for you. Ratchet and his group are looking for the girl, but we don't know why. Care to shed any light on that?"

My truck starts rolling forward, and I make a gut decision. "The girl who was killed was trying to get us video evidence of the night one of our guys was killed a couple of years ago. It's an unsolved murder."

Ryder side-eyes me as he drives us onto the boat.

"Whose murder?"

Creed won't tell me what I want to know until he gets everything he wants first.

"Grayson Scott."

Ryder's jaw ticks with tension.

"Should I know that name?" Creed asks.

"Probably not. He was one of Ryder's guys. It looks like he

was checking into something the night he was killed, but we don't know what it was." I decide to be more forthcoming with my answers in the hopes Creed will give me something to work with.

The line is quiet, and we roll to a stop beside a family in a small car. I watch as they get out and the mother fusses over her two little girls.

Creed finally speaks again. "So here's where I'm at. If Ratchet is hot for your girl, we are of the opinion it has to do with Elia's heir." There's a short pause followed by a deep sigh. "We can't let this go, Cole. Who is she to you?"

Fuck.

Creed's question carries weight. He wants to know where we stand. If Harlow is no one to me other than a mark, they will go forward with their methods of retrieval.

"She's mine."

My answer is heavier than his question.

Creed curses under his breath. "Is she with you?"

"She's safe."

This conversation just took a turn toward strained.

We value our business with Creed, and I'm sure he does as well.

"I'm going to need to talk to her, and I want to see that video. If you bring her to me, I guarantee she will not be harmed, and you will both be free to go. Not only that, she will have our full protection." We both sit in silence for half a minute before he says again, "I can't let this go, Cole."

I understand where he's coming from. He's in a turf war with a small faction of bad apples who believe they are the rightful successors to the Lucciano crime family. There's a mad rush to find and sway the heir so they can take control of the organization.

If I were in his shoes, I would do the same thing.

He's extending us a huge courtesy by sharing this information and attempting to cooperate, and his offer of protection is appreciated.

I don't know why I'm so relieved to hear Creed tell me he wants to meet with Harlow. Maybe it's the added layer of protection we can give her, or maybe we are finally getting some answers, and she might be out of danger soon.

"Give me some time to talk to her and get back to you."

"You have until tonight. I don't know what's going on, but word is they are close to finding her, so I suggest you start moving around while you think it over." Creed ends the call with that, and Ryder looks at me impatiently.

"Being down here makes me seasick, let's go." I get out and lock the truck up to head above deck. Then I recap my conversation, and Ryder and I discuss the possibility of moving everyone to our home in Seattle for a few days.

It's not exactly hiding out, but we have the benefit of added security, and most of us are comfortable and know our way around on familiar turf.

We could also make the drive directly to Creed in Portland and try to settle everything, but I want to make sure Harlow agrees before we make that decision.

When we get to the top deck, the ferry is already pushing out from shore, and Ryder looks over the water as he considers all of our options.

"I don't get it. Why is Ratchet looking for a video of Grayson's murder? Do you think Grayson found out about the heir?"

"No idea. Don't you think that's information he would have come to you with first?" I answer a question with a question.

"Probably. I just wish I knew what it was then." Ryder's frustration is evident.

That's been the million-dollar question since the day he died.

What was Grayson looking into that he felt he couldn't share with any of us first? He would have talked to us if it was about the missing heir.

When my phone vibrates in my pocket, I pull it out to look at the screen.

"What is it?" Ryder asks as I stare at it dumbly.

"The alarm at my place went off. One second. I'll call Dag."

His phone goes to voicemail. I disconnect and try again, only to be asked once more to leave a message. This time, I tell him to call me as soon as possible.

When I look at Ryder, his concern is written all over his face.

Amara is with them.

Ryder pulls out his phone and murmurs that he's sending Amara a text to check in.

I call Dagen's line once more.

He answers on the last ring before voicemail.

"Hey, man. What's up? I'm just getting out of the shower."

My shoulders relax a fraction at his voice. "Just checking in. We're on the ferry coming back. My house alarm went off. Someone opened a door."

"Okay. Give me a second. Getting dressed." The connection rustles as Dagen sets the phone down, and he picks it up less than a minute later. "I'm back." A door opens then closes before he talks again, his voice hushed. "Amara and Sloane are still sleeping."

Another door. I imagine he's making his way down the hall to make sure everyone is in their room before searching the main floor.

"Harlow must be up. I smell coffee." He answers as he

walks, his voice strained by my early morning call and the pace he's at to get downstairs. "We saw some deer off the back deck last night. She probably went out to feed them and forgot about the alarm."

For as much as I know about Harlow, this sounds like a probability, especially after I caught her outside feeding the birds.

Dagen's voice is muted as he calls Harlow's name.

I don't hear a response.

"The back door is locked, and coffee is on. Gimme a sec." He says her name a couple more times, then—

"The front door is unlocked. Getting my shoes on."

A long minute passes before—

"Shit—Cole, my car is gone."

"What?"

"Just a minute."

I listen to a flurry of sounds, and I assume Dagen is running through the house when I hear a woman's voice in the background. It sounds like Sloane.

"Get in your room, and stay there until I get you." Dagen's voice is strained; he sounds out of breath when—

"Shit—she took the keys. FUCK!"

My gaze zeroes in on the island we are still about twenty minutes away from, and I imagine I could probably walk on water right now if I used the anger rising inside of me as fuel to keep me afloat.

"What is it?" Ryder looks pale as he takes me in. "Amara?"

"She's okay. She's at the house. It's Harlow. She took Dagen's car and ran, and—I don't know why." Rage, disappointment, and worry battle to be my dominant emotion, and the result cripples me.

"How long has she been gone?"

"I checked on them maybe forty-five minutes ago. Just

before I got in the shower. She was asleep. She seemed fine when I talked to her last night. She said she hadn't heard from her brother, but it was late, and then she went to bed. Fuck, Cole, I'm sorry. If I thought—"

I cut him off. "Be ready to go when I get there."

I'm not mad at my brother. I gave Harlow a lot of leeway over the last few days myself. I thought we had an understanding, and I'm disappointed I was wrong.

I dial James's number and wait.

It goes to voicemail.

Then my thoughts land on Harlow.

I made myself abundantly clear: she was to remain where I left her. This was not an open-ended invitation, and she knew her place.

There is something horribly wrong.

James isn't picking up, and Harlow is running.

Something happened between yesterday morning and now, and it was bad enough that Harlow broke her promise to me.

"FUCK!" My impatience rears its ugly head, and the few people closest to us stare when I yell.

I want off this fucking boat—now.

But I'm in the middle of the bay, and the fish are swimming faster than we are moving.

By the time we dock and I get to my place to grab Dagen and drop Ryder with the women to wait for another ride, Harlow will be almost two hours away.

I'm not sure if I'm outright growling or if my head is about to implode. I pull up Harlow's number and wait for her to answer.

Voicemail.

I dial again and set it to speaker. Ryder crowds in close.

She picks up on the third ring, and I settle my ire until—

"Hey, Cole. Um...how are you?"

What. The. Fuck.

"I'm good, Socks. How are you?" I ask incredulously.

Fine. If she wants to play games with me, I have about fifteen minutes left on this stupid boat. I'll play.

"I—I'm good. Uh, did you get the file you need?" Harlow wears her heart on her sleeve, and shame clearly laces her words. She's trying to buy time.

"Where are you, Harlow?" I cut to the chase. She has to know I know.

The line is quiet for a moment before she hiccups.

Is she crying?

"They—they have my brother." Her voice lowers into a helpless whisper. "They called me from his phone, and they sent this picture of him, and they'll let him go if I—" She sniffles. "I'm so sorry, Cole."

Whoever is after Harlow hit her right in her Achilles' heel. There is only one thing she would have left the security of my cabin for, and they have it.

"Hey. Listen to me. Stop wherever you are and wait for me. I will help you get him back." Softening my voice, I try with all of my strength to pacify my demons.

I sit in silence. Only the sound of her breathing on the other line tells me she's still there.

"I can't. I have to be there in four hours, or they're going to kill him."

"Baby, they'll kill him anyway. Then they'll kill you if you don't have what they need."

Ryder and I exchange a glance as we wait for her to talk again.

"I know. I'm sorry. I won't leave him alone." Her tortured cry breaks my heart. Harlow is laced with unresolved guilt over Genie's death. "I wish"—she sobs—"I wish everything were different."

"Harlow, listen to—"

The line goes dead.

"Harlow? Socks?"

Rage boils through me. I want to throw my phone as far as I can see. The only thing stopping me from tossing it over the side is the fact that it's the only connection to Harlow I have left.

"So she stole *my* car?" Ryder asks, and I nod, too angry to speak. "Man, I will never let Dagen live this one down." Ryder chuckles, and I freeze.

"What the fuck are you laughing at?"

"You, brother. I told you you'd meet someone who'd drive you batshit bonkers, and you were like, 'Never gonna happen little brother!'" He does what I think is his impression of me. "And now look at you, losing your shit. It doesn't feel good, does it? But you're hooked, aren't you? I recognized it the first time I saw you look at her."

I stare blankly at my younger brother. "I can't talk about this now. I don't know where she is."

Ryder laughs again, and now I'm thinking about throwing him overboard.

When he finishes with his stupid giggle, he says, "Man you are so far gone." Then, leveling a stare at me, he talks to me like I'm five. "Have you forgotten how we tracked Amara when Nash took her?"

We found Amara because the car had a—

Motherfucker!

Harlow took Ryder's car, and she doesn't know all of our family cars have trackers.

This time, I chuckle along with Ryder, but mine isn't jovial. It's dark, twisted, and filled with the knowledge of all the things I'm going to do to Harlow when I find her.

23

HARLOW

It's a little after noon when I reach Portland's city limits. My stomach growls, but there is no way I'm stopping for anything to eat. I won't waste even a minute when my brother is in trouble.

Today was supposed to go very differently.

When I fell asleep last night, Cole was trying to find a way to get me out of this mess, my brother was safe and recovering, and my biggest plans included waking up and feeding deer off the deck so Amara and Sloane had something cool to see in the morning.

I woke up when Dagen checked on me. His footsteps down the hall were loud. After he explained to me how he finds things, I kind of thought he'd move more like a ninja.

I got dressed and went downstairs to put on a pot of coffee, then James returned my call from last night with a text.

Only it wasn't him.

It was a photo of him bound to a chair, his head held up by a fist gripping strands of his hair to show his beaten face to the camera. It was followed by five words: **Come alone or he dies.**

Then they asked if I was in Portland. When I responded I wasn't, they asked how far away I was.

I told them five hours.

They gave me four.

Then came the instructions and a request for confirmation: I was to accept a video call while I drove as proof I was alone and on my way.

The rest blurs together.

I left the kitchen, went to the room I shared with Cole, grabbed my backpack, and left something for him on our pillow. Then I made my way down the hall to Dagen's room.

I was prepared to start going through his pockets, but the stars aligned, and I found the car keys lying on his dresser.

I was gone before the water in the shower turned off.

Then I slipped out of myself, driving as if on autopilot until my phone rang.

It was Cole, and he knew what I did.

We always have a choice, Socks. His words haunt me.

My last conversation with him plays over and over in my head, drowning out the radio station and everything else around me.

I know they're probably going to kill me, and I know they are probably going to kill James, but he is the only family I have left, and I won't let go without a fight.

James and Genie were the ones who always fought for me. Back then I was too young to fight for myself, but now I'm older. Now I can be there for him, even though I wasn't there for Genie.

My stomach twists on itself, and I'm not sure if it's my nerves or my hunger. It might not matter soon.

My heart hurts.

The farther I get away from where Cole is, the more it aches. For someone who was meant to be a temporary comfort, he's somehow carved out a permanent place for himself in my heart.

I wish so much were different, but all I see are two roads in front of me. One leads me back to Cole. The second takes me to James, and I can't see myself on any road that doesn't have my only family left standing on it.

This is my choice, and I hope in the end Cole knows that I'm still choosing him, even though I'm not staying with him.

It's for the best that Cole doesn't know where I'm going. This way, he and his family can't be hurt as well.

I wait until I find a stretch of road with a good-sized shoulder to pull over on. Then I double-check my phone, matching the address to a location on my map app. My stomach sinks when I zoom in to the surrounding area.

James is being held in an industrial park.

No witnesses.

I got here in record time—the address is about ten minutes away. I'll be five minutes early.

Pulling onto the road, I turn up the volume on my phone and follow the directions.

My confidence is bolstered when I pull onto the street leading into the park. I pass office buildings with cars parked out front and notice a couple of trucks in loading docks.

The place isn't deserted. Maybe this will be a real trade-off. Maybe they will take me and let James go, as I can't imagine anyone shooting us so publicly. Surely someone would call the cops with all of this traffic.

You have heard of silencers, right? I remind myself.

Doubt rears its ugly head when I continue on, following the map through the bustling buildings toward an isolated area.

Many of the buildings on this side are boarded up, and I'm confident the only vehicles parked in these lots have been dumped here.

The place feels like one giant mausoleum. Maybe it is.

The voice on my phone tells me the destination is straight ahead.

As I approach, I scan the doors to the building. I find the one I'm supposed to go in instantly; a man stands from a bench out front, tossing his cigarette to the side.

I turn off the car and leave the keys in the ignition, certain I won't be needing them again. Then I shoulder my backpack and make my way up to the guy.

He's beefy, muscular almost to a fault, and he has about a foot of height on me, but that doesn't stop him from manhandling me and exerting his strength when he pushes me up against the wall to pat me down.

Seriously, it feels like a lion pushing a rabbit around.

He removes my backpack from me and steps aside, opening the door.

I don't feel the loss when he takes my bag. It's probably because I left anything of value behind with Cole, and the only things left are the items I won't be needing anymore.

After I enter, I see James right away. They're holding him in the front area, and I can't see past the closed door at the back. From the outside, this place is huge. Now it's reduced to one little room.

James groans, lifting his head at our footsteps.

As soon as his eyes meet mine, he jerks in his binds, anger etched across his face.

Is he mad because I showed up? Of course he is. I would be too if the roles were reversed.

The guy at his side steps in front of him. Raising his arm, he clenches his fingers into a fist and brings it down across James's face before telling him to settle down.

Forgetting my place, I yell at the guy and step forward. The man at my back wraps his meaty fingers around my upper arm and holds me back before tossing my backpack at the third guy standing in the room.

My brother is a big guy, but he's outnumbered and recovering from being shot.

My gaze lowers to his stomach. Blood soaks through his shirt where the bullet ripped into him. His wound must have opened up. I imagine my brother didn't go with them willingly.

James quiets and stares at me while the one with my bag takes it into the center of the room and dumps out the contents before everyone. Crouching down, he fingers through my things, tossing tampons and deodorant aside. I won't brush my teeth with that toothbrush again. Not because it's sitting on the floor in a layer of dust, but because I probably won't be alive when the sun goes down today.

The man chuckles at my brick, drawing his fingers along the red rock.

"Y-you said you'd let him go." My feeble tone threatens no one, and I'm sure I feel the man at my back shake with amusement.

"We're looking for a file." The man who dumped my bag stands and crosses his arms, staring me down.

"I don't have any files." I'm not lying.

"That's not what we heard."

Who the hell are these guys?

"Whoever told you I have anything is lying. Go back to them."

The guy in front of me stares at me for a long time before huffing and shaking his head. "Can't."

"Why not?"

I really want to know who gave me up. No one knew I was with Genie except her and that sack of shit who wouldn't let her go.

"We gutted the bastard last night. He sang like a fucking bird before he went. Then he led us right to you." He tilts his head toward James.

There is no remorse in his tone. This guy looks like he'd kill his own mother if the price was right.

I'm going to hell for this, but I take comfort in knowing the asshole who sent Genie to her death got it worse. Not only was he responsible for Genie getting killed, he gave up James and me without a care in the world.

"I had the file." I blurt out, and James stiffens in his seat.

This gets everyone's attention.

"Do you know what's on it?" The guy pulls out a gun and holds it by his side.

"No. It's"—what's the word Cole used?—"encrypted."

"Where is it now?"

His voice has gone eerily calm, and I worry that once he gets all of his answers, James and I will no longer be useful to him.

"It's with a friend of mine." Maybe I can make another trade and get James out of this.

"And that *friend*—it wouldn't happen to be Cole Saint, would it?"

Dammit. How does he know this?

"Um."

I finally nod.

He thinks over what I've told him for a minute while his two buddies stand around. Eventually, he comes to some type of agreement with himself.

"That settles it then." He lifts the gun and points it at James's head.

Without another thought, I jerk into action. Pulling hard, I get out of meathead's grip and run toward James, yelling at the man with the gun. I make it around the man who hit him and plaster myself across my brother's body. He groans in pain when I crush into him.

"Please. Wait. Don't kill him." I hold on with everything I have and plead, tears pouring down my cheeks and soaking my shirt.

Strong arms wrap around me, prying me away, but I don't budge. I dig in, and after a moment, the man with the gun tells him to stop.

"I don't need him. I'll trade you for the file." Pointing his gun at me, he tells me his plans like he's discussing the stock market, and a chill runs through my body.

As soon as I release James, he's going to die.

James drops his head forward onto my shoulder. His arms are bound, and he can't hug me back. His voice is low, muffled by the cloth they stuffed into his mouth and secured around his head, but I make out his words:

"Let me go. I love you."

"No." I turn my attention to the man with the gun. "Don't do this. Trade *him* for the file. Kill *me*."

James tenses again, lifting his head to shake it furiously.

The man with the gun is already swiveling his head slowly from side to side.

His mind is made up.

Unforgiving hands return to my upper arms, and I brace to fight again when a loud sound out front catches everyone's attention.

The man who walked in with me moves to the front

window to look out before turning back and shrugging his shoulders. "There's nothing there."

"Go out and make sure we're alone. I want to get this done."

The guy looks put out, but he listens and leaves the way we came in.

Everyone stills, waiting for an update, when a thud against the outside wall startles everyone in the room. It sounds like a bag of rocks fell against the side building.

"Check it out," the guy with the gun says to the one who was just manhandling me, and he takes a tentative step away.

He's halfway out the front door when the door behind us bursts open, and my instincts kick in. Tightening my grip around James, I push us both back and over in the chair, and he grunts when we hit the ground and I land on him. I lay myself across his body, covering him just in time to hear the first gunshot, followed by two quick shots, and I screw my eyes shut tight. My body shakes uncontrollably.

I wonder if my senses are heightened, because I swear I feel the air pressure change when the front door is pulled open, but I don't look up. Another shot blasts from behind me, followed by a harrowing scream, then rustling, and I hear a baritone voice behind me.

"Stay down."

I nod against James's chest. It's not a voice I recognize, and I'm not going anywhere, but I use my time to look at my brother to make sure he survived.

His panicked eyes say a thousand different things to me at once.

"Not you. Get up." The same low voice speaks with a hint of irritation, and I look to see who he's talking to.

Glancing up, my eyes zero in on the barrel of the gun pointed at James and me.

Me. He's talking to me.

I lift myself off my brother and place my body in front of him, turning to face the man who's now staring at me.

The familiarity in his eyes hits me first, the resemblance second.

"Lennox?"

24

COLE

Everyone was up when we arrived at my place on the island. Amara and Sloane stayed in the kitchen as I tore through the house.

In my head, I knew she was gone.

In my heart, I wanted to be wrong.

When I entered the room we shared, the last of my hope fell away.

It wasn't a mistake that her teddy bear was on my pillow.

She didn't lose him this time.

She left him like she left me.

We're supposed to take care of each other now.

Underneath him sat some photos of a younger Harlow, smiling with an innocence that hasn't yet seen the hell she'll go through.

She left me her memories.

I returned to find everyone standing around and staring at each other. Dagen looks like he's beat himself up over this, and Ryder is talking with the women.

Since Harlow took his car, they have to wait for a member of our security team to get over here to retrieve them.

Jamming my hands into my pockets, I retrieve the two memory sticks before handing the original to Ryder for safekeeping.

We both know I'm going to use this one as leverage—if I can.

Ryder refused to hand over my keys until I promised that Dagen would do the driving. I was reluctant, but eventually I agreed. I know myself well enough to know we would have been pulled over for speeding well before we reached city limits.

Still, my brother pushed as best as he could, and we made good time.

I check my text messages.

Since we don't have a GPS tracker on us, Yuri has been texting me location updates from Seattle.

"The car still hasn't moved from that spot. It's been sitting there for the last thirty minutes. I have an address." I relay the message to Dagen.

He's pinching his lips together, and his eyes remain trained on the highway in front of us. "Listen, Cole, I'm—"

"Don't. I'm not mad."

I've had a lot of time to sit and think.

I'm tired.

I'm worried.

But I'm not mad at Dagen—or Harlow.

How can I be, when I would do the same thing to protect one of my brothers or their loved ones?

I am, however, furious at whoever is behind this, and once I find them, I will make them watch as I tear apart everything they care about before I kill them slowly.

Dagen doesn't say anything more. Instead, he responds by

upping our speed as we near city limits, and I give him directions until we pull up to Ryder's vehicle, which is parked in front of a derelict building.

Dagen and I check our guns before exiting my truck, and the first sign of life I see is, well, already dead.

A man sits slumped against the side of the building, his head lolled to the side at an odd angle. Without checking, I'm betting his neck is broken.

Harlow couldn't have done this. His size alone would have overpowered her in seconds.

When I look at Dagen, I sense he's thinking the same thing.

One of the doors to the building creaks on its rusty hinges, and we walk toward it to check it first.

Inside, a man lies on his back, his limbs splayed in a star pattern. Blood pools around him from a shot to the head. There's a second wound in the center of his chest.

I've never seen the guy before, but that doesn't mean anything.

My breath hitches when I catch Harlow's backpack lying open, its contents all over the floor, including her phone. This was almost everything she called her own.

I turn my attention to a body bound to an overturned chair and walk over. My throat tightens on itself when I recognize James.

He's been beaten, and his clothes are bloody all over again. I reach out to confirm there's no pulse when he opens his eyes and gasps.

The shock sends me flying backward on my own ass.

Dagen turns, drawing his gun, and I bounce up, holding my hand out and crawling in front of James to keep him safe.

"I know him. He's with me." I lower my attention to James's wide eyes before reaching behind him to untie the blood-soaked cloth from his mouth. "Is she here?"

"She was, but then—" He snaps his mouth shut mid-sentence and glares at me, his eyes jumping briefly to Dagen.

"Then?" I prompt.

A war wages behind his eyes. I don't know what happened here, but there's something he isn't telling me.

I haven't untied him yet, and I won't until he tells me where Harlow is. I know she cares about him, but I care about her, and one overrides the other.

James winces in pain before sighing. "Your brother took her. He killed that one and took a third guy with them."

"Lennox?" Dagen asks from behind us, and James nods his head.

"I recognized him from a photo."

I exchange a hard look with Dagen.

No answers, only more questions.

Without thinking it through, I pull out my phone and send a text to Lennox.

Cole: You have something of mine. I want her back.

Turning my attention to James, I work the binds around his wrists loose, and Dagen joins me to help him stand.

He groans each time we move him.

"Can you walk? We need to get you out of here before anyone else shows up."

James takes a tentative step before telling me he'll try. I lean over to grab Harlow's backpack off the floor, stuffing everything back into it, including the brick she carried around for protection—a lot of good it did her here.

Dagen and I settle ourselves under James's arms and act as crutches, walking him to the exit.

"I can call my guys. They'll come and get me." James's words are forced.

I shut him down. "No. You're coming with us."

James stops walking at my announcement, but it doesn't matter. Between Dagen and I, we are mostly just carrying him at this point.

"I can't—"

"It's not up for discussion. James, this is my brother Dagen."

Dagen nods from his other side. I've already filled Dagen in on him.

James swivels his head from me to him. "But—"

We lean him against my truck, and I prop him up before lifting his shirt to take in the damage. Bruising around his gunshot wound has already started. Someone hit him hard enough to tear his stitches, but the bleeding is minimal. It looks like it's already stopped.

"Here's what's going to happen. You are now with us, and you are not leaving our side until we find Harlow. This isn't up for discussion either."

James looks from me to Dagen and back again a few times. The guy looks like he's going to crack. His teeth are clenched, and the muscles along his jaw tick as his chin trembles.

How different would everything be for me if I didn't have my brothers to back me up? If I was doing this all by myself? I imagine I would be James.

The guy looks exhausted.

"Thank you."

That's all the acceptance I need.

I look at my brother. "Check Ryder's car."

Dagen is gone for seconds before announcing the keys are in the ignition.

It didn't matter. Either one of us could have hot-wired it to start, but the fact she just left them there is very telling of what was going through her head when she got here.

We squeeze James into the front seat as best we can, but he groans as he shifts to settle in place, and I buckle him in.

"Where are we going?" Dagen asks.

I look around the parking lot. Our options are decreasing. I won't leave Portland until I know Harlow is no longer here. I can't risk going home, as my address is known to some of our connections, Creed included.

"Take my truck and follow us. We'll go to ReBar. There's no one there until four. Go around back."

Dagen curtly bows his head and walks toward my truck. I settle in with James and start the car, checking the rearview mirror to make sure my brother is behind us.

"What's ReBar?"

"It's a nightclub of mine about twenty minutes away from here. Caters to the college crowd. I need to make a few calls, and we can get you cleaned up before we leave."

"Leave for where?"

I don't answer his question because I have no idea where the hell my brother took Harlow. But once I find out, that is exactly where I'm going.

"Why the hell didn't you call me sooner? I could have gotten there in minutes." It sounds like Creed punches his fist on something as he yells at me through the phone.

That's exactly why I didn't call him, and he knows it.

Harlow is mine, and there's no chance I was giving up her location without being there to protect her. The whole situation was too volatile to begin with.

"Where's the girl now?"

"She was gone when we got there." I hold on to the additional information I have for a long moment before I lock it away. "I don't know where she is, but I'm looking for her."

I know tensions are as high as the stakes are on Creed's end.

"I have the file she was carrying."

There's a long silence on the other end before he says, "I'm listening."

"I can't hand it over in case I need it—for a trade—but I'll show you what's on it. And I can get you a copy if you want, but we're only here for a couple of hours before we start moving around. And you are to agree it will not be used against the person in the video in any way."

"Tell me where you are."

<hr>

Forty-five minutes later, Creed and two of his men walk through the back door. Creed nods to Dagen and me. He only glances at James.

I used the time before they arrived to talk to James. I told him under no circumstances is he to disclose that Harlow is with Lennox.

The tension around us is strained as Creed's two guys take spots around the room and Creed joins us at the monitor. I slide the stick into a port, and everyone looks at the television on the wall as the video I watched with Ryder plays.

Dagen is as affected by Grayson's murder as we were, but the rest of the men watch with morbid curiosity until I fast forward it to—

"Is that your brother?" Creed steps toward the screen.

"Yes. It's Lennox." I glance at James. Realization dawns in his eyes.

The man who showed up after a murder is the same one

who took his sister. I slowly shake my head, and he doesn't say anything.

"Shit." Creed catches my attention once again, and we all watch until Lennox leaves the frame.

"That's all that's on there until the video cuts out about an hour later."

Creed looks at his guys, and they return confused stares. He turns, taking two addled steps before lifting his hands and shaking his head. "What's this got to do with us?"

"I don't know if it has anything to do with you," I answer honestly. I'm as puzzled as he is as to why Ratchet would kill for this video.

Creed considers my words, his eyes falling on James. It dawns on him that he's out of place. "Who are you?"

James looks at me, and I shrug, telling him he can answer. He tries to stand and clutches his stomach. "James Levine, sir."

Creed straightens at the show of respect.

I can tell when he likes someone, and people don't often get beyond first impressions with Creed.

"And what are you doing with these two?" He waves his hand in our direction.

I step in.

If James keeps deferring to me before he answers Creed's questions, he's going to start looking guilty.

"James is Harlow's brother. He was taken and held as a trade for her."

Creed nods knowingly, looking from me to James. Then he waves one of his guys over. "I've got a picture of someone. Was he one of the ones who took you?"

Creed's guy shows James the front of his phone, and James instantly shakes his head.

Creed looks deep in thought. "So it wasn't Ratchet." Creed talks to his guy, who shakes his head.

James perks up at that. "Ratchet. The guys who took me said that name."

Everyone's attention returns to James.

"They say anything else?" Creed squares himself on James.

"They said if they could be the ones to get"—he lowers his voice—"*that bitch*"—his tone returns to normal—"to Ratchet, then their standing is as good as gold."

Creed takes in James's words like they are the missing piece to a treasure map.

Maybe they are. Who the hell knows at this point?

My take is that Ratchet has the word out he's looking for Harlow and the file. Why he wants them is unknown, but the people who took James thought they'd climb a little higher in Ratchet's pecking order if they were the ones to deliver.

"Thanks—James." Creed tilts his head at James before turning his attention to me. "And thank you for..." He points to the screen. "I don't know what the hell I'm going to do with it, but I want a copy—and if your girl shows up, I want to talk to her."

"I still want protection for her until I know she's safe."

Creed smiles at that.

He's someone who enjoys being on the side of the lender when it comes to debts owed.

Waving to his two men, Creed makes his way to the door. Before they are out of the building, he turns and looks back at me.

"I've never seen you care." He leaves off *for someone else.* "It looks good on you."

Dagen releases a held breath once we are left alone.

"Who was that?" James looks between us.

"That was Creed. He's Elia Lucciano's second."

James's eyes go wide. Yes, the Lucciano crime family that was supposedly looking for his sister. He's up to speed, except—

"There's some things you don't know about their organization. There's a turf war going on right now. You aren't on the Lucciano radar. Ratchet is the leader of a group that's trying to take over their business. They are the ones looking for Harlow, and we don't know why."

James sits in silence as he takes it all in, and I pull out my phone to text Ryder with an update.

A message on the screen makes my heart stop.

Lennox: We need to talk.

"So what do we do now?" Dagen asks.

I show him the text when I say, "Now we get Harlow."

25

HARLOW

My fingers tingle as the rope tied around my wrists slows the circulation into my hands. I stare dumbly down at them, rubbing my palms against each other to get my blood flowing.

From my seat on the passenger side, I watch life go on in the city around us as Lennox drives us away from the industrial park.

I guess I should count this as a win, considering the other guy Lennox dragged out of the building is out cold, tied up, and in the trunk.

Exhaustion creeps in as my adrenaline drains out of me. I'm not tired; I'm depleted, worn out.

I was right there, moments away from watching James die and being killed myself. I can't get the visual of the two dead men out of my head. Everything else blurred together. In my recollection, the events melted into each other.

The next thing I knew, I was riding in this car.

I snapped back to reality when Lennox casually pulled into

the drive-through of a fast-food restaurant and cautioned me to keep quiet.

I listened.

Now we aren't in the city anymore, and dread creeps down my spine.

My fingers are so cold they ache.

Reaching into the paper bag on his lap, Lennox pulls out the only item he ordered and hands it to me.

I must be glaring at him like he's ridiculous, because he takes one glance at me then drops the burger in my tied hands resting on my lap.

"Your stomach is growling. You saw me order it. Eat."

Lennox is a man of few words, but he gets his point across. It's his way of telling me it isn't poisoned.

And damn am I hungry.

He pulls off the highway onto a dirt road, and I fidget with the wrapper then lift the burger to my mouth to have a taste.

Portland is still close enough that I can clearly see its downtown buildings. I take two more quick bites, trying to look as least gluttonous as possible.

I steal a glance at Cole's brother as I give up and practically inhale the last few morsels.

He looks much older than his brothers, and I'm not sure if it's because of his age or the life he's lived through.

Something tells me the years he wears on his face have, sadly, been earned.

He is also giving off conflicting vibes.

For someone who is going to kill me, buying me lunch would seem really low on his list of priorities.

"Um. Thank you." I crumble the wrapper into a ball and hold it between my hands.

He doesn't respond, and I make no further attempt at small talk. Instead, I look out the window and think about James.

When I left him, he looked defeated, but I couldn't stay. Not after I told Lennox I wasn't going anywhere with him, and he pointed his gun at James as a threat.

It worked.

I willingly followed Lennox out of that building to get everyone with a gun away from my brother.

One of the guys made it out with just a bullet to the leg. He's the one in the trunk now.

I wish I'd told Cole where I was going. He could have helped James.

Instead, I'm left with only the hope that he was still strong enough to get himself out of those binds.

The car stops in front of an old barn, and Lennox gets out without a word then heads toward the back.

Lowering myself in the passenger seat, I peer through the back window as Lennox opens the trunk and fights to lift the guy out. His low groans make their way in through the back seat of the car.

When Lennox closes the trunk, I see that the guy has something wrapped around his mouth, and he limps as Lennox pulls him along the passenger side of the car.

He stops at my door, and I freeze.

Lennox taps on the window near my head, and I jump at the sharp sound, leveling my attention on the gun he's rapping against the glass. He reaches down and opens the door, tilting his head toward the barn, silently telling me to follow him.

My feet won't cooperate.

"Let's go." I shudder at his low tone.

I shake my head, my fear building inside of me. "Are you going to kill me?"

He glares daggers at me before his face falls. Closing his eyes, Lennox takes a deep breath and exhales, looking down at my hands tied at my front.

As he does, I look at the man in his custody. While my hands are simply tied in my lap, his are bound behind his back. He is gagged, I can speak, and only one of us got lunch.

"No."

I swallow hard when I meet Lennox's stare.

For some asinine reason, I believe him.

Swinging my legs out of the car, I walk a little behind the men as we approach the barn.

It looks like it's been a long time since this place was in good shape, and the red painted on the outside looks more like a rusty orange with the years it's seen.

Lennox leads me through the barn and toward the back. When he stops, I take in the area around me. Light pours in through the cracks and open windows, and there is nothing to this building except for some musty-smelling hay and a few stalls.

Lennox points his gun at one. "Stay here. You won't be harmed."

I look from Lennox to the other guy, then into the stall, before nodding and stepping inside.

Lennox drags the guy away, and I'm surprised he isn't locking me in.

Their voices rise from the front of the barn, and sounds of struggling catch my attention. I step near the entrance of the stall to listen better.

The unmistakable sound of punching catches me off guard as Lennox's muffled voice asks questions. Each one is followed by another punch. Before I know it, I've left my spot and taken a few steps toward where the men are.

The first clear sentence I hear is Lennox asking the guy about a wrench, and I freeze in confusion as the punches continue. After a minute, I realize Ratchet must be a nickname, and Lennox is trying to find out who they are all working for.

The guy waffles between answering Lennox and yelling profanities at him, and Cole's brother stands over him, dealing harsh blow after harsh blow at every defiance.

I've seen this look before.

The day Cole walked into James's room and grabbed the man who was about to kill us, this same look was etched into his face like war paint.

Lennox is relentless.

The way he stalks around the guy, the way he speaks—every move makes him look like an apex predator.

While I believed him when he said he wasn't going to kill me, my blood runs cold when I watch him circle the man on the floor. Broken and clutching the gunshot wound in his leg, the guy no longer stands his ground.

He cowers at Lennox's feet, his eyes wide with panic.

His bravado is gone.

Does he know he's about to die?

Is that what's going to happen here?

I should have listened to Lennox and stayed where I was.

I should have listened to Cole and waited for him.

I ramble aimlessly back toward the stall, my arms now numb with an overload of emotion.

I don't feel right.

The sting of tears pricks my eyelids. With my bound hands, I grab a large pail from the corner of the stall and turn it over. I sit on it and stare at the wall, fixated on a sliver of the sun's rays in between the cracks, which blind me when I angle my head just right.

When I close my eyes against the light, I can almost picture a beach with the kind of fine sand that slips like water through my fingers and waves that crash against—

The echo of a gunshot startles me out of my thoughts, and the shock sends me a foot into the air and off of the bucket.

I stay frozen in my spot on the ground, waiting for signs of life.

There are none.

I don't think that guy is alive anymore, and I think I might bring up the burger I just ate.

One set of footsteps comes closer at a casual pace toward my stall. Then Lennox steps into my area, the gun in his hand. His eyes flit to the overturned pail by my head, then down over my body as he takes in my situation before joining me in the little cage.

The space between us is so quiet that I can hear the soft vibration of his phone, and Lennox pauses mid-step, pulling it out and glancing at the screen. Whatever he sees gives him pause, and his forehead wrinkles as his eyebrows pinch together before he takes a long look at me.

Securing his gun in his jacket, Lennox stretches his shoulder muscles out as if shaking his demons loose and takes a step toward me. He lifts the bucket, sets it down, and lifts me with no effort, sitting me on it before crouching in front of me.

Then he reaches into the shoelaces of his boots and pulls out a knife.

It's a challenge not to flinch, but I think I stay steady when he pulls my hands toward him and slices the rope.

"What's your name?"

This is interesting. Unlike almost everyone else, he isn't looking for me because he knows who I am or what I have.

So why was he there today?

That's a question I am definitely in no position to ask, so I just answer. "I'm Harlow."

He nods, but he looks like he's mentally miles away. "And you—know my brother Cole?" Judging by the way he's asking the question, he already knows the answer.

"I—yes. How do you know that?"

His resigned chuckle is a stark contrast to the machine who questioned and killed a guy just minutes earlier. "Because he just sent me a message demanding I return you to him." He holds my stare for a moment before he lowers his head and mutters to himself, "Shit."

James once told me I wear my emotions like cheap perfume, and he can always smell me from a mile away.

I bite the inside of my cheek to stop myself from grinning at an obviously really bad time. I'm in a world of trouble, and the fact that Cole is demanding my return makes me feel like he's here with me. Cole knows where I am, and he's coming for me, and I'm not alone out here.

Lennox stands, turns his back to me, and takes a step away. He looks like he's working out some secret math equation in his head.

"What were you doing there today?" he asks over his shoulder.

He doesn't need to elaborate, and I now realize he wasn't after me. He was after *them*, the guys who took James. We just happened to cross paths.

"I was supposed to deliver a memory stick in exchange for my brother's life. But I don't have it."

"What was on the memory stick?"

I wish I had the answers, because none of this makes sense.

"Cole said it might be a recording of a murder from a few years ago. That's all I know."

The weight of the world is visibly crushing this man in front of me.

None of the three brothers talk about Lennox like they talk about each other. In the short time I've known everyone, I get the sense that Lennox is more of a black sheep.

He lowers himself to my eye level. "Where is the memory stick?"

"Cole has it."

I try not to stare too closely at the man a couple of feet away from me. Those are the same eyes that looked into the room where I hid the night Genie died, and I don't want to let on that I know anything about that.

If he finds out I'm a witness to that night, my fate may change.

Lennox rises to his full height, extending his hand out to me, and this time I do flinch. I don't mean to, but the buildup of everything is getting to be too much.

Lennox pulls his hand back before trying again, slower this time, and I take his hand and allow him to help me stand.

As we walk toward the entrance to the barn, lifeless feet sprawled out in the center of the room catch my attention. I don't follow them up to the guy's face. That's one image I don't want burned into my nightmares.

Outside, I watch as Lennox pulls out his phone and taps at the screen before slipping the phone back into his pocket and looking out at the city in the distance.

"How did we get here?" he mutters to himself, and I catch it on the wind.

I pretend I don't hear him.

If the question was meant for me, he'll ask it again.

He doesn't.

26

COLE

I should have Harlow back by now.

Instead, all I got was a text that basically asked for patience—the one thing I don't possess when it comes to her.

Lennox: She's safe. I need time to think. Message in the morning.

James has been quiet since we met with Creed, but he hasn't been passive. The guy has been paying attention. He listened while Dagen and I talked about Ratchet, Creed, and Lennox. I feel his eyes on me whenever Harlow's name is mentioned, and he's been committing our location to memory.

Oddly, he reminds me of Grayson: protective of his sister, loyal, and astute.

In the end, we decided to crash at my place. I know my property inside and out, and I have a cache of weapons and gear if we need. I'm in no danger of Creed showing up, and

Ratchet wouldn't dare make a move that rash. Not after they found the bodies of his men. They'll be trying to figure out what happened and regroup.

James finally and reluctantly allowed us to bandage him up, but not until he tried and failed to do it a few times on his own.

I get it; he's not used to having help. He's a lot like his sister.

Dagen took our orders and left to grab dinner from my restaurant a few minutes ago, and the silence has become obviously awkward now that there are only two of us sitting around.

I hadn't realized how empty my place felt before, when it was only me here, but I feel it when I walk to my fridge to grab two beers instead of one. The place seems more active, even if the other person with me isn't talking.

"Here. You okay?" I hand a beer to James.

He looks from the bottle to me then takes it, twists off the cap, and mumbles a thank-you before taking a gulp. "I'm good."

I stare at him for a few seconds, making it clear I'm not impressed.

"Give me more than that." I take a drink of my own and wait.

I'm used to my brothers calling me out on my shit. I imagine James is not. His glare tells me this is difficult for him.

"Fine." He shrugs, clearly frustrated. "I can't believe she did that. She could have gotten killed. After everything that's happened. She just walked right in there." The pained look on James's face tells me he is more worried than angry.

James lowers his gaze to the opening of his bottle before swallowing another sip.

These two have been on their own for far too long. To James, a worse fate than dying would be watching his second sister die first.

"I can't believe she did that either," I commiserate, and he nods in agreement as I continue, "I mean, it's not like you'd do that for her." I shake my head.

He's still nodding when my words register. "What? No. I mean. I would, but—"

"Then why are you mad she did it for you?"

He blinks a few times before slouching in defeat. He's letting what I've said sink in.

I decide to share some of my own personal shit.

"I watched my brother throw himself into a freezing body of rushing water a couple of months ago. In that moment, there wasn't anything I wouldn't've given to trade places with him—without thought or consideration for myself. He went in because he didn't want his life if it meant living without the woman he loved. We do some really fucked-up things when we love someone."

I give him more to think about, and the crease on his forehead tells me he is doing just that. "And what about your brother?"

"He saved her. They saved each other, really."

"Not that one." James takes another drink.

I look at the door, thinking about Dagen, and James clarifies.

"The one who has my sister."

Lennox.

"He's—complicated."

"Give me more than that." James throws my words back at me.

"Our relationship with our oldest brother is fractured. There's just something"—I hold my hand in front of me—"there. I don't know how else to explain it." I make eye contact with James as I answer the question I know he wants to ask. "If he says Harlow is safe, then she's safe."

This time, the silence that settles between us is comfortable. It gives me time to think about our situation.

Without going into detail, I've made it clear that Harlow belongs to me, yet Lennox is holding on to her. While I believe she is safe, I don't like that he hasn't made plans to release her back to me.

Lennox was on the video, and he was the one Harlow saw the night Genie was killed. My stomach drops in worry. I hope she hasn't let that tidbit of information slip out. It may be the only thing keeping her safe with him.

"Maybe he's trying to save you." James startles me out of my own worries.

"What?"

"Lennox. Maybe the thing that is in between you guys is his way of jumping into freezing water to stop all of you from going under." He shrugs like he knows he's probably way off base, but it's my turn to consider James's words.

Before I wander too far down that rabbit hole, the door opens, and Dagen walks in fisting three brown paper bags.

"Who's hungry?" He makes a straight line for the counter in my kitchen, and James and I stand to help him.

Well, I stand. James sort of claws his way up then hunches over, propping his weight on the arm of my couch.

"Sit down. I'll get yours."

He takes a step to do it himself, but I stop walking and glare at him until he settles into the couch with a wince.

Dagen lowers his voice when I get to him. "You guys good?"

Looking back over my shoulder at Harlow's brother, I say, "Yeah. He's stubborn."

Dagen smirks at that. "He'll fit in around here then."

"Touché, fucker." I spoon our meals onto plates, and Dagen helps himself to a beer, pulling out extras for me and James, which he sets on the counter.

"Listen, I was thinking that maybe I should meet with Lennox tomorrow." Dagen doesn't look up from his plate as he spoons out some garlic mashed potatoes.

"Why?"

"Well, it's just that you and Ryder are both really close to this."

He means we are deeply invested because we each have someone else we're worrying about—unlike him, who doesn't have a care in this world.

He's detached. He's thinking with his head, and he's the least emotional of all of us.

I am worried about Harlow, but I can be rational. I haven't told Dagen yet what James said, nor how it's taken hold and is refusing to let go.

Maybe he's trying to save you.

I imagine this new possibility is going to keep me up most of the night.

Dagen leaves the counter and makes his way to James, handing him one of the beers and leaving mine on the table.

I'm pretty sure my brother refuses to use the coasters just to mess with me.

I follow along, setting his plate on the table in front of him and moving each beer to the coasters that are inches away from the bottles.

"Hey, Cora was on shift tonight. She was asking about you." Dagen winks at me, catching James's attention, and I shake my head with a smirk. "She stuck an extra piece of pie in there and told me to keep my dirty fingers off of it—so naturally I ate it on the drive home."

"Naturally." I laugh. "She probably knew you were going to eat it. I wouldn't be surprised if she laced it with something."

Dagen laughs at that but pauses a second later to consider

my words. Dropping his hand to his stomach, he shifts, uneasy in his seat, and James smiles beside him.

It's the first time he's relaxed and joined our conversation like he's one of the guys.

"Damn that old bat. She probably did." Dagen leans forward, taking a swig of his beer then staring at the bottle before shuddering. "I better wake up here in the morning—and in my own clothes."

We joke, but Cora is not someone to cross. She's been around our business longer than we have. It's rumored she worked for Elia Lucciano before she joined my father's payroll. She always kept to herself and never asked for anything until she approached me a couple of years back looking for a change of scenery. It just so happened I had a new restaurant here that needed a ballbuster in the kitchen.

When the room settles down, I decide to ask James about his past.

"Harlow mentioned the three of you grew up in foster care. You started out together, but then you were separated. What happened?"

Dagen leans over the table to finish his meal. His worries about being drugged are apparently no longer a concern.

"I happened." James lets that linger for a few seconds before he says, "I fucked up."

"What did you do?" I ask.

"Have you ever noticed that smile Harlow gets on her face when she's trying to mask her fear? Like, just looking at her is—"

"Unsettling," I offer, and James nods, stewing in his thoughts.

That damn smile.

It makes me want to burn down the world around her and protect her.

"That's the one. Harlow doesn't know a lot about why we were split up, and I'd like to keep it that way."

I weigh what he's not saying. He's asking me not to share this with his sister. She mentioned he never talks to her about their past, but I sense it weighs heavily on him.

I dip my head, telling him to go on.

"Our foster *dad*"—he says the word like it's sour—"was abusing the older girls under his care. He threatened them. Told them if they ever said anything, they'd be out on the street, where it was worse. Genie knew better. She knew she'd just be sent to another home, but she also knew we'd most likely be split up. So she didn't say anything to anyone for over ten months."

"What changed?" I'm still asking the questions.

Dagen isn't looking our way, but he's listening very closely. He's clasped his hands together in front of his face, his elbows braced against his thighs.

None of us take kindly to abuse.

"The other girl was moved out of the system. Genie noticed he was starting to watch Harlow. She was only eleven. As soon as Genie realized what was going to happen, she came to me and told me what he was doing." James drops his fork on the plate. I don't blame him. I've lost my appetite as well. "I switched rooms with Harlow. Told her it was a secret game. I slept under her covers holding a hammer for almost a week before he snuck in in the middle of the night. I beat him until he passed out, then broke the bones in his hands."

"What happened?" This time, the question doesn't come from me.

I'm too stunned to find the words, so Dagen takes over.

"I got a juvie record, and we were all moved out and split up. The only good thing was that he was investigated and charged. He couldn't explain what he was doing sneaking into her room at three o'clock in the morning. The authorities were more open to hearing Genie's accusations after that, and they got in touch with previous girls under their care."

"But you still think you fucked up?" I ask.

"Harlow is like this ray of light. She has a big heart, and she is everything that is good in our lives." He pauses for a long time while he reconsiders his words. "*My* life. But she's also fragile, and I'm the reason we were split up."

Now that I know more, James and Genie's roles in Harlow's lives have become clear. They weren't just her siblings. They took on the responsibility that should have been treasured by a parent. They protected her, shielded her from all of the shit they saw, and I wonder if, on some level, Harlow already knows this.

"I want his name." Dagen's casual tone is deceiving.

"What?" James swivels his head to glance at my brother.

"The foster guy." Dagen's disdain sours his expression. "I want his name. I'm going to look into him after we're done frying these bigger fish."

I sip the last of my first beer then crack open my second.

James looks between us in confusion, and Dagen decides now is a good time to be himself.

"Look." Dagen points at me. "He's *schtupping* your sister, and personally I think they're good for each other. You're her family, so now you're my family." He leans back, all smug, like he just told us one plus one equals two.

"Dammit, guy. What the fuck, man?" James recoils from Dagen, but I catch the unmistakable look on his face. He's either thankful we moved on from the more serious note or he's enjoying the banter, and an odd rush of relief hits me.

"Well, I think that's enough excitement for one day. My bed is mine; everything else is up for grabs." I stand, clearing our plates and turning my back to the room.

Schtupping.

When I get Harlow back, she's going to wish we were only *schtupping*. She's racked up many a punishable offense, and I intend to collect as soon as we're alone.

27

COLE

By the time we pull up to the old farm, I've had twelve hours to think about what James said the night before.

Maybe he's trying to save you.

I used his theory and ran through every interaction I remember having with Lennox since we were kids.

I'm thick as thieves with Ryder and Dagen, just like brothers should be, but there is that disconnect when it comes to our oldest brother.

The sight of an old barn cuts into my thoughts. It sits in the middle of a huge parcel of land and off to the side and back from a farmhouse.

Both have seen better days.

Dagen parks Ryder's car in front of the house beside the only other vehicle on the property, and I pull my truck in behind him.

"Do you see her?" James asks as he looks out the passenger side window around the sprawling property.

"Not yet." Cutting the engine, I step out and slide my gun into my belt at the back.

I won't relax until I have Harlow with me.

We join Dagen and take a few steps toward the house when a gunshot rings out, surprising all of us, and Dagen and I go for our guns.

I don't wait for James or my brother. As far as I understand, only Lennox and Harlow are out here.

Hurrying around the home, we round the back just in time to see Lennox with his arms around Harlow. Their backs are turned to us.

I lose my shit.

"LET HER GO!"

They both startle and turn to us, and I catch the remnants of a smile dropping from their faces.

I don't want to, but I train my gun on my oldest brother.

Dagen cautions me from behind to stop me from going off the deep end, but I keep advancing toward them.

Harlow steps in front of Lennox.

The selfless act is confusing, and I stop fifteen feet away from them.

"Don't—wait. He's not hurting me." Harlow's eyes are as big as saucers as she points the gun toward the ground and holds her free hand out between us in surrender.

Lennox stays still behind her, and I understand how Ryder was so passionate about ending him to protect Amara when he felt she was in danger.

Dagen steps beside me and lowers his gun first. I side-eye him.

He shrugs and points at Lennox. "What? She has his gun," he says in a matter-of-fact tone.

I return my attention to Harlow and the gun in her hand before meeting her gaze, and she takes a step toward me.

"He's teaching me how to shoot." She points over her shoulder at a line of cans set up in the distance.

It isn't lost on me that Lennox isn't asking for his gun back, nor does he have a second one of his own. I tuck my weapon back into its spot when Harlow notices her brother standing behind us.

"James!"

Dagen steps to the side and allows her to move between us to hug him. He hisses at the contact but doesn't back away from the embrace.

As she asks him how he came to be with Dagen and I, the rest of us listen on in a tense silence.

Lennox wanted to talk, and now we're here, but how do we start when we've spent our adult lives as strangers?

I search my head for a conversation starter. "You taught her how to shoot a gun?"

"I gave her my gun to hold on to, so she would feel safe overnight, but then I became worried about my own safety. She should know how to handle one." Lennox is admonishing me, and I get the message. None of us lead safe lives. Our girls should be able to handle themselves.

Noted.

Lennox looks at Harlow as she fusses over James's wounds. "She's a really good shot. Picked it up fast." Even though he lowers his voice, I still make out a hint of pride. She's impressed him. "Let's go inside. We can talk in there." Lennox lifts his chin toward the farmhouse.

Harlow hears him and steps away from James. She reaches out, attempting to hand Lennox his gun, but he declines it to show he isn't a threat. She holds onto it.

When my brothers meet up, Dagen reaches his arm around Lennox's shoulder and pats him on the back as they leave Harlow and I alone.

Being the two oldest brothers, Dagen has a closer relationship with Lennox than Ryder or I do.

My gaze settles on Harlow. Shifting her weight from foot to foot, she waits for me to approach her. Her doe eyes and slouched stance say it all.

She knows she's in trouble.

Reaching out, she hands me Lennox's gun, and I take it.

"You have a bad habit of not listening to me." I reach my fingers to her forehead, combing a strand of hair off her face before tangling my hand into the back of her hair and tugging her face up to meet mine. "I'm going to break you of that, Socks." In my grip, she's unable to move, but her eyes travel toward the men before snapping back to mine.

She's worried her punishment will start here. "I—"

Crushing my lips against hers, I devour everything she was going to say. That is a conversation for another time.

Her whimpers make me wish we were alone.

Instead, I break the kiss and look at her. Things could have gone very differently. At a few points, I wasn't so sure I'd see her again.

Lennox was right to teach her how to shoot.

I was so focused on protecting her that I didn't think to teach her how to protect herself.

I pull her body flush to mine. Loosening my fingers from her hair, I wrap my hand around the back of her head and tuck her cheek into my chest, kissing the top of her head.

For better or worse, Harlow has managed to ignite a spark deep inside of me, and I almost lost her.

"We need to get inside." I talk into her hair, and she nods her head against my lips in agreement.

By the time we enter the house, everyone is seated around a table.

The place looks like something out of a history book. It's

like the previous owners just up and left sometime in the eighties, and this place has been lost to the outside world ever since.

I take a seat at the table, and Harlow joins James near the couch.

"Let's—um—I'll show you the place." She tugs at James's arm, leading him out of the room and giving us some privacy.

Dagen and I turn our attention to Lennox.

He's seated at the head of the table, his forearms resting on top. I can't place the look on his face; I've never seen it before. Lennox has been many things: guarded, gruff, determined, but this is—new.

He lifts his hands to his head and drags them over his face. Then he takes a deep breath. "I can't do this anymore."

Is this a confession?

I dare to glance at Dagen, and his eyebrows are high on his forehead in confusion.

"I don't know where to start. It's been so long."

Silence slips between us, and I suddenly feel angry. I'm mad that I don't have a close connection with Lennox like I have with my other brothers. I'm hurt that Lennox spent all of his adult life pushing us away.

"After all of this time, why should we listen to anything you have to say?"

The front door opens as I ask my question.

Lennox doesn't answer. I don't think there is an answer when Ryder steps into the house, leveling his gaze over the three of us.

"I say we hear him out."

Dagen stands. "How the—?"

Ryder tips his head at Lennox. "He called me last night and asked me to be here." He takes a resigned breath. "I'm not saying I'm fully on board, but I think we need to listen to what he has to say."

That does it for me.

Of all of us, Ryder has the most to lose with Amara, Sloane, and Henry all in possible danger. So if he is willing to listen, then so am I.

I set Lennox's gun on the table and slide it toward him. He doesn't make a move to pick it up. Instead, he nods to Ryder to take a seat.

Ryder steps to the table then pauses, squaring himself on Lennox. "Did you kill Grayson?"

This conversation is going to end really fast if we find out Lennox is Grayson's killer.

Lennox looks him dead in the eye. "No."

"Do you know who did?"

Ryder flinches when Lennox says, "Yes."

Ryder pulls out a chair and drops his weight into it. Grayson was Ryder's best friend. He was Amara's brother. At one time, Grayson and Lennox wanted the same girl. The answer to Ryder's next question is going to be the literal nail in someone's coffin. Ryder knows this. The answer comes with consequences, and we've all waited years to get to this point.

"Wh—" Ryder clears his throat and tries again. "Who?"

Lennox circles the table, looking each of us in the eyes before he returns to Ryder and answers.

"It was Dad."

I spend the next twenty minutes suspended somewhere between reality and the nightmare we've just strolled into as Lennox explains what he knows about the night Grayson was murdered.

A sickening knot forms in the pit of my stomach as Lennox gets into some of our background. "You know how each of us was given twelve percent of the family business when we turned eighteen?" We all nod, and he continues, "That leaves Dad with fifty-two percent—except he doesn't own fifty-two percent. He owns forty-eight percent. Someone else owns four percent of our company."

"Who is it?" I hear the unease in Dagen's voice without looking at him, but when I do, the expression on his face matches his tone.

Of the three of us, Dagen is the most easygoing. I used to envy his decision to go out on his own. He works for himself. He comes and goes as he pleases, and he answers only to those he chooses.

But not right now. Now, he's as invested in this as the rest of us are.

"Elia Lucciano."

"How did you find that out?" Ryder crosses his arms, leaning back in his chair.

Being the youngest and oldest, Ryder and Lennox have the largest wedge between them. They've always butted heads.

The color drains from Lennox's face, sucking the air out of the room. I can count on one hand the number of times I've seen Lennox afraid of something, and this is one of those times.

"How did you find out Elia owns four percent, Lennox?"

Ryder and Dagen look from me to Lennox when I ask the question, and he bows his head, his eyes going to the table in between us.

"Grayson figured it out."

"What?" Ryder jumps to his feet, leaning over the table. My brother looks like he's about to climb across it and strangle Lennox. "Is that why he's dead? Why didn't you come to us?"

Lennox raises his hands in surrender, speaking over his

youngest brother. "I didn't know he was looking into it at the time, or I would have told him to back off. Besides, he got it wrong. That's why he died."

Dagen and I stand on either side of the table to get in between the two. I meet Ryder's stare, and he's on his last shreds of control. We owe it to Amara and Grayson to find out what happened, and killing each other isn't going to get us those answers.

Lennox speaks from his seated position. "The night Grayson was killed, I heard through one of Dad's employees that something didn't sound right. She had overheard a call from Grayson to Dad. Grayson was talking about missing money, and he thought it was me who had stolen it from our family business." Lennox looks at Ryder. "He didn't want to involve you until he was sure. By the time I got to the address to sort it out, Grayson was dead."

"Why did he think it was you who had stolen it?" I ask.

"Because it was my name and signature on the documents. Except I never signed them. Dad was setting it up to look like I was the one stealing in case he was ever caught." He levels all of us with a stare before continuing, "You don't know him like I do. Dad will do anything to get what he wants, and none of us are above being spared."

"That's kind of diabolical of him. To sign everything as you. Why not the rest of us?" I challenge him.

Lennox laughs at that, but his chuckle carries no humor. It's dark and filled with years of pain.

He reaches into his jacket and slides a folded piece of paper over to me.

"None of you are clean in all of this." Lennox waves his hand around the room as I unfold the paper. "You're on the deed to this house, Cole. Technically, you own fifty percent of this place and the acres all around it. Along with Dad."

I scan the official document in my hands. It's as close to my signature as one could get, but I never signed it.

"That doesn't make any sense. If I owned this, I'd know about it."

"Not if you're using the family lawyer and accountant. They've been on Dad's payroll since I was a baby."

The ground drops out from under me. How complacent and trusting had I become that I used them, year after year? They have access to everything. When I look at the matching looks of despair on my brothers' faces, I realize they are both in the same boat as me.

Lennox looks at each of us as he keeps going. "By the time I found out about this, he had already signed you all up to be his scapegoats. And whether you want to be a part of the entire family business or not, if he goes down, we all go down. We all own twelve percent, and we are listed on countless properties that are currently being used for trafficking, drugs, weapons, you name it. I wouldn't be surprised if there were bodies out here on this land." Lennox pauses before adding, "I mean, other than the one I left in the barn."

The three of us look out the window to the building near the tree line before exchanging glances with each other. That's a topic for another time, and Lennox is still talking.

"Dad raised us to take over the family business, but we started doing things our own way. Dagen, you left, and we were all interested in working aboveboard. We ceased being his assets and became his liabilities instead. We didn't serve the purpose he intended for us, and we became expendable in his eyes. The businesses we know about and run are legal, but there is a graveyard of lies below the surface."

Then Lennox looks toward the back room. "It's thanks to your girl that I found out a little more. The Lucciano group aren't the only ones fighting themselves. Dad isn't retired. He's aligned himself with Ratchet's side, and if he's trying to represent the Saints, and he's going against Creed, then—"

Son of a bitch.

"We're all on the wrong side of their war." I finish Lennox's thought, and everything just got a shit ton worse.

"So, if Ratchet takes control, what does Dad get?" Dagen asks.

"The guy in the barn gave up what he knew before..." Lennox shakes his head. That last part is irrelevant. "He said Ratchet is desperate to get his hands on the memory stick to use in trade with Dad. Harlow and I talked a bit yesterday. She mentioned you had it. Was it Grayson?"

I nod, and Lennox swears under his breath.

"Have you seen it?"

Ryder tells him we did, and Lennox asks him what was on it. When we tell him the shooter isn't captured on video, but he is, Lennox looks like he's going to pass out.

"Dad can never know he isn't on it. I saw the camera the night I found Grayson. When I heard the footage went missing, I took a chance that Dad didn't have it and used it as leverage to keep him from—" Lennox takes a deep breath, shaking his thought out of his head and replacing it with, "I started to see Dad for who he really was when I turned sixteen. I didn't want that for any of you. It—there's no good in him. It's too late for me. He's already tied me to everything. When he goes down, he'll take me down with him, but there's still time for you."

I get the feeling we are going to need years of conversations like this to get to the bottom of everything our father has done.

James was right. Lennox sacrificed himself to protect all of us. In the absence of our father, he pushed us all away to keep us sheltered, but it didn't work.

My mind swirls with all the questions I want to ask. Each one is more important than the next.

"You said Harlow told you about the memory stick. Did she say anything else? Like how she came to have it?"

I'm curious how that conversation played out.

"She hasn't, and honestly, if you didn't message me to speak up for her, I would have pushed it, but I didn't think it would gain me any ground with you. I can't do this on my own anymore, but Dad can never know that we've talked. He isn't above killing everyone here just to save himself."

"That might be a bit of a stretch. Do you really think Dad is capable of killing any of us? His own family?" I ask.

I've caught glimpses of my father's ruthless practices, but this seems a little too far-fetched for him.

Lennox stares me down. His eyebrows pinch together as he clears his throat.

The next thing he says makes my blood run cold.

"He's already tried to kill you."

HARLOW

I explored this house last night while Lennox heated up some stale tea. By the sounds of the raised voices in the other room, he's more talkative with his brothers than he was with me.

After I lead James through another couple of rooms, we finally reach the back of the house. A large velvet green couch sits in the middle of the room in front of an old box television that doesn't work.

I wrapped myself up in a knit blanket and sat in here to watch the sunrise this morning. I'm sure I would have enjoyed it more if the barn wasn't the building it rose behind. Knowing a man died there yesterday cloaked the bright morning rays in haunting disparity—even if that man was intent on killing me first.

I walk James to the couch and wrap him in the same blanket I used earlier. He looks like he didn't sleep much last night. I can't imagine any of us did. I stared at the ceiling in the room where Lennox left me until I fell asleep in the early hours of the morning, although time became blurred after the first couple of hours in the dark.

I fuss with the blanket then look at my brother. The lost expression on his bruised face says it all. What is happening here has nothing to do with us, yet we are cursed to play a part.

Judging by the number of bodies on the other side, so far, our chances of surviving are good.

I shouldn't have run to James when Genie died. I'm the one who brought all of this trouble and infected his life.

"I thought—" James takes a deep, shuddering breath instead of finishing his sentence.

"I know." I sit with him and nudge close.

He thought he was going to die, or he thought he was going to watch me die. I lower my gaze to my lap and let myself go. Lowering my head into my hands, I cry.

I cry because I lost Genie. I cry because I almost lost James, and I cry because I drove away from Cole, and I never wanted to do that.

James wraps his arm around me, tugging me into him, and he sits with me in silence for a few minutes while I weep against his chest.

When my sobs turn into short gasps, James brushes the hair off of my face. "He cares for you."

I meet James's eyes and force a smile.

On the one hand, I've managed to screw things up. On the other, I didn't.

I don't know where we stand. Not after he pleaded for me to wait for him and I disconnected the call like he meant nothing when I know that is so far from the truth.

"I care for him."

That's not what I want to say. I think it's still too early for what I want to say, but I know I won't walk away from him again. Leaving him, defying him, goes against my very nature, and every time I've done it, I've walked away from my heart. I felt it. It hurt.

I sit up straight, wiping the tears from my cheeks. "Will you stay here? I'm going to go and see what's going on. Rest. I'll be back."

James leans into the couch, all too happy to stay where he is, and I stand and walk back to the front of the house.

It isn't my intention to eavesdrop.

I mean to make my presence known and join the conversation, but as I near the room the brothers are in, my footsteps slow.

Then, when I hear Cole's doubtful voice asking if their father could be capable of killing his own family, my feet stop moving altogether until I hear Lennox's response.

"He's already tried to kill you."

I take the last half step to the entrance of the room. I remain hidden in the shadow of the half-opened door. All of the brothers are seated around the table, their attention on Lennox. From my spot at the door, I am able to see Cole and Lennox and the backs of the other two. I didn't hear Ryder come in.

Whatever Cole's previous expression was, it's already slipping from his face. Nausea rolls through me as Lennox's words settle into my head.

The silence is deafening until Ryder cuts the tension with his question.

"What? When?"

Lennox looks briefly at his youngest brother before returning to Cole. "The night you got your scar. It wasn't random. Dad sent someone after you."

I fight off the vertigo threatening to knock me over at Lennox's revelation. Cole's own father tried to have him killed, and from what I remember him telling me, his scar is really old. He was just a kid when it happened.

"Why?" I think it was Dagen who asked the question, but their voices are starting to bleed together.

Lennox looks like he doesn't want to say any more. I don't get the impression he is trying to protect their father. I think he's trying to protect his brothers from whatever this truth means.

"Dad gave up control over the company when he handed over that four percent to Elia. When the time came for Dad to buy it back, Elia was happy to hold on to it. He didn't want to hand it over." Lennox points to Dagen. "It was around the time you left to go into business for yourself. We didn't know where you had gone for about a year, remember? It made you hard to target. Dad was pissed you left. He saw it as a slight against him. Then, Cole, you started talking about going out on your own when you graduated. I had hoped you were going to go. I thought if all of you didn't want to stick around, it would be just me and him, and I could handle that. Then Dad decided he'd just be done with you and take back control of the company. If any of us dies, our shares automatically revert back to him, and he has his majority."

"How did you find out about it though? I thought you had just stopped by that night." Cole's subdued voice breaks my heart.

"You have a guardian angel. She overheard the conversation between Dad and the guy he hired to kill you and called me. After that, you know what happened. I showed up and—"

Lennox doesn't need to share what he did with his brothers. Their forlorn expressions tell me they are all aware.

Cole props himself on the table with his elbows and drags his hands down his face. "Who called you?"

Lennox shakes his head. "You know they're as good as dead if it ever got out."

"What happened after? Why didn't Dad try again?"

"I threatened him. It was the first time and the last time I ever stood toe to toe with him. I told him if anyone was harmed, his life was forfeit. Even if I had to kill him in front of Mom. When Grayson came forward thinking it was me who had given away the company, Dad must have decided to cover it up knowing he'd go to you guys once he figured it out. You'll remember Dad moved Mom out of the house shortly after Grayson was killed. He moved to protect himself from me because I had access to the house, and he knew it was no longer safe for him. He knows there is a rift between the four of us; he nurtures it. I'm convinced it's the only thing keeping everyone alive, and this is why he can't know about this."

"So in exchange for Dad's loyalty to Ratchet, he gets the video evidence and the four percent of his company back when Ratchet takes control. Then he can push us all out and go back to the business he wants to run." Dagen wraps everything up, and everyone looks over to him.

Then they see me, because I'm standing past him in the doorway.

"Harlow." Cole straightens in his seat, trying to correct the tortured look on his face when his eyes settle on me.

I thought I had held back my tears, but they still slipped down my cheeks. I wipe my face as I join them at the table.

There's only one question I want answered.

"Do you have a picture of your dad?" I'm looking at Lennox, but the question is meant for everyone, and it is Ryder who pulls out his phone and starts swiping.

"Just a minute. My mom texts when she feels well enough. Here's one." He hands his phone to me, and I scan the image in my hand.

The light in the room diminishes as quickly as the air is pushed out of my lungs.

I'll never forget those soulless eyes.

"He's the one I saw. I think he killed Genie."

I don't notice Cole stand, but he's immediately at my side, his arms pulling me into him as he mutters apologies against my hair.

"Who's Genie?" The voice sounds faint, but I know it's coming from Lennox. He's the only one who doesn't know.

Cole keeps his arm around me but breaks away to answer him. "The night we met with Dad at the house, a woman was killed. Harlow was there. It was her sister."

Lennox meets my stare, and realization dawns in his features. I close my eyes and push my face into Cole's jacket. The comfort of his familiar scent surrounds me.

The scraping of a chair on the floor draws my attention back to him.

"I didn't know. You need to know—I didn't—"

"I know. I saw you after." I blink rapidly to hold back the next wave of tears that threaten to spill out.

Then Dagen speaks up. "I saw you too. What were you doing there?" His words are a surprise. Cole never mentioned Dagen was there too.

It's clear Lennox didn't kill my sister, but there is still so much we don't know.

"Dad's been on edge ever since the Scott girl joined us for dinner and started going on about how she was going to find Grayson's killer." Lennox shoots Ryder a glare, and I'm not sure why. "Dad was acting strange at our meeting. He said he was going home after, but when he pulled out, that isn't the direction he drove in. I decided to follow him. I hung back when he went into the building, but then I heard two gunshots. I waited until he left then went in to check it out. I didn't know who she was or what was happening. I'm sorry."

I pinch my lips into the ghost of a smile, accepting Lennox's condolences.

Ryder draws our attention when his body stiffens. "That night, Sloane said she heard Nash say he was texting Mr. Saint. We thought that meant he was texting me. He was texting Dad."

None of this makes sense to me, but it sobers the room into a haunting silence.

"So how do we all get out of this alive?" Dagen stands, stretching out his legs.

It's Lennox who responds. "Dad raised us to compete against each other so we would be four sides of his foundation and loyal only to him. We were never meant to work together. Everything he did was with the sole goal of pitting us against each other for scraps of his praise, and it only served to make him stronger. The only way you will all get out of this is if we work together and keep quiet."

His last sentence rubs me the wrong way. I sense Lennox doesn't think he's going to get out of this. He's trying to give his brothers their best shot of breaking free from everything.

Cole's chest vibrates against my cheek as he speaks.

"There's one thing we can do that will help. We need to find the heir before Elia dies. If we can help Creed secure Elia's successor, then that four percent will be kept out of Dad's hands."

"Are Sloane and—" I want to ask if she and Amara are safe, but Cole cuts me off.

"Sloane is Ryder's fiancée, and she is his concern." His tone is sharp, and I catch Lennox stiffen at her name.

I decide to let it go.

Cole told me only a few people know the truth, and it isn't my place to speak up.

Although Ryder and Lennox don't talk to each other

directly, they both decide they will drive back to their homes in Seattle separately and return to business as usual. That way, their new alliance will remain off of their father's radar.

The glares they level on each other seem tense.

When I break free from Cole's embrace, I find James standing at the door, taking in the situation, and I walk over to join him.

"Um, what about us?" I ask, pointing between my brother and me. "James mentioned he had a friend in Nebraska. Maybe we could still go out that way for a while. You know—lay low."

All of the brothers stop and look at me like I've amused them.

When my eyes meet Cole's, I know why.

He's already stalking toward me, determination etched into his pinched eyebrows. Gripping my upper arm, he leads me away from the group and cages me against the wall. He leans into my space, his lips tickling the shell of my ear.

"Do you really think you're going to Nebraska?"

There's something in the way he asked the question that makes me think it might be rhetorical, but I answer him anyway.

My answer sounds like a question. "Uh, yes?" My cheeks flush because he's too close to me.

His smirk turns wolfish. "I don't know how it is where you're from, so I'm going to spell it out for you. When I say you are mine, that means *we* are in this."

Then he raises his voice, catching everyone's attention. "*We* are in this." He repeats himself. "And that means *no one* sacrifices themselves or runs away for the good of the group anymore. We are strongest when we're together."

He returns his attention to me, lowering his voice so only I can hear him. "Besides, you and I have some unfinished business, and I'm aching to get you alone, Socks." His hot breath against my neck makes me shudder.

When he steps back from me, Lennox is already walking out the front door with Ryder close behind him. Dagen catches Cole's attention, and he looks away. As Ryder passes us, he smirks at me, as if to tell me he knows I'm in trouble.

My face warms again.

Cole steps away to talk to his brother, and James takes his spot.

"I'm not going anywhere, Harlow. I want to help—for Genie."

It's settled then. We're all in this up to our eyeballs.

I catch Dagen and Cole's attention. "What are *we* going to do next?"

The brothers exchange a glance before Cole settles his stare on me.

"I'm taking you to meet Creed."

COLE

We all have our jobs now.

Lennox is heading back to gather an extensive list of everything our father purchased under our names, and Ryder is working on a list of everyone who is still loyal to our dad.

And we're all doing this without raising any flags.

We need to know the extent and depth of our father's dealings. We've been betrayed at our core and—

He's already tried to kill you. The memory of Lennox's words steals my breath.

Shit.

That cuts deep.

In my own father's eyes, my life is worth twelve percent.

To think, all of this time, I walked around with a false sense of security.

I thought being a Saint meant we had each other's backs. We weren't protected; we were ignorant, but it was that ignorance that kept us alive all these years—that, and the sacrifices Lennox made.

None of us have the luxury of time to sit back and consider what all of this means. We are now at war with our own, and decisions need to be made to bring us back onto the winning side.

It took us an hour to dispose of the body Lennox left in the barn, and another to make our way into town.

I sent a message to Creed requesting a meeting at my restaurant.

We've been here for forty-five minutes, and the meeting isn't for another fifteen. I know Creed and his guys are around here somewhere, checking the place out. I'd do the same, especially since weapons are not allowed inside.

Harlow looked hungry, and I wanted time to get her comfortable, so I made extra concessions for a meal. Cora was more than happy to feed us.

Well, most of us.

Watching Cora and Dagen bicker back and forth makes me chuckle. Their banter has captured Harlow's attention as well, easing some of her anxiety.

Since Creed will match the number of men we have around the table, I had James sit off to the side, on his own. I don't want more than Creed and one other with us.

Cora set him up with an extra-large plate of pasta, and he's been making his way through it.

Cora ambles toward us with two plates before I've had the chance to ask Harlow if she wants any dessert. She sets the larger piece of cake down in front of Harlow, places the smaller piece in front of Dagen, and digs forks out of her apron with a grin.

Dagen reaches across the table, switching his plate with Harlow's, and Cora's smile drops off her face, replaced by a scowl. She switches the plates back and glares at him.

"What?" Dagen pretends to be hurt. "It's the only way I'll

know for sure if you messed with my dessert. Which, by the way, isn't cool."

He tries to switch them again, and Cora leans over the table, her hand landing on a stray knife, causing Dagen to abort his mission.

"The bigger piece is for the girl." Then she smiles at me and Harlow. "I gave you two forks, dear."

I stifle a chuckle, and Harlow thanks her for her kindness.

Cora warms right up at that.

"Dammit, woman. I can't tell if you're fucking with me, and I really want that cake."

That gets a soft laugh out of Harlow, and I catch Cora winking at her before she responds to Dagen. "We take our lives into our own hands every minute of the day now, don't we?"

She struts away without another word, leaving Dagen there to assess his odds as he stares at the piece of chocolate cake in front of him.

Finally he mutters, "Fuck it!" to himself and lifts his fork.

I know our company is here when the smile on Harlow's face becomes forced and awkward. She hasn't met him yet, but there is no mistaking a man like Creed. He's close in age to Lennox, and they both move through a room aware and ready at all times.

I glance at the door and nod at the group of four men who entered. Creed returns the gesture then looks around the room.

Turning to his men, he sends one back outside, and another makes his way casually over to James's table to join him. I recognize him as one of the people we met up with at the club yesterday. They exchange a glance, and James leans back in his seat, dropping his fork on his plate.

Creed walks over to us with one other guy at his back, and they take their seats. "You know Ghost."

The man nods once.

While Creed is Elia's second, Ghost is Creed's.

Creed looks over at Harlow and smiles. He's waiting for an introduction.

"This is Harlow." I place my hand on her thigh under the table to calm her, and she smiles sheepishly and lowers her fork to the table.

"By all means, sugar, keep eating. We're just talking." His tone isn't threatening. I get the sense Creed doesn't want to draw any attention to our group.

She runs her fingers over her fork but doesn't pick it up.

Cora walks over without a word, sets two mugs on the table, and fills them with coffee before doing the same for the guy now sitting with James.

Not much gets past that woman.

Creed cuts the small talk. I'm the one who contacted him, so he looks directly at me. "What's this about?"

"Some sensitive information has come to our attention, and it affects you as well." Leaning in, I continue, "We know why Ratchet wanted the video Harlow had."

His eyes flit to Harlow before returning to mine, and I take a deep breath. This is the part I wish I didn't have to say.

"Our father has aligned himself with Ratchet's crew."

Creed looks like I've slapped him. Clenching his hands into fists on either side of his mug, he takes a hard look at me. "If your father is aligned with them, then you all are aligned, and we're done here." He jerks his head to the side, and they prepare to stand.

"He doesn't have majority." This stops him. "Right now, we're split. Forty-eight and forty-eight percent. Lennox is on board with us."

Creed looks at me like I have two heads. "You can't be that bad at math, kid. You know you're missing four percent?"

"It's not missing. Elia Lucciano holds it. When he passes, that will go to his successor."

My breaths come in slow as I wait to see what Creed is willing to do with this information.

"I need to verify that." Creed looks at me, but it is Ghost who reacts. He lifts his phone, types something out, then sets it on the table.

"From my understanding, our father owed Elia a debt, and he paid with stock in our company. He wanted to buy it back, but Elia decided to hold on to it. Our father has been trying to regain control of it ever since."

Creed's chuckle is dark. "You know why that is, right?"

I shake my head.

"Fuck those old bastards." He shakes his head. "A long time ago, they both wanted something, and your father ended up getting it. It's bothered Elia for as long as I've known him. Of course he's going to hold on to that four percent. There's no way he'll let go of something that important to your dad while he's still alive."

"What did they both want?" Dagen finally joins the conversation, drawing Creed's gaze to him.

"Your mother."

I try. I try really hard not to react to that, but I'm sure I've failed when I recoil in my seat. Today has been one long string of revelation after revelation, and I don't know how much more I can take when soft fingers run along my own thigh.

I glance down to see Harlow's forearm disappear under the table. She's trying to mimic the comfort I showed her earlier. Picking up her fork with her free hand, she cuts out a slice of cake and takes a bite, attempting to look normal.

The effort makes me smile.

Creed breaks the tension when he speaks again. "Here's the thing. Elia doesn't give a shit about your old man, but he does care about Kristianne." My mother. "If you're going through the same...restructuring as we are, then we have mutual enemies. We are not loyal to your father, but we will remain loyal to you. What do you need from us?"

"Has anyone seen the video I turned over yesterday?" I ask. Creed shakes his head, and I continue, "Our father believes he's on that video, killing the kid you saw. Lennox is holding that over his head. He can't know he isn't on it."

"I won't destroy it, but I will make sure your father never knows what is on it." Ghost lifts his phone and types another message at Creed's words. "What else?"

"The brother." I tilt my head toward James. "He has a bar here in town he needs to get back to. There's no need for Ratchet's crew to target him anymore, but I don't want to leave his back exposed."

Creed glances at Harlow's brother before turning his attention to her, the corner of his lip twisting up. "Well, it's a good thing some of my boys like to drink then, isn't it?"

I meet Creed's eyes. "Appreciate it."

"And what else do you want?"

I spoke briefly with my brothers before we parted about what we were going to come to the table with and what we wanted to take away, and we are all in agreement.

"We want the agreement we've already settled on. You have the backing of the four Saint brothers. We won't ask for the stock to be signed over; however, we'd request the successor support our efforts to keep our father from destroying us further. And this conversation never happened. You don't know anything about my father's plans. It's important he doesn't catch wind of anything."

Creed looks like he really doesn't want to honor my last request. We do not handle betrayal well in our line of work. If someone disrespected us like this, they would be dealt with, so looking away, even for a short time, is a tough ask, but it is necessary.

"In our line of work, betrayal seems to come with the territory. We expect it." Creed lowers then shakes his head. "But we don't expect it from family and that's what hurts the most." He leans back in his seat. "Done."

The survival of both of our groups depends on us working together because our enemies are working together.

Creed leans back in his seat, crossing his arms in thought. "It'd be easier if we had the birth records." He speaks more out of frustration than anything else.

Harlow licks the icing off her fork, reminding me I still want to get her alone, and soon.

"Why can't you get them?" she asks innocently.

"The paper copies were destroyed a long time ago," Creed answers.

"That's rough," she commiserates, and he nods in agreement. "Did they destroy the microfiche as well?"

Creed stops nodding. "The what?"

Now we're all staring, slack-jawed, at Harlow.

"The microfiche." She looks at all of us around the table as she says the word slowly, like she's teaching us a new language. She explains, "When I turned eighteen, I tried to find out who my birth father was, but the hospital records had been destroyed in a fire. I ended up getting sent to a storage facility, and they had the original certificate of live birth on microfiche, but my dad's name wasn't filled in." Harlow shrugs when her eyes meet mine, and she must realize she's started rambling, because she straightens in her seat and corrects herself. "I mean. That was up in Seattle though, so I don't know how it is here."

Creed and I meet each other's eyes at the same time.

Their search for Elia's heir is narrowed to Seattle.

"Little girl, if you didn't belong to this one right here—I'd kiss you." Creed has a new fire lit under his ass. He turns his attention to my brother, then to me. "Dagen, Cole, this has been a fucking pleasure." He points to James. "Text me his address. We will be in touch."

He stands, not bothering to look at the men he walked in with, and strolls out of the restaurant. Ghost nods once then follows him out with the man who was seated with James.

Harlow releases a long breath beside me, and I swivel my body around in my seat to face her head-on.

"What?" she asks, her eyes bouncing between me and Dagen, and I zero in on a fleck of icing on her lip.

"You're brilliant!" my brother chimes in. Harlow grins at that as James joins us at the table.

Cora sets a tray down and loads the empty plates and cups onto it. She side-eyes me. "You guys all good? I was worried I was going to have to intervene there for a minute."

My chuckle is full of relief. Our meeting went better than I hoped it would.

It's good to know there are people like Cora around who have my back. For as long as I can remember, she's always been like a—

Guardian angel.

The thought subdues me.

That's the term Lennox used to describe the person who sent him to save me that night.

Everyone chats around the table as I sit with my thoughts and watch Cora make her way to the kitchen with her tray propped against her hip.

She worked for my father first.

It had to have been Cora who told Lennox where to find me that night.

She's the reason I'm alive.

HARLOW

Cole has been quiet since we left James and Dagen back at his apartment.

We made sure they settled in, and James and I watched with great fascination as Dagen managed to push every single one of Cole's buttons.

When we arrived at Cole's place, Dagen walked in with his shoes on. He acted like it was a mistake, but I caught the giddy glint in his eyes as he glanced at Cole before he did it.

James just shook his head and rolled his eyes. His laugh was easy.

Then Dagen accused Cole of having a sweet tooth and hiding candy all over the house. When Cole denied everything, Dagen crossed his arms, saying, "It's like you don't remember what I do for a living."

I find things.

Cole stomped off down the hall, leaving us standing around to stare at each other before he returned with a fistful of small plastic bags, stuffing treats into his backpack and muttering under his breath.

Now the sun is almost gone, and our drive is reminiscent of the last time Cole drove me out of Portland.

The car is just as quiet.

While everyone believes the attention has moved off of finding me, my safety isn't a surety, because I am aligned with Cole. Someone wanting to hurt him could go for me. The realization that losing me would hurt Cole fills me with a whole new set of emotions.

I wait as long as I can before my curiosity gets the better of me. "Are we going back to the island?"

Cole's eyes stay on the road, but he smiles. "Did you like it there?" He answers my question with a question.

I shrug, then, realizing he isn't looking at me, I answer, "I liked being with you there."

He sits with my answer for a long time before speaking again. "I'm taking you somewhere else."

We slip into a vulnerable silence for the next half an hour while we continue to drive north.

I sneak glimpses of Cole, and he is always deep in thought. Now and then, his features twitch with the same pained look he had when I overheard his brother tell him how his father tried to have him killed. How a parent could reduce their child to dollars and decide to cash in on them—I just can't fathom it, and my heart breaks for Cole.

I'm jostled out of my thoughts when Cole pulls onto the shoulder of the highway, then turns onto a dirt road.

There are no lights out here, and the scenery in front of me now takes on a different familiarity.

My heart jumps into my throat at a fleeting thought.

Could we be?

I shift in my seat, looking out every window, trying to place something that will jog my memory.

Most of that night is a blur.

I recall that time felt warped and distance distorted.

I spend five minutes trying to recognize curves in the road or the spacing of the trees until Cole slows then turns at a boulder on the side of the road.

I cover my mouth with my hands to stop myself from squealing when he pulls up the little driveway out front.

"Now all I need to see is a car with big flowers painted all over it parked right over there." Cole points to where I parked the first night we met and smiles at me from the driver's seat.

"I can't believe you rented this place again."

Everything looks both new and old at the same time. I was running scared that night. I remember this place like I watched it in a movie.

I was going through the motions until I met Cole.

"We," Cole corrects, and I pause, replaying my last words in my head. He rephrases my sentence for me. "We rented this place again. It isn't *me* and *you* anymore, Harlow. It is *us* and *we*. And we didn't rent it—we are buying it. Welcome to our new secret hideout."

I have no words.

That night, I lived the life I wanted.

I dared to open myself up to someone, thinking it would be my only chance to feel that way, and life had other plans for me —for *us*.

Cole's scent hits me when he turns in his seat, reaches into the back seat behind me, and drops a bag into my lap.

My backpack.

"I would have given this to you sooner, but you left everything that mattered with me, didn't you?" Cole doesn't ask the question in anger. His glossy eyes watch me as I wrap my fingers into the fabric of the bag and nod.

He doesn't say anything else. We both know I don't own much, and I value the little I carried with me.

Unzipping his jacket, he reaches along his chest into an inside pocket. When he pulls his hand out, he's holding my teddy bear in his fist.

I run my hand over his worn fur, and Cole hands him over to me. Setting my stuffed animal on my lap like I used to when I was younger, I straighten his tie and pull the ends to make sure it stays that way before I take a deep breath.

"Back at your place on the island, Amara told me that we don't choose our family. We choose who we love, and we make them our family."

Surprise flashes across Cole's face before he settles on a smile.

Did I just tell him I loved him?

Do I?

Lifting his hand to my face, he brushes the hair out of my eyes, and I lean into his touch.

"She is a smart woman. Come on. I want to show you what I like best about this place." Cole pockets his keys and opens the driver's side door to the fresh air.

I stuff my bear into my backpack and sling it over my shoulder to join him. "And what's that?"

"That no one will hear you scream." Cole's words can be taken a few different ways, and his face is unreadable.

A zing of excitement at all of the possibilities rushes through me as we grab some bags from the back and walk up to the quiet place.

This is what it was like when Cole arrived here that night. The lights were out. The place was nothing more than a lifeless fixture. When I arrived, he had already filled this space.

I like it even better now that we are stumbling into it together.

Last time we were here, Cole made me stew from scratch.

This time, he asked Cora to make him some meals we could take with us before we left the restaurant.

I immediately liked Cora. She reminded me a bit of Genie in how she fussed over me, asking me if there was anything I didn't like to eat. Even though she went back and forth with Dagen, she still told him to watch his back when we left. Although, now that I think about it, that could have been a threat.

She loaded us up with bread, soup, meat, and potatoes— and another huge helping of the chocolate cake I devoured.

I unpack everything while Cole brings in some wood from outside. I prefer a real fireplace to the kind you can turn on, and, judging by the occasional hint of a smile on Cole's face, he enjoys roughing it as well.

He sets the logs up then says he's going to start the heater for the shower. I had almost forgotten that we don't have the luxury of just turning it on.

When he returns, he opens the box of matches and turns his attention back to the fireplace.

The room warms with the first crackles of the fire, and Cole stands, stepping back to the couch to appreciate his mad boy scout skills.

"Are you hungry?"

That is a loaded question.

I shake my head. I want a lot of things—food isn't one of them.

"Tired?"

"Not particularly." That answer sounded a little huskier than I would have liked, and Cole's lips tick up in a wicked smirk.

"Well then, let's talk." Cole sits down on the couch.

My high hopes take a nosedive and crash down around me. "Um—yeah—sure."

I advance to where Cole is sitting, and he holds up a hand, stopping me. "You'll be having this *talk* naked."

I used to read romance novels that would say, "her nipples hardened instantly," and I always used to chuckle, thinking it was a load of crap—until right now. I'm pretty sure I could cut glass with the pressure building behind these babies as Cole sits there, staring me down, without a care in the world.

Excitement bubbles up from deep in my belly, and it isn't until Cole raises his eyebrows at me that I realize I giggled out loud.

I'm thankful I can't see how red my cheeks have flushed as I lift my hands, my fingers fumbling with my bra under my shirt. I release the clasp and pull it off with my top all at once.

Now it's my turn to wrinkle my forehead questioningly when Cole doesn't move to take his clothes off as well.

"Uh. Aren't you gonna—"

GET NAKED! a voice screams inside my head.

Cole leans forward, placing his elbows on his knees and running his thumb along his lower lip. "I'm not the one who ran off and almost got themselves killed, now am I?"

Right. That was all me.

The humor in his face slips when I unbutton my jeans and slide my pants down to my ankles, along with my underwear.

I'm not above using my own tricks to get what I want—I leave my fuzzy socks on, fully aware of what it does to Cole. I clench my thighs at the look of appreciation spreading across his darkened features.

His eyes meet mine with a hard hint of accusation. He knows I left them on on purpose.

I'm playing with fire, and I don't care.

The outline of Cole's cock is clearly visible as he strains against his own pants. Leaning back against the couch, he curls his forefinger in my direction, calling me the rest of the way to him.

I obey.

Stepping in between his parted legs, I curl my toes inside my socks to wring out some of the anxious energy building inside of me.

His hand leaves his lap to trail up the inside of my thigh. His eyes hold mine in rapt attention before lowering to stare at my hardened nipples, which are now pointing right at him.

God, how I want his mouth on them.

I shift, spreading my legs apart to grant him easier access.

In my head, I'm silently willing his fingers to keep going as they trail higher along my sensitive flesh to my—

The room tilts as Cole wraps his free hand around my wrist, pulling me down and over his knee. My face is now pressed into the old couch, and I lift my head, turning it to the side to take a breath when his palm lands with a sharp slap across my ass.

My groan is borderline embarrassing. It's depraved and wanton, and it's laced with an urgency, reflecting the fire building inside of me.

Cole spanks me again, not bothering to check on me. We both know I'm more than okay.

Every smack warms me a little more, until I'm brazenly lifting my ass for his next contact.

"Needy, greedy, little thing, aren't you?" He drops his hand to my ass, then between my legs, spreading my slick lips open and exploring my folds.

"Yes. Please." I buck my hips up, spreading my legs further.

Cole moves his free hand to my ass while his fingers continue to glide through my slick, delving deep into my opening.

"Please *what*, Harlow?"

Fuck, I love my name so much.

"Please take care of me, Cole."

His free hand grips my punished ass, sending jolts of pain to mix with the pleasure. I whimper into the sofa as I desperately hump my hips against his hand working my clit.

Locking his legs around mine, Cole moves his hand into my hair, holding me as he wants. Now that I'm fully on board and pliable, I'm easier to move.

"I'm going to take care of you, baby. I just don't think you're going to like it very much." His dark chuckle sends shivers rippling through my body.

I'm not in the right frame of mind to be scared.

I should be.

A little voice in my head screams at me to slow my roll and talk to him, but this horny heart of mine still thinks she's gettin' some.

With Cole's legs wrapped around my own, I can't shift my body enough to open myself to his touch, nor can I give myself the friction I need to get off.

His open palm slaps down on my ass once again, but there is no offsetting pleasure to wind me up. There is only the sting of his—discipline.

Oh no.

"I did say this was a punishment, didn't I?" Cole's tone is laced with feigned confusion.

Like an idiot, I pathetically shake my head to silently answer no.

"Because it wouldn't be nice if I went off and did my own thing without telling you about it when you thought we were going to do something else."

Son of a—

My body deflates against the old couch.

Another smack lands on my ass with no sign of relief on the horizon.

"Here's the thing, Socks." He thrums his fingers on the fleshiest part of my ass. "And nice job trying to get me with the fuzzies, by the way." His body vibrates underneath me with what I think is a chuckle before he continues, "I'm not mad that you went after your brother because I know how fiercely you love your family."

Another spank lands sharply on my ass.

"I'm livid that you made my choice for me. You hung up on me without giving me the address and the chance to decide for myself to be there for you like you were there for your brother." There is no playful humor in Cole's tone.

He spanks me again, but this time I only hear it.

My heart aches at the crushing disappointment I feel in myself. Cole is brutal, but he is also vulnerable, and I took away his power. I held his control hostage when I made those decisions for him.

I try to blink away my tears, but it's too late.

The logs crackle as they succumb to the fire. It's the only sound in the room. Cole doesn't move underneath me. Being left to think about what I've done is worse than being punished. Or is it part of my punishment?

Either way, I don't like it.

"More." I'm too cowardly to ask any louder than a whisper, but Cole hears me.

"What?"

"Please spank me harder, Cole. I need to—"

"You want to feel better?" His fingers trail tenderly over my ass, and I sob, nodding against the couch.

"I need you to take care of me."

31

COLE

I'd be outright lying if I said I wasn't enjoying this.

Watching Harlow hesitate and fumble as she removed her clothing tested my resolve. Then she left those socks on, and it took everything I had not to give her exactly what I know she wants.

But right now is about clearing the air and making my expectations known.

I've been thinking about getting through to Harlow since the moment I knew she was out of harm's way.

I was raised to be loyal and demand the loyalty of those around me in return. Granted, I was raised by the very man who tried to have me killed.

I spent the drive out here thinking about Lennox and his detachment from the rest of us. In the end, I arrived at the only conclusion that made any sense.

Lennox didn't put up walls, he created boundaries. He knew who our father was a long time ago, and he made the choice to step up and try to be the father figure we deserved.

Many of the conversations that once felt like him asserting his will over us were merely him trying to guide us—as a real father should have.

When I think about it more deeply, I learned loyalty from Lennox and my brothers. I learned subjugation from my father, and I rejected it. I wanted to follow Dagen away from the family business because of my dad—I just didn't realize it at the time.

He disguised his iron fist well, and he pitted us against each other. We were too busy vying for his approval to see the losing game he had created. He attempted to groom his own sons into following him, and if it wasn't for Lennox, we might have done just that.

Lennox went out on his own to protect us, and I'm still upset about it. He should have come to us a long time ago, but that's something we'll have to work out another time.

Right now, I have a slate to clear with this one lying limp over my knee.

Harlow's whisper drags me from my thoughts. I didn't catch what she said, so I ask her to repeat herself.

"Please spank me harder, Cole. I need to—"

The sadness in her voice tugs at my heart and begs me to help her.

"You want to feel better?" I ask as I caress the blushing splotches on her ass.

Harlow has a big heart, and it overrides her head at the worst of times.

I know she didn't think she was hurting anyone by running to help her brother, but she could have died many times over by now, and I won't lose her. Her actions affect more than just her and her brother now, and she needs to be made aware of how important she is.

"I need you to take care of me."

This isn't just for Harlow. This is for the both of us.

I raise my hand from her ass, and she doesn't tense waiting for the impact.

She stays still on my lap in surrender—in submission—waiting for me to help her make things right.

I tighten my calves around her legs, locking them together and holding them firm against me so she can't take any pleasure from her discipline until I am done.

My hand comes down, cracking against her bottom, and her skin under my palm goes white before filling in with a pink hue.

I spank her again.

Her ass jiggles on impact, and she chokes on a sob against the cushion.

I'm lucky I have her here to punish. It could have been so much worse, and my mind drifts to what I would have done if I'd arrived to find her with bullets in her instead of in the guys that Lennox killed.

My hand lands harder than I would have liked when that image floats into my head, and I blink rapidly, pulling myself out of my daze when a hot tear rolls over my cheek.

It's only a tear, but it's more than I've ever given any woman, and I quickly wipe it away before Harlow glances up at me.

Harlow's body is easy to move, and I slide her up, angling her bottom to land a spank on each of her sit bones. She'll feel the sting for a couple of days after, but she doesn't move. While she whimpers, she doesn't object.

Her discipline is over when she exhales into the couch, her body sinking further into my hold, and sobs.

It's the sound she makes that alerts me. Her cry coils in my gut and wrenches my heart clear out of my chest.

Lifting her from the couch, I turn her over, and she immediately climbs into my lap, burying her face in my chest.

Cradling her head, I comb my fingers through her hair as she curls into me. Her small fingers grab at my shirt as I shush her.

"I was so scared. I th-thought they were going to kill him. But then—but then when I was there and I thought they were going to kill me, all I could think about was y-you."

I understand the helpless fear of the moment you realize you might actually die. The day I almost died, I remember lying on the ground in my own blood, my back torn open from a knife wound. Apparently, I wasn't just meant to die. I was meant to suffer for what my father saw as a betrayal first. I was meant to be made an example of.

I still carry the lesson around with me, etched eternally into my back.

I thought about my brothers and my mom. I thought about the people who I loved most and who I was about to leave.

"I know you were. You're safe now. If you give me the choice, I will always choose you, Harlow." I kiss the top of her head before inhaling her scent deeply.

I will never get enough of her smell, her smile, her laugh, her socks, or any other part of her.

"I'm sorry, Cole."

I tilt her face up to mine. Her puffy eyes meet my own.

"I know."

Leaning in, I claim her tear-soaked lips in a kiss, and she opens for me, allowing me to control our connection while she moans into my mouth.

Her hand finds its way to my cock, straining against my zipper, begging to be freed. I cover her fingers with my own.

"You won't come tonight. I want to make sure you understand, your punishment isn't done."

Denying Harlow an orgasm is also a punishment for me because I crave the sound she makes when she lets go and tumbles over that edge, but I'm still driving my point home.

It isn't just about her realizing the danger she was in. It's also about her learning that it isn't fun when our choice is taken away from us.

Harlow studies my eyes for a few seconds before she nods. "I understand."

"No, Socks, I don't think you do. If you want to do this, you will only be satisfying me, and I will edge you then put you to bed. There is nothing for you. But I am going to give you the one thing I didn't get, and that is a choice. You can choose to go to bed with me now, and neither of us will get what we want. Or you can pursue this and go to bed frustrated."

Biting her lower lip in thought, she flicks my hand off hers, and I think she's going to choose to cuddle and go to sleep when she returns to rubbing my cock through my jeans.

A growl rumbles from my chest at the touch of her hand.

"It's not about me." Harlow slides off my lap, landing on the floor to kneel between my knees. She winces when her bottom comes to rest on her heels.

Her little fuzzy socks jutting out from underneath her freshly punished ass are fucking with my sanity.

Dragging her teeth over her lower lip, she nibbles the plump flesh as her fingers travel up my thighs to my zipper. When her eyes meet mine, she smiles bashfully.

I may not survive this, but what a fucking way to go.

I shift my hips, allowing her access, but only enough so she can release my length from my pants. My clothes will stay on for this so she understands the difference between true punishment and the stuff we will do for fun. Judging by how my girl enjoyed herself earlier, there will be a lot of the latter in our future.

Harlow's wide eyes follow her fingers as she strokes them down my shaft to my balls, squeezing and rubbing her way to the base.

When a drop forms at the tip, she leans over and licks it up before she looks up at me again.

God, those eyes are going to be the death of me.

I'm almost ready to throw in the towel. I want to flip her over and fuck her into the rusted old springs of this couch when she opens her mouth to suck me in, and my hips thrust up to meet her.

Pulling back her head, she looks at me. Worry that I pushed her too fast rushes through me.

Her hands wrap the girth of my cock, and she tilts her head back.

"I want you to fuck my mouth."

My first thought is, *Isn't that what we're doing?* but I quickly realize that isn't what she's asking.

She wants me to take control.

Opening her mouth again, she sticks her tongue out and drops her hands away from my length.

Profanity slips from my lips, and I stand to take charge of her better. She backs away but keeps herself open and ready.

Cupping the back of her hair, I hold her in place while I fist my cock and bring it to her face, running it around the rim of her lips, marking her with a trail of precum before sinking myself into the warmth of her mouth.

She hums, sending vibrations through me as she allows me to guide myself deeper to the back of her throat.

"Just relax. Tap my thigh if you need me to stop, baby." I move my hands to the sides of her head, tilting and pulling myself into her.

She settles and relaxes herself into my palms, and I thrust

myself in and out at a slow pace a few times to learn how to take her.

Harlow shifts under me, catching my attention and drawing my eyes to her legs. She's spread her legs open at the knees; her hands remain at her sides.

She knows she's being denied tonight, and I think she's adjusted her sitting position to ease any friction she knows she isn't allowed to enjoy.

As much as I'd like to enjoy this all night, I've made my point. I pull out once more before increasing my pace to chase my own finish without holding her here to suffer on her own for much longer.

My thrusts become rigid and relentless as I tighten my grip in her hair. Her wide eyes, filled with tears, stare up from her place at my feet.

The image sends me over the edge, and I release myself into her throat with a growl, holding her head in position to take all of me on my final thrust.

The sight of the entire length of my cock slipping out of her puffy lips is mesmerizing. Then she licks them, and her tongue sneaking out of her mouth to taste me off her bottom lip makes me curse again.

I now owe her an edging.

Lifting Harlow to her feet, I smash my mouth down on hers and kiss myself off of her sweet lips before hugging her naked body into mine.

"The water will be hot now. Let's get cleaned up."

Tangling my fingers in hers, I lead her out of the room and through the bedroom. I had forgotten how small the bathroom was.

She hugs her arms across her body while she watches me undress, then I remove her socks and pull her under the warm spray with me.

When I'm done washing her hair, I soap her up and clean her off. Her eyes remain on mine the entire time, a shy smile gracing her lips.

I have enough hot water left to finish her punishment in the shower. Lowering myself to my knees, I nudge her back against the tiled wall, spreading her legs open to access her pretty cunt, and I dive in, aching for a taste of her surrender.

I'm so enthralled with her that I almost forget she isn't allowed to come. Her hips writhe, grinding her pussy into my mouth, but her fingers in my hair start tugging me off. The pull becomes frantic when I realize she is actively participating in her own discipline by denying herself.

Harlow has more restraint than I do at this point.

I rise, releasing her legs to stand on her own weight. She wraps her fingers around my upper arms, her body tensing as she forces herself to reject the orgasm I know she desperately wants.

I edge her two more times with my fingers before the water runs lukewarm, and Harlow looks like she's had enough although she never voices her limit.

Wrapping her in a towel, I carry her back to the small bed before leaving her to check on the fire. There's nothing left of it but a warm glow.

When I return, Harlow pulls the covers back for me, and I join her under the sheets.

She murmurs as I pull her body into mine, and I settle us into a comfortable position, my arm wrapped protectively around her naked form.

"Cole?"

"Mm-hmm?" I tuck the back of her head under my chin.

"I—um." She pauses for a long moment, and I wonder what words would have followed had she spoken her thoughts without second-guessing them. "Thank you—for...choosing me."

I smile against the back of her head.

"Thank you for choosing me too, Socks. Sweet dreams."

32

HARLOW

The first thing I see when I open my eyes is Cole staring back at me.

I've somehow wrapped my limbs around him in my sleep in an unconscious plan to make him my little spoon.

His wavy blond hair is tousled in that just-been-fucked look, and I can't wait to see what he'll look like when I really do get to climb him—hopefully soon.

"Mmmm, good morning." My words run together in one big slur. I yawn and try again. "What are you doing?"

"Watching you sleep." His lips twitch into a smirk.

"That's not creepy."

He chuckles at my lame attempt at being witty. "Says the woman who has me locked into some half-assed reverse sleeper hold."

"How did you sleep?" I ask, teasing my fingers along his skin.

"Like a rock."

"Then I'd argue it was a full-assed reverse sleeper hold."

His smile lights up the cozy room, and he squeezes me into him before detangling my limbs and turning me onto my back.

Sucking air in through clenched teeth, I wince when my ass makes contact with the mattress. Cole lifts his head in concern before assessing and coming to the unspoken conclusion that my current pain is warranted.

The pain fades away when his fingers draw circles around my areola before pinching my nipple tight. Biting my lower lip, I will myself not to get too excited.

Cole tilts his head to one side, examining my features. His fingers stop moving, but he holds his fingers around my hardened nipple.

"That was settled last night, baby. Today is a new day." Dropping his head, his teeth replace his fingers as he nips at my sensitive tip. His hand smooths over my stomach and continues until he dips between my legs.

Spreading my legs, I thrust my hips up to meet his touch, moaning involuntarily and drawing Cole's attention to me.

His lips claim mine in a rough kiss as he slides his fingers inside of me, reviving the memory of how desperately I wanted to orgasm last night.

"You can come whenever you want, but it has to be when my cock is inside that needy pussy of yours." Cole's low growl against my ear sends shivers along my body.

Well, then. Let's get this party started! my mind screams as I prop myself onto my elbow and push Cole to lie back on the bed.

Then I mount him like a pro.

Swinging my leg over his body, I settle myself on his thighs, scratching my nails over his chest and abdomen. His muscles twitch under my touch as he lazily draws circles on my legs.

His length is already hard, and I wrap my hands around it,

spreading the viscous droplet at the tip around the head of his cock before shifting my body down his legs and licking him.

Cole is demanding and all-consuming. His fingers comb into my hair like they did last night. His possessive grip sends a thrill through me, and goosebumps prickle along my body, chasing the sensation across my skin.

His fists tighten, lifting my head, and I release him with a slurpy pop.

"You better be getting on this real fast, Socks." His gaze drops to his cock underneath me before returning to taunt me with a wink.

His smirk falls away when I climb him and center his shaft at my entrance before impaling myself on him as I sink down around him.

His hands drop from my hair to my hips as he attempts to steady me on my way down, and I roll my hips, grinding my clit against his muscular pelvis.

I lift off and lower myself with a little more force when his fingers dig into my hips and ass, drawing another wince from me. I'm sure his grip will leave bruises later. I hope it does.

My hands find their way to my chest, and I wantonly knead my breasts while I continue to ride Cole's cock. His eyes jump from my hips to my hands before he drops his head to the pillow and growls.

I should have recognized that as a warning.

Tossing my own head back, I close my eyes and ride him, enjoying every little spot he hits from this angle.

"Jesus fucking Christ, Harlow."

I'm flipped over and on my back before I open my eyes.

Staring down at me is a driven man.

His eyes bore into mine demand obedience.

His hand wraps around my throat.

"You pinch those nipples good and hard for me, and don't stop until you come."

His grip tightens, and pressure builds in my face. I'm still able to breathe but it's reduced, and his cock feels larger inside of me. Every sensitive nerve ending fires and glitches at the restricted oxygen entering my lungs.

"Open your legs for me, baby." Cole's punishing pace ticks up, and I unhook my legs from his hips, spreading them as high and wide as I can for him.

Euphoria swirls in my head as Cole lowers his gaze to my chest, and I pinch myself harder to please him.

The thumb of his free hand slides along my labia and around my clit.

The pain I'm causing myself is delicious against the stimulation of his touch.

"I love—the look on your face when you come, baby. Give it to me. Let me hear you."

"Fuuuu—Cole, yes—I'm commmmm—"

I open my mouth wide, but no sound comes out. My words are reduced to grunts as waves of bliss consume me. Cole watches, his own lips parting, mirroring me.

"Fuck, Harlow. Mine." Two hard thrusts, and Cole's body seizes up around me as the bed shifts underneath us and tilts with a loud crash.

We lie still, our feet angled downward, clutching each other as we manage both our orgasms and our collective surprise.

"Shit, Harlow. I think we broke the bed." Cole looks very pleased with himself. "That settles it. We're definitely buying this place now."

Tucking my head into his chest, I laugh, and his arms bracket my body, his fingers pulling the sweaty hair off my face.

When I meet his eyes, there's something about the way he's looking at me, but I can't place it.

"Wait, were you serious about buying this place?"

"*We*, Harlow. *We* are seriously buying this place." He looks around the room. "I mean, it needs a lot of work, and some updates—and a new bed." Then he returns to me, his eyes bright with a smile. "How can you think I wouldn't want us to own all of this?"

I get the feeling he isn't just talking about the little cabin.

I know what it's like to lose love. But I've never experienced gaining it, and my heart aches in a different way. It feels stuffed full. I've closed myself off and limited my heart to Genie and James, then it was just my brother. This is new to me, and fresh tears fall fast.

"Socks?" Cole draws his fingers through my salty anguish, his face dropping into concern.

"I—I'm okay. I think I'm happy," I blubber.

"You don't look happy."

Then I laugh because I must look like a real-life oxymoron.

Cupping his face, I pull his lips to mine. He settles his weight on me, and I love the feeling of being cocooned by him.

"I am. This is just—a lot. It's amazing, but it's a lot."

He leans in for a swift peck, followed by a bite on my lower lip, before he shifts himself to lie beside me. "I understand. Everything turned *extra* really fast." Cole slides me into his side, settling my head on his shoulder and wrapping his arm around me.

The covers have slipped off us, but I don't mind one bit.

"What are you going to do—about your dad?" My voice lowers to a whisper at the second half of my question.

We lie in silence for a few minutes while Cole draws his fingers along my arm before he talks again. "Right now—

nothing. He can't know we know. This means I need to deal with my anger and resentment on my own until it's time."

I jolt to sitting, ignoring the pain in my ass, and glare down at him.

"What? You're still happy, right?" He eyes me cautiously.

"How could you, Cole Saint?" I ask, crossing my arms under my chest. The action draws his attention with a hungry smirk, but I'm not having it. "You're not dealing with anything on your own. You said it's 'we,' and it goes both ways."

He stares at me, open-mouthed, for a long time, considering my words, and I stare right back. How can he think he's going to carry this on his own?

"You're right, Harlow. I love you."

"You're damn right I'm right. How could you—"

I blink stupidly at him.

Once.

Twice.

Three times.

The warning sting of tears builds behind my eyes.

Did he say—

"I love you." He speaks more slowly, softly. "I wanted to say it last night. I should have. You're crying again, baby."

"I love you too, Cole." Dropping my face into my hands, I sob, and he chuckles, pulling me onto his chest.

"You're a handful, Socks, but I wouldn't have it any other way."

We stay tangled in each other for a few minutes. Then I close my eyes, and the heaviness in them starts to win out. I've almost drifted back to sleep when Cole kisses my head and moves underneath me.

He stands and pulls on his jeans, not bothering to zip them up, and I get a little show.

"I had Cora pack a carton of eggs. I'm making you breakfast."

With the new angle of the bed, I pretty much roll out of it. The two legs at the bottom have snapped and folded under the weight of the old wood frame.

I exchange a guilty look with Cole, and he shrugs, a smug look etching across his features, and I swear he struts out of the room.

I grab a pair of leggings, stumbling as I put them on while I follow him out, asking for instructions to heat the water for a shower. He tells me he'll do it later, saying, "I want you to smell like me for a while."

I like that. Hearing it makes me want to try a strut of my own.

While Cole opens the little fridge, I grab his shirt off the couch and pull it on, then kneel in front of the fireplace and start building the fire like I saw Cole do it last night.

The matches sit in a little box on the mantel. I strike one, then reach underneath the iron grate to light the newspaper I set under the logs.

It goes up as easily as it did last night.

"Can I ask a question—about your brother?" I lean back on my sit bones and wince. Last night's spanking still stings, but it's dulled into a pleasurable reminder.

"Sure," Cole answers while he starts the woodstove.

"Why didn't you tell Lennox about Ryder and Amara being married? I mean—if you aren't keeping secrets?"

Cole doesn't lift his head from his task, but his eyes rise to take me in. "So you know how I—*we*," he corrects "have a lot of work to do so I can deal with my father's deception before I see him?"

"Yes." I take a seat near him at the table, where he's

chopping and mixing what looks like the start of a delicious omelet.

"Well, there's something in knowing about Ryder and Amara that I think will send Lennox off the deep end, and right now, we need my oldest brother to believe things are as he believes they are." He stops what he's doing for a moment and leans on the table. "Trust me, I see the hypocrisy in telling him we work together while keeping this from him, but it has the potential to go nuclear if the right person doesn't tell him at the right time, and I'm not the right person. None of his brothers are."

"Do you mean he needs to hear it from Amara?"

Cole is shaking his head. "No. He needs to hear it from Sloane."

Cole resumes chopping some mushrooms, and I sit with what he's told me. I know I'll learn more over time. I trust Cole, and I've come to trust his family, so I let it go.

"There's one more thing you need to hold on to. Sloane and Amara can't know that our father killed Grayson yet. Grayson was Amara's brother and Sloane's boyfriend. The same thing will happen." Cole brings his hands up and flexes his fingers out to indicate an explosion, and I understand his meaning. "They won't be able to hide their feelings in front of my father, and their lives are at stake."

I wouldn't be able to be in the same room with the man who killed my brother. Then the thought hits me:

Cole's father killed Genie.

"I won't have to see your dad, will I?"

"No. You, above everyone, cannot be in the same room as him. You are an open book. There's no way you can hide your beautiful heart, and the harder you try, the more obvious it is."

A ding from the other room catches Cole's attention, and he wipes his hands on a dish towel before excusing himself.

When he returns, he's looking at his phone while he types. His lips are pinched together, and I instantly recognize the look of concern on his face.

"What's wrong?" I ask.

He steps back to his spot at the table, slides the phone to me, and picks up a whisk to beat the eggs he's cracked when he says, "Playtime is over—for now," with a wink.

The message on his screen is short.

Dagen: We have a problem.

33

COLE

As soon as breakfast was over, Harlow and I took turns in the shower. I didn't trust myself not to take advantage of us being naked in an enclosed space together, and judging by Dagen's texts, we needed to get to Seattle as soon as we could.

The drive into town was different than any other time we've been in my truck.

I hadn't planned on telling Harlow I loved her this morning, but seeing the way she got angry with me for attempting to deal with my shit on my own broke something apart inside of me, and I spoke my heart instead of my head for once.

We made one stop before meeting up with Ryder and Dagen at our family home.

Lennox is keeping his distance since it would be unusual for us to have too much contact, and we don't want to let our father know we are onto him.

Since Dagen and Lennox have always been closest, he's been keeping Lennox apprised of our updates.

I don't believe Harlow is still in danger, but I won't bet her life on it, so she came with me to meet up with Dark Webb.

Dagen had dropped into the storage facility where all of the city's birth records are stored on microfiche, along with countless other city records.

During the day, the only ones who can gain access are those who have appointments or approved legal or court documents granting access, as well as employees. Security had been upgraded due to a data breach a little over a year ago, so everything is locked tight.

We decided the best time to access the information we needed was going to be when they were open for business, and we needed Leonard to get us into the building.

It would have been so much easier if everything were digital. Our guy could have just hacked his way in and grabbed what we needed, but the fact that it's analog is probably what has kept that record from being destroyed, if in fact it is still there.

Now Harlow and I are rushing to check in with everyone back at Ryder's place with all of the new information we've gathered, and not all of it is good news.

"This is where you grew up?" Harlow's head swivels around, taking in the property as we drive through the gate and pass security.

When I was younger, I took all of this for granted. We know what we're exposed to, and this was my baseline for normal. I know Harlow's version of childhood is vastly different from mine.

"It is. I'll show you my old room later." I wriggle my eyebrows at Harlow, and she shies away from me.

Dagen's car is parked out front, and I pull in beside him.

Ryder opens the front door before we reach it. "What did you find out?"

Harlow stops walking at his brash greeting, and I nearly run into her.

"Don't mind my brother, Socks. His emotional growth was stunted in his earlier years, and he never did get the hang of how to say hello without making it sound like 'I'm an impatient little shit.'" I narrow my gaze on my younger brother.

Ryder steps back from the door, allowing her to enter, and I shake my head as I pass him.

"I apologize, Harlow. We are all happy you're okay. Amara and Sloane are excited to talk to you." Ryder points in the direction of our father's old office. "They're down the hall with Dagen."

Harlow glances at me over her shoulder, and I lift my chin, telling her she is good to go. She wanders down the hall, and I hang back with Ryder.

"I'm sorry. I'm on edge. I want this all to be over." Ryder turns to walk toward the office, and I join him, slapping my hand on his shoulder.

"I know, little brother."

"Does—um, does she know not to say anything?"

Ryder is referring to everything that Harlow knows about who killed Grayson. Now that Amara is back, if this got out, he'd have to deal with both her and Sloane's wrath, and none of us are ready for that yet.

"She knows. It's my bet she'll be pretty quiet during our meeting today. She doesn't like the secrets, but she gets it."

When we get into the office, Amara and Sloane have already pulled Harlow over to the couch and sat her down in between them.

"How is James?" I ask as soon as I see my brother.

Harlow leans forward, breaking away from the women flanking her to listen to Dagen's response. She flashes me an appreciative smile.

"He's staying at Cole's place until he hears from us. I talked to him a couple of hours ago. Creed sent one of his guys over to work the bar, and a few have dropped in." Dagen looks at Harlow. "Creed owes you a lot for the tip about the microfiche. He'll hold up his end of the deal."

I walk to the desk my father used to sit at and lean against the front of it. I start talking so the women don't have enough time to question Harlow much.

"I have some good news and some bad news." Everyone stops chatting and looks my way. "The good news is our tech guy can look into getting us access to the storage area, but it will take a couple of days to create what we need. The bad news is we aren't the first to ask him about this place. He was contacted yesterday by someone else."

We've always had Sloane in on our plans, and since the night she almost died, Amara's been brought in as well. And now Harlow is sitting here too. The number of people in our inner circle is growing, and it is both a good and bad thing.

"Maybe it's someone with Creed?" Ryder offers, and Dagen shakes his head.

"No. When I checked in with Creed to tell him we were going after the information, he said he'd wait to hear back from us. He's pretty tied up with Ratchet at the moment, so he's happy for our help."

None of the guys question if it might be our father who contacted Dark Webb. Amara and Sloane would ask why we are just now considering him when we never have before.

"Does your guy know who it is?" It's Sloane's turn to ask.

"No. The call ended when Leonard told him it would take a couple of days. He doesn't know who it was. So that either means that this mystery man has someone who can do it faster or—"

Dagen cuts me off. "Or he's going to make a run at it, what? Today?"

"That's my guess. I thought a couple of us could go down there and see what we could find. Maybe we'll get lucky." Everyone in the room looks around at each other, trying to decide who will go.

"I'd like to go." Harlow's voice startles me, and everyone looks at her. "I mean, I've been there before, and I know how to use their system to pull up the location of what you need, if it's in there." Her eyes meet mine, and I'm proud of her for inserting herself into our family.

"I'm going too."

"Me too."

Sloane and Amara both speak up, and I look at my brothers to step in. This isn't a fucking field trip.

Ryder squares himself on his wife. "You're getting your brace off in a couple of days. I will not have a repeat of the last time you decided your life wasn't enough of a fucking adventure." Amara looks guilty as she settles back into the couch. Then he points at Sloane. "You and I will join Cole and Harlow."

"Maybe this will lead us to who killed Grayson." Amara sounds hopeful, and Harlow pales beside her, staring at me in silence.

This is as close to a poker face as my girl is going to get.

"We're leaving in fifteen minutes. Be ready to go." I end the meeting fast before Harlow breaks.

Sloane turns to Amara and Dagen, telling them Henry's schedule for the afternoon. His day care doesn't let out for another few hours. She writes instructions on a piece of paper before reminding Amara she added her to his pickup information, so she can get him if we are not back in time, and Dagen offers to drive her if needed.

Harlow stands and joins me at the desk without a word. I brush her hair off her shoulder, put my arm around her, and lean over, whispering into her ear, "Come on. I'll show you my room."

I leave everyone else behind and lead Harlow out of the office and up the staircase toward the second floor.

Our parents kept each of our rooms as they were when we left, so we always had a place to stay when we came to visit. That was my mother's idea.

I took most of my stuff with me when I moved out. Now, my room looks just like a spare bedroom with only furniture left. The sheets were stripped off the bed the last time they were washed, and I only put them on when I'm staying here, which is rare. I opt to stay out in the guesthouse now, away from the main house.

"This house is huge." Harlow sounds uncomfortable, and I don't blame her.

I feel out of place here now, especially knowing my own father tried to have me killed. It kind of sucks the warmth out of the joint.

"Here. This was me." Harlow misses the double meaning in my words.

This was me.

This room belonged to who I was, not who I am.

I had a nice view of the backyard and the pool on the other end of it just before the guesthouse out back.

The room feels smaller than I remember, but, then again, I've been living in my own place for ten years now.

A wooden ruler still sits on the floor near my closet. The latch on my window would lock on its own when it shut, so I would use the ruler to prop my window open on nights when I would sneak out. It worked like a charm, until Dagen stumbled upon my empty room and pulled the ruler out just to get back at me for something I'm sure I didn't do.

"Thank you for offering to help us." I walk over to sit on my old bed, which is also smaller than I remember.

Harlow spins in place and closes the distance between us to join me.

Sitting down, she rests her hand on my thigh. I follow her gaze down to her small fingers delicately splayed across my jeans.

How did I ever come to deserve someone this raw and pure? Maybe I don't deserve her, but that won't stop me from keeping her regardless.

"I have butterflies in my stomach," she confesses. "Is it stupid that I'm scared?"

Wrapping my arm around her waist, I slide her closer to me on the bed. "No. We're all scared, but that's why we're doing this. We can't live like this anymore."

Harlow looks around my empty space before launching into a story.

"I used to think my mom didn't love me." Her eyes scan the wall in front of us as she continues as though she's speaking to a ghost in front of us. "She was always gone, and when I was younger, Genie and James hated that they got stuck with the baby all the time. I felt like a burden—no one wanted me." I don't like this story, and I cover her fingers with my hand. "But then my mom died, and I realized too late that she loved us, and she did her best. She worked two jobs and she—um—saw men. She had no one else, only us, and she did everything she could to feed us and dress us. We were all in school, we were all safe, we were all together, and it was because of her. She did her best."

Harlow's eyes meet mine, and I process her words.

"Are you trying to tell me my dad is doing his best?" I ask.

"No. Your dad is a piece of shit, and he doesn't deserve any of you," she deadpans, and I stare at her for half a second longer before I toss my head back and laugh.

"But you have the rest of your family. When my mom died, James and Genie were the best siblings I could have asked for. They took over roles that they shouldn't have had to, kind of like Lennox. Your dad may be too stupid to appreciate what he had, but I'm not. I know how lucky I am, and I will fight beside you until we are all not scared anymore."

Damn. This girl knows how to knock me down and build me back up in the same sentence.

A knock at the door catches our attention, and Dagen ambles into the room, looking around.

It feels like a lifetime ago since all four of us lived under the same roof. I don't often feel regret, but I wish I could go back to those days and change the path Lennox felt he had to walk on his own.

The way Dagen looks around makes me think he's feeling the same way. Dagen was closest to Lennox. I remember chasing after them when I was a little kid. I wanted to do everything they did when I grew up. I wanted to be them.

"When we're gone, can you get in touch with Lennox and tell him where we're at? Ask him to try to find out if Dad hired whoever this guy is? He might be able to access some of his records. I'd like to know who we're dealing with. Then, can you check in with Leonard and see if he can hack into the cameras at the facility? I'll send him a message letting him know that I approve the contact so he'll work with you."

Dagen digs his hands into his jeans and nods. "I might be able to find out some things through my channels as well. I'll let you know what they have."

Standing, I reach for Harlow's hand, and she rises with me.

Ryder and Sloane are waiting by the front door, ready to go.

We need to get out to that place before anything goes down, and everyone knows this. We might be about to find the last piece of evidence linking an heir to Elia Lucciano.

34

HARLOW

The records storage facility is located in another industrial park, which does nothing to settle my nerves.

Flashbacks of James beaten and defeated rise up until I close my eyes, blocking out the buildings outside.

A warm hand on mine pulls me out of my thoughts before I begin my descent into panic, and I look up, meeting Sloane's stare next to me in the back seat.

"It's going to be okay." She doesn't look like she completely believes her words, but I smile anyway.

From the front seat, Cole points to a familiar building on the left side, and Ryder pulls into the lot. Whatever security Cole's tech guy told us about earlier must be located inside the building, as there are no vehicles or additional men on the grounds.

There's no grand entrance at the front of the building.

This place isn't built for the public.

It's been a little over five years since I've been here. It still looks the same.

"Those are the doors I went in."

Ryder follows my finger to a metal door around the right side of the building, and he steers his car in the same direction. He drives past the door and parks a little bit away. We're partially hidden by a dumpster.

By habit, I pull my backpack out with me and sling it across my back.

I'm standing close enough to Cole to hear the vibration in his phone when he gets a message.

"That's Dagen. Webb can access the security feed. Dagen is driving there with Amara to check it out." Cole pockets his phone while we approach the building.

The door groans on its hinges as we walk into the main area. Some of the chairs are in different spots, but the room looks the same as it did the last time I was here.

Once we enter, we all look around to collect ourselves.

The walls are painted off-white and decorated with a few generic pictures I'm sure I've seen in every government office I've been in. I think these types of buildings are designed to turn people away, but none of us are going anywhere.

When I look back to Cole, his expression says it all.

We don't have a plan. All we know is someone else is looking for access to this same building, and tomorrow is too late for them.

Ryder and Cole take two seats in the middle of the room, and I take a step to follow them when Sloane hooks her hand around my arm and guides me to the only other door leading to the back of the building.

I meet her gaze, and she gives me an uncertain look and shrugs her shoulders. Then, glancing back at the two brothers, I realize what she's trying to do. If we stick together, we have one shot at getting into the storage area—if we separate, we have two.

The front door opens, and a stream of light from outside follows a man in, catching Ryder and Cole's attention. They stiffen as they size him up.

This kid can't be more than twenty years old.

Is this who we're looking for?

I glance at Cole, but there is no recognition on his face.

The inside door opens while everyone is staring at the guy who just entered, and Sloane tenses in the seat beside me as an older woman walks out, and the door closes behind her with a click.

"Too fast." Sloane quietly chastises herself as she looks at the closed door. We weren't ready for the door to open, and now it's locked again. Sloane slowly leans over. Her words come out on her hushed breath: "Be ready."

My heart rate picks up, and I nod, completely unaware of what she's talking about.

The old lady sets a small basket on the counter near the door deciding to deal with the kid standing in the middle of the room first.

"You are?"

"Um, Ewan Tanner. I'm with the temp agency."

She responds with a curt smile. "You've done this before?"

The kid nods. Without looking, she points to the basket she just set down. "Grab a key card from the basket and head back."

Sloane waves to Ryder then points at the old lady as she makes an urgent face. Ryder jumps to his feet, drawing the woman's attention while keeping her back to the two of us. The kid saunters past the woman and grabs a key, swiping it on the pad at the door. The lady turns her focus to Ryder, and Sloane wraps her fingers around my arm again, whispering, "You are the only one who knows what to do in there." It sounds like an apology, and I look at her in confusion.

The lock to the back area clicks, and the kid opens the door wide and steps through.

Sloane stands, dragging me up with her, and Ryder's eyes go wide before he recovers with a slick smile. Cole stands behind him, and his eyes settle nervously on us.

Ryder introduces himself to the woman, but he sounds different. Maybe I've just always talked to him in a casual setting. He is abrupt and domineering, yet the woman warms to him.

Before the door shuts, Sloane grabs the handle and pulls it open slowly, careful not to make a sound. Reaching into the little basket, she stuffs a key card into my hand then pushes me through the door.

I'm in.

The thought fills me with more butterflies, and I'm not sure if I'm excited or terrified. Whatever I am, I'm now on my own, and they are all depending on me.

The last thing I see before the door closes behind me is the worried look on Cole's face.

I don't have time to process what just happened. There is only one door leading back here, and that woman will walk through it as soon as she's done with them.

I could do this one of a few ways.

I could wait for the woman to come back and then tell her I'm with the temp agency and I got lost, but then she might drag me into some area I don't want or ask me for ID.

I turn and take the hall to my left, following the signs leading me toward the warehouse. When I was here looking for my birth records, I checked in at the front desk and gave them my name. They easily pulled up my court documents to confirm my access, then a man showed me how to use the search monitor and walked around with me to help me find what I needed.

As I near the warehouse, I decide this plan won't work. First off, it's an old court ruling. I don't know how long they stay on file, and my story will fall apart if they ask too many questions. Not only that, but if they walk around with me, there's no way I'll be walking out of here with something that isn't mine.

I turn the last corner, and the area I need is beyond the door at the end.

I won't let Cole down.

I've got this.

With every step I take, I straighten myself a little more until I'm exuding confidence I definitely don't feel on the inside.

Flipping the key card in my hands, I slide it along the pad and open the door, walking through it like I own the place.

The middle-aged man behind the counter doesn't even look up from the book he's reading. I falter in my step, but it's subtle. Taking my attention off him, I head toward the first row of boxes.

I don't remember this place being so intimidating. It's probably because last time, someone else was doing all of the work, and they knew exactly where to go—also, I wasn't breaking in.

Metal shelving stands at least twenty-five feet high, and each shelf has the same-sized cardboard boxes on it. Each box has a storage identification number and some other information printed on a label that's stuck to the front. The shelves seem to stretch on, row after row.

I retrace the steps I took the first time I was here. At the end of the first row is a monitor and a small section of binders. Each set of files is documented in the binders if you know what you're looking for and on the monitor if you don't...so monitor it is.

I click the mouse a few times and a lock screen pops up.

Shuffling loose papers around on the desk, I scan the area and behind the computer for the information I need. Written on a sticky note on the back of the monitor is a username and password. Typing it in brings the monitor to life.

I step back to look around my area. I'm alone with nothing more than the odd sound here and there. This is where files come never to be seen again.

A window opens on the screen automatically, and I stare in silence at all of the words displayed before I realize this must be a portal to all of the files. It looks like a long list of government agencies, businesses, charities, and other organizations. These must be all of the places who use this storage facility, and there are hundreds, maybe thousands, of names here.

I'm going to get caught before I find what we need.

I click the letter S at the top of the page to jump to the section, hoping it'll be under "Seattle Hospital Records," but it isn't. My heart sinks when I realize I might need to search each hospital one by one. I check two random hospitals only to find it isn't sorted that way either.

Staring up at the mountain of files around me, I chastise myself for not paying closer attention the last time I was here. As a new idea comes to me, I search and repeat the process for another five minutes before I find the words I need.

Listed under "Public Health" is a link for birth and death records, and clicking it takes me to a screen with search fields. I type in Elia Lucciano's name, click "Birth Records," then wait.

This system is as archaic as the microfiche the warehouse stores. It beeps an odd retro sound that makes me think the system is actually old-school dialing up to the internet, then two records pop up with their own box, file, and microfiche numbers.

I remember from looking up my file number that the first four digits of the file are the birth year.

The first file is dated too long ago, and I'm pretty sure it is Elia's own birth records. The second gives me hope in the form of a file number that is the same as my birth year.

The heir is my age. My chest tightens at the thought.

I tear off a corner of paper sitting beside the computer and grab a pen, writing down the information. This was the easy part. Now I need to navigate that maze of boxes out there and find what I'm looking for before someone finds me.

I decide to walk along the back wall, sinking myself further into the labyrinth before I start making sense of these files. Each shelf has a paper taped to the bottom of it with a list of boxes and their numbers down the aisle.

Passing by a few rows, I notice the digits are climbing, but I'm not near the box number I'm looking for. A thud in the distance startles me, and I stop moving for a moment to make sure no one is heading my way.

I allow a full minute to pass before the clicking of boots sounds on the cement floor. The sharp but light clacking sound makes me think it is a female before I see her. I hide myself at the end of the aisle, staring down it, waiting for the woman attached to those heels to pass by.

An employee clears the far end of the aisle, and I wait until she's gone a few more rows and her footsteps no longer sound in my vicinity.

When I don't hear anything else, I keep moving. With each row, my nervous energy builds inside of me. Trepidation sends the butterflies in my stomach into a flurry of flutters.

My pace picks up, and I fly down the aisle, only stopping to check the number on the lowest shelf against the one written on the paper in my hand.

I check the numbers once more—too low.

Another row—too low.

Another row—too high.

I freeze.

Backtracking, I step into the previous aisle, and I instantly know I'm too late.

My heart sinks at a box that lies open on the ground at the far end, its contents thrown around the middle of the aisle.

As if on autopilot, I run toward the box, not bothering to check the numbers on any of the shelves. My heart clenches with every step I take. I already know before I get to the box— I've failed.

Kneeling down, I hold my paper to the box to check the number.

It's a match.

I move to the file numbers. The files in the back half of the box are still intact, but I'm not looking for them. The numbers on the folders are too high. I scan the ones strewn on the floor.

The box is here.

The whole file is missing.

I don't waste any more time.

I pull my phone out and send a message to Cole.

Now I need to make it out of here without getting caught myself.

35

COLE

I leveled a hardened glare on Sloane when the door closed Harlow away from me. She met it with an apologetic shrug and a wince.

This was not the plan I envisioned. No part of any plan I ran through in my head included Harlow being separated from me and on her own, but I can't deny that she and Sloane just managed to do the one thing Ryder and I could not, and that is charm our way into the records area.

After a couple of different approaches, we gave up trying to access the records area and hoped our distraction would give Harlow enough time to get farther into the building unnoticed.

Considering she wasn't kicked out as soon as the old lady left us, it must have worked.

Ryder thanked the woman for her time, and we left, making our way to his car so we could watch the front of the building for Harlow.

I turn my attention to Sloane.

"I can't believe you just pushed her in there. She's on her own."

"You don't give her enough credit, Cole."

I cross my arms, offended. I give Harlow a lot of credit. I know what she's faced and handled on her own. I just don't like that I'm not there for her. "I know she's strong. We just didn't plan for it and—"

"What was your plan then? Smolder the old lady to death? Because you two were laying it on so thick, I need a shower to get all the smarm off me." Sloane dramatically shudders, shaking out her arms from the back seat.

Ryder chuckles from the driver's side.

Sloane is so good at zinging all of us, I'm convinced she's a long-lost sister.

When Ryder looks over and sees that I don't share his humor, he defends himself. "What? Sloane is right. We weren't getting in there today. Your girl is our only hope."

I pause at his words. Not at the part where he said Harlow is our only hope, but at the acknowledgement that Harlow is my girl. Hearing that settles my fire.

A delivery truck pulls past us, turns the corner, and heads toward the back. The logo on the side matches the storage facility logo, so we let it go, but if Harlow takes too long, I will wander around and check them out.

"Anything from Dagen?" Sloane asks as the front door opens, and a woman walks out, heading toward a car in the lot.

I'm happy for the distraction.

Pulling out my phone, I check my messages. There are no updates, and I shake my head, focusing on the door to the building once more.

I add up the time since we've last seen Harlow. She should be coming out, either on her own or escorted, soon. But it's more time than I'm comfortable with, and my phone vibrates on my lap.

Socks: The file is gone.

I don't have time to process the information. It's immediately followed by a text from my brother that doesn't make sense.

Dagen: STOP HER!

"Dagen wants me to stop Harlow." My heart races.
Is she in danger?
"Why?" Sloane asks from the back.
I'm ready to tear into the building after her; my hand is on the passenger door when my phone rings. Dagen's name flashes on the display, and I put him on speaker.
"Why do you want me to stop Harlow? Is she okay?"
"Not her. The other woman. She's heading to her car right now. I see her on the video."
We all look out the window at the empty lot.
"There's no one else here."
"What the fuck are you talking about? She's wearing a dark brown leather jacket. SHE'S RIGHT THERE. DON'T LET HER LEAVE." I've never heard him so panicked before, and I look at the lot again.
Sloane answers Dagen. "There was a woman wearing that jacket. She left almost a minute ago."
Dagen makes a noise that falls somewhere between a growl and an angry groan, and the three of us exchange confused glances with each other.
"DAMMIT! There's a delay on the video." The rest of his sentence is a long line of curses.
The door to the building opens once more, and Harlow scans the lot before walking swiftly toward us.
"Harlow's out. We'll see if we can catch up with the brown

jacket. Call you back." I disconnect and step out of the car, closing the distance between me and Harlow until we're in the middle of the lot.

"The box was already open. I checked three times. The file isn't there." Harlow looks disappointed.

"It's okay, baby. I'm so proud of you. We think we have a lead, but we need to go."

I want to pull her in and kiss her, but I can't let Dagen down. I don't know what he saw on that video, but it rattled him to his core.

When we are a few feet away from Ryder's vehicle, I glance up, meeting my brother's gaze, and the first thing that registers is the look of dread in his eyes as he opens the car door.

Tires screech to a stop behind me, and a male voice draws my gaze away from my brother.

"HEY!"

Spinning, I turn in time to see the barrel of a gun pointed at me, and the loud pop sounds like the crack of thunder in the quiet lot.

I reach out to push Harlow away, but my hand doesn't connect with her as my eyes close and I go down. My head hits the pavement with a crack.

Tires scream, and the car drives away. Ryder hovers over me, his own gun drawn and pointing in the direction they went before lowering his attention to me. He looks terrified.

I struggle to sit up and go after whoever it was when a heavy weight holds me down.

"What the—" I freeze when I realize it's Harlow's body lying limp on my own that is pinning me to the ground. "Harlow?"

She was standing beside me when we turned around. The only way she would have ended up on me is if she stepped in front of me.

Rage blinds me as I yell random words and struggle to get out from under her so I can see where the bullet went. Sloane cries from behind us, but she gives us space to work.

The door to the building opens and a few people step out, but I don't pay any attention to what they are doing.

Ryder helps me to turn Harlow over—there's no blood. He looks at me confused.

I pat my front, searching for a wound before leaning in to check her pulse. As I do, her eyes shoot open, and she sucks in a sharp breath of air.

"Son of a bitch, that hurt!" Ryder and I jump at Harlow's raised voice. She groans in pain and winces before looking at me.

"Where? What hurts?"

I'm relieved Harlow is alive, but the memory of Amara almost bleeding out right in front of us sends fear through me.

"My back. I feel like someone hit me with a sledgehammer."

I lift her, pulling her onto my lap, and Ryder moves her backpack and jacket out of the way.

"There's an odd bruise forming but no bullet. She's okay." His voice is oddly positive. Then I realize he's trying to comfort me like I did for him that night on the bridge. "Wait a minute."

Ryder rustles with something at Harlow's back, and I wait patiently, just happy to have her in my arms. When he sits back on his haunches, he's holding two pieces of a brick that's been cracked in half.

It's not just any brick.

It's the same brick Harlow once called her "personal bodyguard." When Ryder puts the two halves back together, there is no mistaking the circular hole in its center.

My guess is the bullet meant for me is somewhere in Harlow's backpack.

"Guys. If everyone is okay, we need to get out of here." Sloane jostles Ryder's arm and points to the couple of people standing by the door. One of them sounds as though they are staying on the line while help is on the way.

I stand and carry Harlow to the back seat, and she protests the few steps of the way, telling me she's okay to move on her own. I motion for Sloane to take my place in the front so I can be with Harlow in the back.

Ryder peels around the building and out of the lot, heading in the same direction as the shooter's vehicle.

I don't have time to deal with what this means for us.

I pull out my phone with shaky hands and unlock it to a slew of messages from Dagen that are just coming in.

He must have seen what happened on the video feed.

With the delay, I'm not sure if he knows I'm okay, so I message him back, telling him we are alive and to get back to the house.

Tucking Harlow into my side, I wrap myself around her this time.

"FUCK!" Ryder slams his palm against the steering wheel, and I glance out the windshield from my place in the back seat.

We're on the street leading out of the industrial park, and there's no sign of any other vehicle or this mystery woman that Dagen is losing his shit over.

I pull up the memory of her; she is no one to me. I'm sure I've never seen her before, but that doesn't mean Dagen hasn't.

"Let's get home. Cops will be here any minute." At my warning, Ryder slows to the speed limit and drives us away from the storage facility.

I sit beside Harlow in silence, subdued by the shock of almost losing her all over again. This time, she sacrificed herself for me. The thought creates conflicting emotions, and I squeeze her closer to me.

"Before you say anything. I'd do it again, and I won't ever be sorry." She leaves off *for saving my life.* I bury my face in her hair and inhale, using her strands to hide the start of a smile on my face.

She's already attempting to reason her way out of a punishment, but it isn't necessary. The next time I punish her, she'll like it.

"What were you thinking?" I murmur so only she can hear.

She sits in silence for a long time before she answers.

"It never occurred to me that I could lose Genie. That's why I let her go in on her own, and why I froze when she was shot. I can't take something like that back. I won't make that mistake again because now I know how it feels to live through the death of someone I love. I would rather it be me. I don't care if it makes me selfish."

I pull her away from me to examine her face.

She's serious.

She's ridiculous if she thinks that makes her selfish, but she's serious just the same.

Then she looks up at me and smiles.

By the time we get to the house, Dagen and Amara are already there. We find them in the sitting area. Amara is sitting on the back of the couch with her feet where we would normally sit, and she's watching Dagen pace the room.

When he sees us enter, he walks a straight line toward us.

"This should be good," Ryder mumbles to me when he sees the unhinged expression on Dagen's face.

"Who is she?" I ask.

Dagen looks like he wants to slap my head clear off my

shoulders at my question. Shaking his head, he stops walking then turns and stalks into the middle of the room.

When the women join Amara on the couch, she says, "You're not going to believe this."

Amara looks like she wishes she had popcorn for this conversation.

"*She.*" Dagen says the word like it smells bad. "That woman is my rival. She's the one who left me tied to a fucking tree in the desert and took off with my money five years ago."

"No way." I say the words without thinking, and Dagen glares at me as Ryder chuckles under his breath.

The woman wearing the brown jacket in the parking lot is Dagen's archnemesis. They are in the same line of work, yet she bested him in a job, and he hasn't been able to let it go.

Rather, I should say, he hasn't been able to let *her* go, but he would deny it.

Ryder and I have heard the whole story. If I'm being honest, I'm secretly impressed by her, but I'd never say that out loud. I've never seen a woman get under Dagen's skin before, and this one has been living in his head rent-free all these years.

"What do we do now?" Ryder asks, drawing Dagen's ire, and I swear his eyes flash with maniacal delight.

"Now I'm going to hunt her down and take back what's mine."

The way he stakes his claim gives me pause, and I exchange a glance with Ryder before returning my attention to my older brother. Ryder meets my gaze out of the corner of his eye, his eyebrow raised with an unasked question.

I feel what Dagen is saying on a visceral level. It's how I felt when I went after Harlow. I imagine it's how Ryder felt when he went after Amara, but there's no way I'm voicing it to my older brother right now.

Dagen is wound so tight at this turn of events that hearing me say anything might be what makes him snap.

I switch gears, asking Harlow, "Can you tell us anything about the missing file?"

All eyes turn to her, and she looks blankly around the room, considering my question. Finally, she pulls a piece of paper out of her pocket and tells us about the file number itself. While it doesn't say which hospital the file refers to, it turns out that the file number includes the year and month of the records within it. Then she says the year and tells us that the month is April.

Sloane sucks in a deep breath. Her eyes go wide, and she directs her response to Ryder when she speaks. "We were all born within four weeks of each other. You and Grayson were born in April."

Everyone but Harlow picks up on the weight of those words. It doesn't take Grayson off the list of possibilities, but we're pretty sure it isn't Ryder, or Creed would have pushed for a DNA test already.

Speaking of which, I redirect the conversation again.

"We need to bring Creed and Lennox up to speed, and then we'll start looking for..." I trail off, waiting for a name, and I glance at Dagen, who looks frustrated all over again.

"Nyla." His answer is clipped, and I notice an angry eye roll at the fact that I'm making him say her name out loud.

I repeat the last of my directions. "Then we'll start looking for Nyla."

I attempt to focus Dagen on the task, and it seems to work, but only a little. Crossing his arms in front of his chest, he plunks himself into an oversized sofa.

I have a feeling that once we find Nyla, Dagen will be more than happy to be the one to go and retrieve her, and I can't wait to see how that shitstorm plays out.

HARLOW

Everything I owned was in my backpack.

Then I met Cole Saint.

Now everything I own is all around me.

Cole framed the few pictures I had of my childhood, and now they sit, framed, amid the new photos we've been taking together. My teddy bear sits on a shelf in our bedroom, and Cole and I have been adding new memories and moments to the few possessions I once carried with me.

Three tense months have passed since someone tried to kill Cole. We found out they were linked to Ratchet, but everything else went as cold as the guy's body was when he was found a week later.

Cole moved us back to Portland. He said it was so I could be closer to James, but I think he wanted to keep me off his father's radar. So far, he's hardly heard from him.

As far as Cole's parents know, he is single, and I am never spoken about.

I don't get to see Amara and Sloane as much as I'd like, but keeping up appearances means me not making an appearance.

Amara put me in touch with an instructor she knew when she lived in Portland, and I've started taking self-defense classes with Cole's encouragement. He's always eager to practice what I've learned with me, but I've come to realize it's because rolling around on the mat usually ends in sex. I'm not complaining. It's my favorite part too.

Last month, I asked Cole to take me to a range so I could learn how to shoot a gun. I don't think I'll ever need to fire one, but I enjoyed the lesson I had with Lennox, and it turns out I'm a decent shot when I'm not a clumsy mess.

A week after we returned to Portland, Ryder somehow got Genie's body released to us. He did it without the proper paperwork that would lead anyone our way, and we finally brought her home.

I cried for three days.

Cole has been making excuse after excuse to be away from Seattle. He's spoken to his father on the phone, but he isn't confident he'll be able to hide his hurt and anger if they are in the same room.

We've heard from Dagen the most out of everyone lately.

Since finding out the woman who took the file is basically the female version of him, Dagen has worked tirelessly to locate her. We don't know if she still has the microfiche. If not, we're at least hoping to find out what was on it or who hired her to take it in the first place.

Creed has taken a liking to James. In the beginning, he sent some of his guys around to keep watch on the bar. It was good for my brother's business. Not just because he has extra customers to charge, but James told me that Creed's influence has changed the clientele, and his bar is always busy—and profitable—now.

Then Creed stopped in a little over a month ago, and they got to talking. Whatever they talked about kindled a mutual respect of sorts. I've started to notice small changes in my brother. He doesn't carry the weight of all our worlds on his shoulders anymore, and I think it's because he's found someone he relates to who can offer him the guidance he should have had growing up.

Cole was true to his word, and we bought the cozy, off-the-grid cabin where we met.

The first thing he did was change out the small and very broken bed with a more sturdy king-size one. It's so large, we only have a foot of space between the bed and the walls on all sides.

When I asked about it, he said we're going to do two things in this room, and all we need is a bed for both of them.

Lights illuminate the back wall of the cabin, catching Cole's attention, and he sets his glass of wine on a side table beside the couch and stands.

"Dagen is here."

He opens the door and steps onto the porch. It's still summer, but the August nights now carry the hint of fall with them, and I pull the knit blanket onto my lap.

Dagen messaged earlier to let us know he was passing through Portland on his way to Seattle, and he wanted to see us. Cole invited him to stay the night out here, and he's been chuckling to himself ever since.

When I asked him what was so funny, he told me there was no way in hell Dagen would willingly sleep on the old couch, then he called him a princess.

Now we have a bet between us.

Cole says he'll end up refusing to sleep on the couch; I say he'll do just fine. It's not like we're roughing it out here. The loser strips the moment Dagen leaves in the morning and spends the next twenty-four hours naked and in service of the winner.

I say I have it in the bag, and Cole says it's a win-win either way.

Dagen's first words chip away at my confidence.

"Holy hell, Cole. You said this place was new."

"I meant it's new to us." Cole laughs as he leads his brother inside, glancing at me with a smug smirk.

I'm not going down that easily. Shaking my head, I stand, a grin plastered on my face.

"Dagen, it's nice to see you again. Can I get you a glass of wine?"

Or maybe the whole bottle, if it will chill you out enough so I'm not walking around in my birthday suit tomorrow.

"Hey, Harlow. This is a nice place. I'd love a glass." He says the word "nice" like it's an insult, but I'll take it. I lift my chin at Cole and do my own little victory strut, which consists of about five steps until I'm in the kitchen.

Dagen drops his bags at the front and hangs his jacket by the door. I half listen while I pour a glass, then I return with the bottle to top off me and Cole.

"So you found her?" Cole nods his thanks and picks his wine up, sitting back in his seat, and Dagen sits in an armchair.

"Sort of. I don't know where she is, but I know where she will be in five days."

"How so?"

Dagen looks like a predator with his sly smile, sure of his kill and ready to pounce.

"I had one of my guys check out some jobs for me to see if she was still active, and it turns out she's been picking up a string of contracts one after the other since the microfiche, which was also a job for hire. I might have had access to who the buyer was if I'd been paying attention to open contracts back then, but we were all kind of busy."

Dagen doesn't need to explain what had him distracted.

They had gone from almost losing their youngest brother to me being on the run and Cole being targeted in a drive-by shooting.

"Anyway." Dagen circles back to Cole's question. "Nigel, one of my teammates, hacked into the most recent contracts, and she's signed on for one that goes down—"

Cole cuts him off. "In five days."

"Yes. So when these contracts come through, they can be open, closed, or assigned. If they are assigned, the buyer specifically requested a certain person or persons and doesn't want anyone else on the job. If they are closed, then anyone can apply, but only those approved can complete the task. It's kind of like a job interview, lots apply, one gets the job. And if they are open, then all you need to do is sign up as an interested party, and the person who completes the task first gets paid."

Dagen leans back, taking a sip. He glances at the fire burning when a log cracks under the heat before turning his gaze back to us.

"But here is where it gets weird."

I snort into my wine, and both brothers look at me.

"*Here* is where it gets weird? It's kinda been weird from the start." I glance at Dagen and Cole with a look that dares them to deny it.

Cole chuckles, and Dagen nods in agreement.

"It has been. But the additional *odd thing* is that this is a hybrid contract. Technically, it is assigned; however, there is a list of people it is assigned to, making it an 'assigned open' contract, and the payday is way higher than it should be. I had Nigel check the names, and they match the same people who signed up to go after—"

"The microfiche." It's my turn to cut Dagen off, and he points at me with a nod. "But what does that mean?"

Dagen considers my question. "Not sure, but if I were a

betting man, I'd say it's a trap. Maybe the buyer doesn't know which one of them actually completed the task. That information is never public knowledge. So someone might be looking for everyone who signed up for the contract."

"But we know who took it," I mutter to myself, but both brothers hear me and nod.

The memory of the woman walking past the far end of the aisle makes me shudder. I didn't get a close look at her, so I didn't see what color her jacket was. I'm still not sure if it even was her, but it affects me just the same.

"Are you cold?" Cole watches me as he takes a sip.

"I'm fine, but I think I forgot to pack my sweater."

The hint of a wolfish smile creeps across his lips. "You won't be needing it tomorrow." Then he winks, silently reminding me of our bet.

When I turn my attention back to Dagen, he looks lost in thought, staring into the fire. Whoever this woman is, Dagen's changed since he found out their paths have crossed again.

"And so you're going to save her?" I ask.

He nods solemnly.

Then, as if catching himself, he shakes off his vulnerability and corrects his response.

"I'm saving her ass so I can punish her myself." He doesn't say it with as much conviction as he had before, and I wonder if he's softened toward Nyla in the time it took him to find her.

"So where's this job?" Cole brings us back on topic.

"Alaska, of all places. I'm on my way to Seattle. I spoke to Lennox about it this morning." Cole nods knowingly, and I look between both brothers in confusion.

When Cole looks at me, he clarifies, "Lennox has a plane; he has his pilot's license." He says it like it's normal to have an extra plane lying around.

"If he can't get away, he said he'll have someone else ready to fly me out."

"You sure you don't want me to come along?" Cole asks, and my stomach twists.

I don't think I hide the worry on my face when Dagen looks my way and smiles.

"No. Ryder asked the same thing. You both have—*priorities* here that need your attention. I'll be fine. It's a quick in and out."

We finish our wine when Cole stands and announces it's time for bed.

My stomach churns when he tells Dagen he can sleep on the couch, and I wait, holding my breath for the outcome.

Standing, Dagen stretches then takes a walk around the small room before glancing into our bedroom. Behind his back, Cole looks at me with a wide grin spread across his face.

"This bedroom is like one giant, sexy bouncy house. Come on, there is clearly room for the three of us on that bed." Dagen turns to wiggle his eyebrows at me, and I flush. Cole's smile is eaten up by a possessive grimace as he steps beside me, wrapping an arm around me and pulling me into him.

"Fine." Dagen resigns himself to the couch, and I pinch my lips together to stop my smile.

Gathering the glasses, I walk away and set them in the kitchen before returning to say goodnight. Cole is already out of the room when I pass Dagen, and he stands to pull me into a hug.

"I knew you were good for him." He lowers his voice so his brother can't hear. Then he says at a normal level, "See you in the morning." Calling over my shoulder to his brother, he says, "Breakfast better be good after this bullshit." He points to the couch, and Cole chuckles from the other room.

I don't bother with pajamas. As soon as the door is closed, I remove my jeans and bra in the dark, then crawl under the covers in my panties and top.

Cole's strong arm wraps around my midsection, and he pulls my back into his front, making me the little spoon. His fingers trail along my skin under my shirt. My flesh prickles with goosebumps as he draws lines, circling my breast then pinching my nipple.

As we settle in, a giggle bubbles up from inside me.

"What are you laughing at, Socks?" Cole asks casually as he nuzzles his lips into the back of my neck and kisses me softly.

"I told you he'd be okay with the couch."

Cole's dark chuckle combined with the tickle of his facial hair along my neck sends shivers down my spine. Lifting his head, he lines his lips up with my ear and whispers, "Wait for it."

I sit in silence in the dark. My eyes are wide open, but it doesn't matter, I can't see a damn thing.

Holding my breath, my heart thuds into my chest until the distant yipping of coyotes breaks the silence outside.

Then—

"I'M NOT SLEEPING ON THIS FUCKING COUCH!"

SHE BEAT HIM AT HIS OWN GAME ONCE.

NOW IT'S ROUND TWO,

AND THIS TIME THEY'RE PLAYING DIRTY.

DAGEN SAINT

Nyla stole two million dollars from me and disappeared five years ago.

Now she's resurfaced and I'm determined to settle her debt...one way or another.

Hiking in the mountains in my underwear while being hunted by hitmen wasn't something I thought we'd be doing when I woke up this morning, yet here we are.

If we can settle our issues and work together, we just might make it out alive—if we don't kill each other first.

NYLA JENSEN

I conned the con five years ago, but he took something I wasn't prepared to leave behind—my heart.

Now I'm stranded in the wilderness with the one person who has every reason to hate me and we have no choice but to work together or we're dead.

It turns out surviving the elements and the men searching for us is the easy part.

The hard part is being close to Dagen, coming clean, and looking him in the eye. Those same eyes I see every time I look at the daughter he doesn't know we have.

ACKNOWLEDGMENTS

I want to thank everyone who helped me get this book ready to present to you:

Cover design: Kirsty Still (Pretty Little Design Co.)
Editor: Caroline Knecht (Reedsy)
Photographer: Wander Aguiar
Cover Model: Josh Mario

Writing a series in its entirety before publishing a word is a daunting experience. It means sitting on finished work that could be financially supporting me while I write the others, but this story needed to be whole and complete before any of the books could be shared. I'd like to thank my family for encouraging and supporting me while I wrote.

Until next time...

ABOUT LUNA

Luna Kayne is a multi-genre romance author located in Canada. She writes dark, explicit, romantic suspense with a hint of humor and angst. Her men are dominant and often stubborn, and her women are usually underestimated. As for tropes and sub-genres, nothing is off the table.

In 2021, she won an IPPY (Independent Publisher Book Awards) award with her novel, *Step Darkly* which earned a bronze medal.

Luna Kayne is the pen name of author *Sheri Landry* who writes non-romance action thrillers and has won awards for her writing under both names.

You can learn more at LunaKayne.com.

 facebook.com/LunaKayne

 twitter.com/LunaKayne

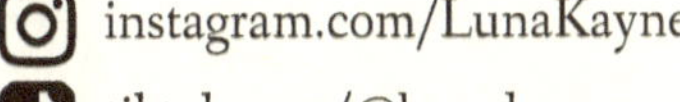 instagram.com/LunaKayne

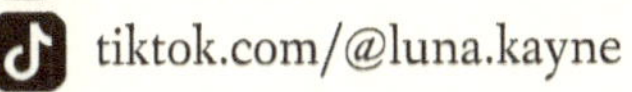 tiktok.com/@luna.kayne

bookbub.com/profile/luna-kayne